DARKNESS
GETS THERE FIRST

Books by John Spencer Perry

Available at Amazon and Barnes & Noble

★★★★★ **Great read for mystery lovers!**
I loved this book! I read it in two days. Couldn't put it down. Entertaining and relevant for baby boomers; mystery fans; Palm Spring lovers; etc.

★★★★★ **Nostalgic page turner**
The story starts as a nostalgic rewind of life in the 1970's and those days when life seemed like it had no ending and/or no responsibilities... Then the story takes a twist and a turn making the book a total page turner up to the final pages.

★★★★★ **Noir classic detective novel**
1966 is the perfect setting for a noir/Hollywood-style detective whose shady background allows him to find clues like no one else.

★★★★★ **Murder, intrigue, sex, the Mob!**
As soon as I started reading this book, I knew I could not put it down until I finished it. A who-done-it in a time I grew up in.

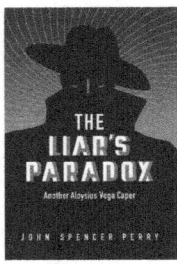

★★★★★ **Great novel within historical events**
"The Liar's Paradox is Perry's best so far. His story-telling skills have grown with each of his novels."

★★★★★ **A great read!**
"An exciting page turner that makes you want to keep reading. Fun mix of fact and fiction to keep your interest."

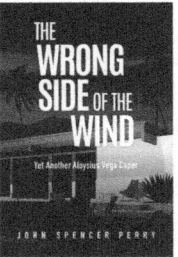

★★★★★ **Best read in a long time**
"Like a James Patterson novel. Easy to read and follow and non-stop action. Not much more you can ask for out of a book."

★★★★★ **A work of great imagination**
"Great historical detail and nostalgia in a romping mystery. If you like Palm Springs, mystery, martinis, and a little sex, this a book for you to enjoy."

DARKNESS GETS THERE FIRST

Aloysius Vega and The Case of the Missing Bride

BY

JOHN SPENCER PERRY

RUSTIC CANYON
PUBLISHING LLC

DARKNESS GETS THERE FIRST
Aloysius Vega & The Case of the Missing Bride

By John Spencer Perry

Copyright © 2025 by John Spencer Perry
La Quinta, CA 92253

This is a work of fiction. Many of the characters and events portrayed in this novel are either products of the author's wild imagination or are used fictitiously.

Published by Amazon 2025
Printed in the United State of America
ISBN: 979-8-9934258-0-1
Library of Congress Control Number: Pending
Cover and Interior design by Anita Williams | Design

All rights reserved. Copyright encourages creativity and supports writers. Thank you for buying an authorized edition of this book and for complying with copyright laws by not reproducing, scanning, or distributing any part of it in any form without permission.

*For those who follow my detective,
Aloysius Vega.
His stories exist because you
keep turning the page.*

Light thinks it travels faster than anything,
but it is wrong.
No matter how fast light travels, it finds
the darkness has always got there first
and is waiting for it.

— *Terry Pratchett, 1948-2015*

PART 1
The Unraveling

PART I

The Unraveling

CHAPTER ONE

Aoysius Vega regained consciousness to the scent of jasmine and lilies. The brew of carnal and rot irritated his nasal cavity, causing his eyes to open, close, then open again. The surrealistic landscape of the dream that consumed his altered state flickered then flashed white like the snapping of broken film in an old movie projector. Awakened from an isolated realm of pure nightmare, a dimension where time and space had lost coherence, Vega realized he had no volition or control of his surroundings. He was at the mercy of mysterious, inhuman specters. Plus a sense that this may...never...end.

From his peripheral vision, shadowed outlines of what appeared to be flowers wavered in the darkness. A timeworn garden? Rows of long-stemmed flowers? Perhaps bouquets placed against the gray granite of a marbled gravestone.

Is that it? Am I dead? Buried in a graveyard? How did I...?

A beep shattered the silence. Then...ticking. Something – or someone – was counting. A steady cadence, one after another, without a lapse. Like a drumbeat. Or the pounding of a heart.

Something...something I recall.

A heartbeat.

A tiny heartbeat.

CHAPTER TWO

On thin plastic chairs that offered little comfort in a room that smelled of antiseptic and stale coffee, two women sat quietly. The overhead paging system offered a muffled call for a doctor. A security scanner crackled with static, breaking the stillness in a room set aside for family members outside the Intensive Care Unit at UCLA Medical Center.

The ICU waiting room was set apart from other waiting areas in the sprawling hospital complex. In those other spaces automatic doors opened and closed with the frequency of a 7-Eleven at lunch hour. Children and adults sat slumped in stiff chairs, nursing broken limbs and bloodied skin, surrounded by weary walls where clocks barely noted the passing of time.

The younger woman fidgeted in her chair, twisting the visitor band on her wrist, crossing and recrossing her ankles, looking about the room at nothing in particular. To her left, silently reading a hardcover print of *Myra Breckinridge*, was her comrade in waiting. The two spoke infrequently except to ask the other to watch a purse before taking the short walk to the ladies room or a longer escape to breathe in the cool ocean air that wafted over Los Angeles that first evening of 1969.

The two women were as different as their thumbprints.

Erika Lake was a former movie actress who married money and divorced for more. She lighted between homes in Manhattan, Milan, and Palm Springs when not traveling to Africa or Southeast Asia. The striking 42-year-old threw lavish parties that raised enormous sums for her favorite charities and splashed the society pages of the *Desert Post*.

Coralina Sanchez grew up in Tepoztlán, a rural village south of Mexico City, raised with two sisters by a single working mother. After the family migrated to Southern California, Coralina learned English, graduated from high school, then began her working life as a hotel maid, cleaning bathrooms and changing bedsheets. Now, at age 23, she was widowed and eight months pregnant.

What the two women had in common was their fierce loyalty to Aloysius Vega and their suspicion of each other. Each owed the private detective a debt of gratitude. Vega had safeguarded Erika's reputation within the Palm Springs social order by securing an 8 mm film that was being used as blackmail. For Coralina, Vega had provided a pathway from her impoverished background. She now managed the Vega Detective Agency as his executive assistant.

Coralina was Vega's companion on New Year's Eve when the private detective was gunned down outside the Whisky a Go Go, shot by a man exposed for cheating on his wife. She cradled her wounded boss on the broken sidewalk outside the famous nightclub, praying medics would arrive before he expired. Erika arrived at the hospital five hours later. She briefly consoled Coralina before confronting staff and administrators about her expectations as a major donor to the medical center. Erika's pull allowed her to ignore ICU rules to decorate Vega's private room with a flotilla of cut flowers.

— • —

The attending physician, Joseph H. Gargery, was among the founders of the Society of Neuroscience, created to advance the understanding of the brain and nervous system. Soft-spoken and with the appearance of a kindly white-haired grandfather, the 69-year-old understood the importance of the relationships between doctor, patient, and patient's family. Although informed that Erika and Coralina were not related to Vega, Gargery treated the two as if they were. Like family members, they were overwhelmed by a situation they never anticipated.

His first meeting with the two women began in a private office on the hospital's second floor. Gargery was brief but to the point. Mr. Vega's vital signs were stable. Bleeding from the gunshot wound had been arrested in surgery. The collapse of one lung had been repaired and reinflated. His respiratory system was being aided by a ventilator. Medications to prevent infection and reduce pain had been administered.

"That is the good news, ladies. However, Mr. Vega is comatose. He is breathing but is non-responsive."

Gargery realized his statement had stopped their world. Experience had taught him that after the initial shock, something more terrifying than death had crept into the conversation.

Coma.

A cruel condition with staggering unknowns. Will he awaken? How long will it take? Will he be the same? Will he need brain surgery? Will he be disabled? Will he be a...

Gargery's next statement was delivered in a manner both honest and compassionate.

"Before we talk about possible recovery or the pace of recovery, it's important that I provide you with basic information on this condition. Coma comes from a Greek term meaning deep sleep. But that's deceptive. Better to say that coma is the opposite of consciousness. Clinically, consciousness refers to two quite distinct things: wakefulness and awareness. Consciousness is at once familiar to us all, and deeply mysterious. All of us lose consciousness every night when we go to sleep, only to regain it in the morning. No one knows where consciousness comes from. There is no specific area of the brain where it resides, unlike speech or other senses. Consciousness is also uniquely human. It's what makes us aware of who we are and allows us to reason."

Gargery paused, giving his audience time to assess his statement before continuing.

"Our understanding of consciousness has been hampered by our historically rudimentary ways of understanding its absence. We can easily determine if someone is awake, because their eyes will probably be open. Awareness is much harder to detect, because the only way we have of knowing whether someone is aware is by asking them. However, unlike someone asleep, a comatose patient remains in an unreceptive and unresponsive state. If poked, their arms or legs might react but the action is a reflex rather than movement done with a purpose. Is this making sense? Am I speaking too quickly?"

Coralina was the first to speak.

"I understand. What caused Aloysius to go into a coma? He did not hit his head on the sidewalk when he collapsed. He fell on me."

"It is true that most comas result from a traumatic injury to the brain, but I could easily come up with a hundred other causes. Seizure, drug overdose, a blockage, environmental causes like electricity, water, ice or heat. But in Mr. Vega's case, his unresponsive state was caused by a severe loss of blood from the gunshot wound. If the blood loss is significant, as it was with Mr. Vega, the heart is unable to maintain circulation and adequate blood pressure. The patient loses consciousness and slips into a coma. Without a transfusion, organs will begin to fail."

Reaching for the table between them, Erika handed Coralina a small box of Kleenex before asking Gargery how much blood Vega had lost.

"A class four hemorrhage. Medics were able to begin a transfusion enroute to the hospital. Once he arrived in emergency, the transfusions were increased. These two actions, we believe, saved his life."

Her voice wavering, Coralina asked when Aloysius would wake up.

"At this point, unknown. The sooner he regains consciousness, the better. Outcomes are often worse for patients who remain comatose for longer periods. Right now, Miss Sanchez, his condition is critical, which is the best we can hope for at the present time."

— • —

For the next four days, the two women would arrive at the hospital together, sitting silently in the waiting room until they were allowed to enter the ICU patient ward one at a time. Visits were limited to twenty minutes twice per day. Each woman approached their time with Vega with differences as wide as their backgrounds.

Coralina would pull the single visitor's chair across the room to sit next to the bed where she held Vega's limp hand the entire time. She spoke in a low voice about mundane office matters and potential cases once he recovered. Mostly, she would sit quietly, squeezing his fingers softly with her right hand while massaging her swollen belly with her left.

When it was her turn, Erika would gently tussle Vega's dark curly hair before sitting by the window that overlooked traffic crawling below on the new 405 freeway. As was her practice, Erika would read aloud from *The Lady in the Lake* by Raymond Chandler. Today, she began where she left off. Philip Marlowe was making his way to the office of a wealthy businessman who wanted the famous detective to find his estranged wife.

"*He handed me a large and very clear snapshot on glazed paper which showed a man and a woman sitting on the sand under a beach umbrella. The man wore trunks and the woman what looked like a very daring white sharkskin bathing suit. She was a slim blonde, young and shapely and smiling. The man was a hefty dark handsome lad with fine shoulders and legs, sleek dark hair and white teeth. Six feet of a standard type of homewrecker."*

CHAPTER THREE

On the fourth evening, like the preceding three, the two women shared a town car for the three-mile ride from the hospital to the Beverly Hills Hotel. Erika insisted they stay at the iconic pink palace rather than make the two-hour drive back to Palm Springs. When Coralina balked, Erika remained steadfast, insisting the mother-to-be required comfort and a wait staff rather than a strenuous 120-mile automobile trip back and forth each day to the desert.

The legendary hideaway had hosted Hollywood royalty since it opened in 1912. Movie deals were made on the back of napkins in the Polo Lounge. The hotel's private bungalows were favored for secret affairs by the likes of Spencer Tracy, Marilyn Monroe, and presidential candidate Jack Kennedy.

Honeymooners Elizabeth Taylor and Richard Burton had a standing room-service order that included two bottles of vodka with breakfast and another two with lunch. Howard Hughes lived at the hotel on and off for thirty years, occupying as many as nine bungalows at once. Staff delivered his favorite roast-beef sandwiches by leaving them in the crook of a tree. Starlets sunbathed in the cabanas by the aquamarine pool as did Rex Harrison who, rather than donning a swimsuit, preferred to cover his genitals with a handkerchief – employing a different color each day.

And so it was that Coralina Sanchez, the former hotel maid, found herself in the lap of luxury in a third-floor suite in the heart of Beverly Hills, on twelve lush acres in the foothills of the Santa Monica Mountains on land once owned by the Mexican government.

That evening, as the two women dined at the Polo Lounge, several Hollywood executives stopped at their table to greet Erika. The last was Robert Evans, the only visitor to maneuver into the booth next to the former actress. Tall, with long raven hair and a deep perma-tan accentuated by the pale turtleneck sweater worn underneath his navy-blue dinner jacket, the legendary producer and head of Paramount Studios quickly kissed Erika on the cheek and acknowledged Coralina before beginning an audacious rapid-fire conversation in a voice as seductive as Kentucky bourbon.

"Just the person I was about to call. I have the perfect vehicle for your return. It's a can't-miss part. We're doing *Love Story*. I got Ali MacGraw as the lead. We're still casting about for her college sweetheart."

"I'm not good at playing the opposite sex, Evans. I can't do vapid."

"Funny girl. I got you down as Ali's mother. Perfect fit."

"I read the book. I don't do middle-aged mothers either. Certainly not middle-aged mothers who are Jewish. I'm still a hot lady, Evans."

"Never change."

"I will and so will you. We all grow older. No one will want to see us that way. Audiences want us frozen young."

"You can play anything, Erika. You know that. I know that. C'mon. I'll get you a good price and maybe a residual or two. It'll be your springboard back to the top."

"I never made the top. I never even glimpsed the top. I washed out."

"Only because of that damn stutter. It's gone. You will be the comeback story of the year. Do this for me, Erika."

"I'd do almost anything for you, Evans. You know that. But I'm not returning to Hollywood."

"We're filming at Harvard. On campus. You love the East Coast, remember?"

"When does filming start?"

"November."

The waiter brought the studio chief a martini. After draining it by half, he returned to his pitch only to be interrupted by Erika, who pointed across the table to Coralina.

"This is the girl you should be courting. Coralina would have made a better pregnant lead in *Rosemary's Baby* than that pixie-haired tramp. Look at those high cheekbones, brown eyes, and long dark hair."

Evans regarded Coralina before returning his attention to Erika.

"Good lord, Erika. We grossed $33 million on a budget of three. The picture was a knockout. Best screenplay. Roman got the Director's Guild award, for Christ sakes. Mia got her share of accolades."

"She got Sinatra. That was her award."

"I detect a hint of jealousy."

"Just a hint. Now, you want material for a screenplay? How about a guy lying in a coma at UCLA? He's a private dick. A handsome Spaniard straight from central casting. He's got a knack for trouble and cracking cases. With a name that sticks with you. Aloysius Vega."

Evans downed the rest of the martini.

"Vega, huh? How come I know that name?"

Coralina answered.

"Aloysius solved the murder of Al Archer, the movie director."

"That's right. It was in the papers. Located the body in a concrete grave in the desert."

"That was Aloysius."

Evans asked Erika why Vega was comatose.

"The New Year's Eve shooting? Outside the Whisky? He was the target. Vega got the goods on a cheating husband. Apparently, the husband took offense."

"Jesus, that's terrible. Is he going to make it?"

Coralina slid from the booth, excusing herself for the ladies room. Evans waited until she left.

"Did I say something wrong?"

"It's okay. She's Vega's assistant and is sweet on the guy."

"She carrying his baby?"

"Nope. Her husband's. Died in a plane crash several months ago. Newlyweds."

"Jesus."

"I told you. There's a screenplay here."

Evans snapped his fingers for another martini.

"I got Townie working on one. Wanted him to resuscitate Capote's disastrous rewrite of *Gatsby*. We met for dinner at Dominique's. Before I could get into *Gatsby*, he began telling me about an original he was working on. About how Los Angeles became a boomtown by stealing water from the Owens Valley. It's set in the thirties. A second-rate detective gets eighty-sixed by a mysterious broad. Instead of solving a case for her, he becomes the pigeon."

"I like Vega's case better."

— • —

By the time Coralina returned, Evans had left.

"Interesting gentleman. How did you two meet?"

"Long story. The short version is we met at a studio party and stayed friends ever since."

"He is very handsome. Is he an actor?"

"He tried his hand in front of the camera, but said he never felt comfortable. He grew up on the Upper West Side and ran a women's clothing business with his brother. Norma Shearer spotted him by the pool, right here, at the hotel. She was so impressed she insisted he play the role of her husband, a studio chief, in *The Man of a Thousand Faces*. A headline at the time read "New York Businessman Dives In Pool and Comes Out a Movie Star." He did a few more movies before making his way up the business end. He wasn't a star as an actor, but he certainly is a star as the head of Paramount."

"And you? You do not have the interest to act again?"

"Not at all. I wasn't cut out for Hollywood. It was the moon I desperately wanted to…I don't know…capture. I learned it's all a fabrication. A paper moon created on the back lot. On the screen and when the cameras are off."

Erika looked out over the top of her martini glass to the flickering lights beyond the Polo Lounge.

"Marilyn got it right. Hollywood is a place where they'll pay you a thousand dollars for a kiss and fifty cents for your soul."

CHAPTER FOUR

"**Good morning. Can you hear me?** Just nod your head yes – or no if you don't wish to talk."

The patient nodded to the uniform standing next to him. The man was a doctor and this was a hospital. He knew that much. And that his throat was very sore.

"Good. I'm a doctor and I'm taking care of you. I know you are feeling pain. We are doing what we can to manage that pain. Mostly, I want you to know you are safe. You're tired, and likely quite confused. Do you feel up to listening?"

Another nod.

"Good. You went through a bit of an ordeal. But your vital signs are good, and now that you're alert, I expect your progress to steadily improve. I am Doctor Gargery. You're a patient at UCLA Medical Center. Do you know why you are here?"

A slight swivel. Negative.

"How about your name? Can you tell me your name?"

The answer came in a raspy whisper.

"Vey...gah."

"Good. Can you tell me your first name?"

Each of the four syllables were pronounced slowly in the same raspy whisper, this time with the patient's eyes closed in a grimace.

"Al...oh...wish...ez."

"Good. I won't ask you to speak any further, Mr. Vega. I know your throat feels like it's on fire. Several tubes were placed there to help in your recovery. Your throat will heal rather quickly now. Let me quickly describe your condition, then we'll get you cleaned up. Okay? Good. Mr. Vega, you arrived here with a single gunshot wound to the lower chest. The bullet entered on your right side where it damaged the number four rib before exiting your body five centimeters below the axilla, your armpit. Your rib was fractured and required surgery to repair it. Are you following me, Mr. Vega?"

The brief nod instructed Gargery to continue.

"The good news is your rib deflected the projectile from its initial path, which was toward your spinal cord. The bad news is two-fold. First, your broken rib punctured your lung. The released air collected in the pleural space outside, putting pressure on the lung, preventing its proper expansion, and causing the lung to collapse. We inserted a tube into the pleural space to draw out the excess air. This reduced the pressure against the lung, allowing it to expand again. You were on a ventilator for several days to ensure your breathing returned to normal."

He studied the patient for signs of comprehension before continuing.

"I see that you are quite tired, Mr. Vega. You'll feel better tomorrow and I will explain more. Okay?"

Vega attempted to speak.

"You...say...two."

"Two?"

"Baa...nooze..."

"Yes. I said there was bad news. The first was your deflated lung and fractured rib. The second, Mr. Vega, involves your condition when you arrived. The gunshot wound, while it did not severely damage any vital organs other than your lung, did cause you to lose quite a large volume of blood. When medical personnel first arrived, you were in hypovolemic shock. Unconscious and experiencing a significant drop in blood pressure. By the time you arrived here, at UCLA, you remained unresponsive even after we stabilized your blood pressure. For four days. You were comatose during that time. You are alert now and, as I said, your vital signs are good. Our initial tests indicate there are..."

    The UCLA surgeon never finished his sentence. His patient had dozed off, returning to a perplexing and frightful dreamscape.

CHAPTER FIVE

Coralina arrived at the hospital the fifth morning unaccompanied by Erika. The chauffeur was unaware of the reason, told only to provide Miss Sanchez transportation to UCLA Medical Center and to ensure her safe return. Unable to enter Vega's room, and without an explanation from the nurse, Coralina circled the empty waiting room, taking slow deep breaths as she paced and holding her belly. The baby was active. A night full of what she thought were fetal hiccups developed into a circus of elbows and somersaults in her uterus. She vowed to remain calm for the baby's sake but questions pestered her. Why won't they allow me to see Aloysius? Had his condition worsened overnight?

Twenty minutes passed before she would learn the answers from Doctor Gargery – answers that both comforted and spooked her.

"Miss Sanchez, I'm sorry we kept you waiting. Please sit down. Miss Lake, is she not with you today?"

"No."

"Then let me provide you with the latest information, much of which is good. Mr. Vega is conscious. His vital signs remain stable. He is able to breathe on his own. He is having difficulty talking, something that is not unusual for patients who have been comatose with a ventilator inserted in their windpipe."

Coralina finally sat. She closed her eyes momentarily to thank God for answering her daily prayers.

"Will Aloysius be alright?"

"It's early and his injuries were severe, as you know. But I am quite confident that his physical prognosis is good. The internal injuries appear to be healing and we see no sign of infection. Mr. Vega can turn his head, raise his arms and feel pain. His nervous system appears sound."

"You said he is conscious."

"Yes. And…"

"Is he… aware? Does he know where he is and what happened?"

"To your first question, Miss Sanchez, the answer is yes. He is aware of his environment and recited his name. I told him why he is here and the nature of his injuries. He appears to understand. But to your second question, he does not recall the actual incident or where he was at the time."

"That is good that he does not remember?"

"In a way, yes. When the brain registers an overwhelming trauma such as what Mr. Vega experienced, it will attempt to protect itself. Much the way the body can wall-off an abscess or foreign substance to protect the rest of the body, the brain can wander off to avoid the memory. Am I making sense?"

"Yes. What you say is helpful."

"Good. The brain's disassociation from a trauma can also be impacted by a coma. People who regain consciousness after being comatose often don't recall what happened. It's like a veil has descended. And when they regain consciousness, they may have difficulty comprehending. Not only the trauma they experienced but also their surroundings or their identity."

"But you said Aloysius knows he is in a hospital and told you his name, did he not? I am not understanding."

"As I mentioned, there are no outward signs of any physical difficulties other than the wounds he suffered. But we are very early in the recovery process. We have not yet tried to get him to walk or feed himself. But I expect he will progress and be able to transition from this hospital to a nursing center and, eventually, home. We are, however, detecting signs of ICU delirium."

Coralina's hand covered her mouth.

"Please. I didn't mean to alarm you. About two-thirds of patients in ICU develop delirium, and those on breathing machines tend to be most at risk. For most patients here in ICU, delirium doesn't last long – usually only a few days. We are prepared to treat delirium in patients like Mr. Vega with medication mostly but also with quiet conversation."

"What are his, his…"

"Symptoms?"

"Thank you. Yes."

"Confusion, mostly. Difficulty focusing. His eyesight. Also his attention span. He is easily distracted and becomes very tired. His symptoms fluctuate throughout a day. We have also observed episodes where Mr. Vega becomes very fearful and thinks that something bad is happening to him. This evidences itself at night. He becomes fearful of falling asleep, believing that if he sleeps, he will die. We assure him he will not. That he is getting the best medical care available. It is not unusual for a patient recovering from a coma to experience nightmares so vivid and realistic that they struggled to differentiate between the dream and reality. They felt trapped in a nightmarish world, an experience that may leave them feeling traumatized long after consciousness. Last night, Mr. Vega awakened and was obviously terrified. We sedated him and he remains asleep as we speak."

"I cannot see Aloysius?"

"When he wakes, and if he appears lucid, I will let staff know to allow you a brief visit. At this point in his recovery, we want to avoid overstimulation."

With a practiced smile, Dr. Gargery placed his hands on hers.

"I have a hunch that you, Miss Sanchez, may be the best medicine I can prescribe for my patient."

— • —

Two hours later, as an apportionment of the morning shift of doctors and nurses made its way to the elevators and the lunchroom on the first floor, Donna Prescott, the chief ICU nurse, found Coralina dozing on a couch Erika had ordered to be placed in the spartan waiting room.

"Miss Sanchez? Miss Sanchez?"

Helping the very pregnant woman get seated upright, the nurse asked if she would like to freshen up before seeing Mr. Vega.

"Yes. I want to look my best for Aloysius. Thank you."

In the ladies' room, as she brushed her hair and attempted to soften the dark circles below her eyes, Coralina considered the woman in the mirror. The past fourteen months had taken an obvious toll. She had married another man after Vega refused to acknowledge that he loved her. The marriage ended before its first anniversary. Juan Morales was killed along with eighty-nine other passengers when their plane crashed in the mountains of El Salvador. After burying her husband, Coralina sought refuge in her work at the Vega Detective Agency and comfort in the arms of its namesake. Someone who, she has been told, may not remember her.

"I am as ready as I can be...in my condition."

"You look beautiful. This way. I will need to remain in the room to observe his reactions."

"I understand."

Prepared as she was, Coralina was startled to see Vega awake and seemingly alert. No longer flat on his back with tubing down his throat, he was propped at a forty-degree angle in the bed. His pale face was charcoaled with five-day stubble. Still connected to a tangle of monitors and intravenous drip lines, his expression could only be described as detached.

"Mr. Vega? You have a visitor."

The detective turned his attention from the nurse to Coralina. His blank stare followed her as she approached the bedside and reached for his hand. He did not return her squeeze. His hand remained limp.

"Oh, Aloysius. You are awake."

His eyes appeared to be mapping her image, like a man attempting to identify a strange shadow. Crestfallen, she turned to the nurse, who returned a weak smile. Determined not to allow him to see the shot of fear that raced up her spine, Coralina let go of his hand for a moment to pull up a chair to his bedside. After sitting, she once again took his hand.

"We have missed you at the office, Aloysius. Nancy has been helping me out. You remember Nancy, don't you? Nancy Randall, she works at the library? Young girl? Very smart. She assisted you on a case. She is very good at research. She comes by each afternoon at three when she gets off work. Sometimes weekends too."

If Vega was connecting the dots, the results were not apparent. His face remained as vague as fog.

"Many people have been asking about you, Aloysius. My mother, that policewoman Lily, and of course all the bartenders in town, especially Jilly. Nancy says he calls at least twice a day. He told Nancy that he will prepare the coldest, driest, and best martini in the world after your release. How does that sound?"

A small grin, Coralina could tell that much.

"And the baby, Aloysius? She...I am certain the baby is a girl. I can tell by her position. She will be a girl. Remember the name I chose if she was a girl? Do you remember? Juliet. I will name her Juliet after the movie we watched together. Remember? *Romeo and Juliet*? It was so romantic. We watched it together. Remember?"

Nothing.

"Juliet is an active girl, Aloysius. She likes to punch me. And stick me with her elbow. And do somersaults. She is very active, this little girl. The doctors here, Aloysius? They are so nice. They took me to a room and allowed me to listen to her heartbeat. They say her heart is strong. Very strong. At night, while I am lying down and the room is quiet, I place my hand here, right here and I swear I can feel her heartbeat."

Still clutching Vega's hand, Coralina placed it palm down on her belly.

"Can you feel it, Aloysius? Heartbeats, tiny heartbeats."

The eyes that had remained so dispassionate moistened.

"Tiny…"

The voice was raspy, but it belonged to Vega.

CHAPTER SIX

Twenty-six days after being cut down outside the Whisky a Go Go, Aloysius Vega was released from UCLA Medical Center. His recovery was spotty. He remained unsteady on his feet, had a constant cough, and suffered joint stiffness. Medication to prevent infection left him nauseous. His sleep remained disturbed, tormented by nightmarish visions. Awake, he oftentimes saw double or only part of his visual field.

Memories of his upbringing in New Jersey and even his early childhood in Ría de San Vicente de la Barquera were sharp. Recollection of his three years in Palm Springs, and his work at the Vega Detective Agency remained, at best, uneven. The events of New Year's Eve, and the people he was with, had vanished. Whether they would reveal themselves eventually was unknown.

Doctor Gargery had warned that there was the potential for depression and apathy in patients recovering from a coma.

"Depression can feel like a heavy cloak, suffocating the spirit and clouding the vision. It can lead to a pervasive sense of emptiness and a struggle to find meaning in life, where the things that once brought joy lose their sparkle. Or Mr. Vega might have episodes of aggressive behavior or panic attacks. His response to other people may be significantly impaired. He might have a very low tolerance for stressful situations, less able to control his behaviors."

The good doctor saw the alarm on Coralina and Erika's faces as he shared this information before Vega's official release.

"Look, it's important to emphasize that Mr. Vega's long-term outcome is a moving target. He's relatively young and was in good physical and mental shape before his injuries. He may reemerge in similar mental and physical condition after rehabilitation. While I'm on that subject, Miss Lake, I remain strongly opposed to your desire to conduct Mr. Vega's rehabilitation at your home rather than at a certified rehabilitation center. Administration has waved off the concerns that I and the other physicians who have treated Mr. Vega have expressed about your plan. However, under the mutual agreement as I understand it, he will remain under the care of Vivian Dy."

Erika had grown impatient with the time it was taking to get Vega out of the Los Angeles hospital to her estate in Palm Springs. And with another lecture by hospital doctors and executives.

"I understand your concern, Doctor Gargery. But as you well know Vivian Dy is one of UCLA's own rehabilitation experts. Her qualifications to care for Mr. Vega are exceptional. She is certified in neurology by the American Board of Psychiatry and Neurology and she..."

"I am well aware of Doctor Dy's credentials, Miss Lake. A decision has been made and I will certainly honor it."

"Thank you. You and the UCLA staff are to be commended for your work. I believe we are finished here."

— • —

Erika arranged for her private jet to bring Vega and Vivian Dy to Palm Springs from Santa Monica Airport. Her secluded estate on West Hermosa in the Old Las Palmas neighborhood, a manor built by a Hollywood mogul and once occupied by Elizabeth Taylor, would serve as his rehabilitation center.

A generous guest suite – one of three – had been prepared for Vega's stay. The room overlooked a private back yard framed by Mexican fan palms and vertical strands of bougainvillea, jasmine and trumpet vines. A large pool lined with Italian mosaic tile marked the eastern end of the property. A smaller reflecting pool was set perpendicular to the other. In its center, a sculpted mermaid reclined.

Doctor Dy was given one of three guest cottages that lined the property's southern wall. An adjoining cottage was set up as a temporary medical office complete with a blood pressure monitor, examination table, an IV set, and a spirometer to track Vega's lung capacity.

There was no shortage of food for the guests. Erika's staff prepared breakfast and lunch. Dinner from Jilly's Restaurant was delivered each night promptly at seven, oftentimes by the owner, Jilly Rizzo, who was anxious to see his old friend.

"You've lost too much weight, Aloysius. You've gotten as skinny as Frank. By the way, he sends his best. He's in Arizona filming a western, of all things. A cowboy comedy! Believe that?"

Jilly was one of the few visitors Erika and Vivian allowed. Others like *Desert Post* reporter Scott Jarvis were allowed brief telephone calls. Among those checking in were members of the Califano crime family, including Francisco "Fat Frank" Majuri. The family capo took Vega into the family's plumbing business just days after the patrolman had been fired from the Asbury Park Police Department for insubordination. The request came from the old man himself, Salvator Califano.

On most telephone calls, Vega listened but rarely said more than a few words. His throat had healed and the gunshot wound was mending. Still, his mind remained disturbed. He had difficulty thinking ahead, whether it was to remember his next scheduled activity or the question he wanted to ask. So he said little. Memories of his time with the Asbury Park Police Department were vivid. So too his marriage and divorce. The cases he investigated as a private investigator were coming into focus. Faces and names became more familiar with each interaction. With one exception: Coralina Sanchez.

— • —

As she did at the hospital, Erika made time each day to read to Vega. He would lounge in a hammock with his eyes closed as she read. Thinking he had fallen asleep, she would stop only to continue after he waved his left hand in a circle. *The Lady In The Lake* had given way to *Playback*, Chandler's final novel.

The voice on the telephone seemed to be sharp and peremptory, but I didn't hear too well what it said – partly because I was only half awake and partly because I was holding the receiver upside down. I fumbled it around and grunted.

"Did you hear me? I said I was Clyde Umney, the lawyer."

"Clyde Umney, the lawyer. I thought we had several of them."

"You're Marlowe, aren't you?"

"Yeah. I guess so." *I looked at my wristwatch. It was 6:30 a.m., not my best hour.*

"Don't get fresh with me, young man."

"Sorry, Mr. Umney. But I'm not a young man. I'm old, tired and full of no coffee. What can I do for you, sir?"

— • —

Vega spent four hours each day with Doctor Vivian Dy. After assessing his blood pressure and lung capacity, she would take him through a regimen of cognitive therapy attempting to tie memory to behavior. As she explained to Erika:

"People commonly believe that memory is just a matter of training. That memory may be restored simply by practicing word lists, pictures or other material. This is a false belief. When remembering takes place, a behavior took place that is linked to what was learned at the time. Accessing that memory becomes an act of restoring that repertoire of specific behaviors."

"You lost me, doctor. But that's of no matter. Aloysius is getting better, I can see that. Still, I wish he would smile, express some emotion. Say what he's thinking."

"I'm confident that will come with time, Miss Lake. Unlike a person who suffers a severe brain injury, the information – the original behavior that created that memory – is accessible."

Erika paused to consider her next comment.

"Aloysius is a detective. A good one. He was trained as a policeman to be observant. He spent much of his adolescence reading detective stories. Sherlock Holmes. The Hardy Boys. AA Fair. Using his brain rather than a gun is his livelihood. I'd even say it's his life. That and martinis and women. What I'm getting to is this: Will he be able resume his ambition? Will he be able to function as he was? As a detective? A talking one."

"I believe he will, though I cannot assure you of that. I'm pleased with the progress he is making."

"But the gaps. There are sizeable gaps in his memory. Will they fill in? Especially when it comes to his assistant, Coralina? You, me, Jilly. He recognizes and remembers us. Even the girl who's filling in at the agency. But he appears puzzled when Coralina is present. That poor girl loves him and it tears her in two to see that vacant look."

"Memory is the slowest part of the conscious mind to recover from a trauma, Miss Lake. The associated amnesia can last three to four times longer than the coma. What Doctor Gargery told you is correct. When the brain suffers an overwhelming trauma, it will attempt to protect itself. In Mr. Vega's case, he has no recollection of being injured or the events leading to that trauma. Miss Sanchez was there at his side when it happened. She is being blocked out with everything else that occurred at that time. Doctor Gargery's analogy is a good one: A veil has descended over his memory of that time. A protective veil."

"And Coralina is behind that veil."

CHAPTER SEVEN

Pushing off from the wall at the deep end of the swimming pool, Vega glided underwater before surfacing for a breath of cool morning air. Instead, he swallowed a mouthful of warm water. Choking, he struggled to find his footing before spitting and coughing. Another wave slapped his left ear causing him to lose his balance. Like a drunk on a poorly patched sidewalk, Vega reached for the edge of the pool to regain his balance. Pinching water from his eyes, he watched in disbelief as the surface of the pool sloshed back and forth.

A magnitude 4.8 earthquake was rumbling across the Coachella Valley, rattling dishes and nerves. Although the quake resulted in little damage, it was a cheeky reminder that, wealthy or not, residents here live atop an 800-mile-long crack in the Earth known as the San Andreas Fault.

The temblor made for ideal cocktail chatter that evening at Erika's soiree. A dozen guests had been invited to celebrate the conclusion of Vega's rehabilitation. He had been cleared by Doctor Dy, who would depart the estate in the morning.

"I've lived with the promise of The Big One since I moved here. It holds as much assurance as the promise to love someone until death do you part."

Erika's declaration resulted in a few snickers but also extracted the sharpened tongue of Claude Binyon, a former screenwriter and journalist known for his "Wall Street Lays An Egg" headline in 1929.

"This is no laughing matter, Erika. An earthquake of a 7.8 magnitude along this portion of San Andreas would be forty-four times stronger than what we felt this morning. There's a forty-eight percent likelihood of at least one such earthquake occurring here within the next thirty years."

Erika glared at her neighbor.

"Thank you for that science lesson, Claude, but the rest of us here are pretending it's a party."

It was left to Robert Evans to break the awkward silence that followed.

"Quarreling is healthy. If everyone has too much reverence for each other, the results are invariably underwhelming. Darling Erika, where is that adventurous detective you are hiding? You led us to believe he would attend a party thrown in his honor."

What the studio head referenced had been lost among the negronis and platters of bacon-wrapped dates. Aloysius Vega remained in his room, sitting on the edge of the bed fully dressed except for the Nino Cerruti jacket hanging on the mahogany valet stand. On the night table to his right, he swallowed the last of his SweeTarts, a craving that had substituted for martinis during his convalescence.

He looked through the balcony's French doors to the mermaid reclining above the pool in the yard. Her dark figure shimmered in gentle reflection from lights hidden within the mosaic tiles below the pool's surface. In the distance, the Santa Rosa Mountains, their granite walls once golden with desert sunlight, receded into silhouettes, swallowed slowly by the evening's growing shadow.

A polite tap on the door announced a doctor's final house call.

"Mr. Vega, may I come in?"

Without waiting for his reply, Vivian Dy entered, closing the door behind her. Unlike most days clad in a soft blue or white UCLA medical jacket and matching scrub pants, the doctor wore a relaxed shift dress with colorful blue-and-yellow diamond patterns.

Vega stood for a moment before she urged him to sit. He complied. Sitting next to him on the bed, she searched his face.

"What is more concerning tonight? Socializing with Erika and the guests down the hall? Or is it the thought of going home tomorrow morning and returning to the life you once inhabited?"

"Both."

"That is normal for..."

"Normal? Normal is not having bullet holes marking your body. Normal is remembering people you encounter. Normal is not wanting to slap someone's face because they said something stupid. I'm not normal, doctor. I'm a fool for choosing this line of business. I had better luck as a cop walking the night beat. I had better luck when I performed odd jobs for Salvatore Califano. Shit, I had better luck when Buddy Holly was still alive."

"Do you realize that you just put together more sentences than in the last six weeks combined? That is progress, Mr. Vega. And it's a sign of normalcy. Let me help you with that jacket. The guests are anxious to see you. And downstairs, I believe, is a very dry, very cold martini with your name on it."

Perplexed, Vega squinted as the doctor held his jacket.

"It's true. You may have a drink once again. One. You've been off medications for pain and infection for a week. You're good to go as far as I'm concerned."

"Doctor Dy..."

"My name is pronounced Dee, Mr. Vega. I've told you that nearly every single day. Surely you can remember."

"Tell you what, how 'bout I call you Vivian and you refer to me as Aloysius?"

"Rather intimate, don't you think, for a doctor-patient relationship?"

"I'm no longer taking your drugs and you're no longer in uniform. That dress, while it doesn't hug your curves, still announces there's a woman underneath."

"You forget that I'm married."

"My memory... not what it once was."

CHAPTER EIGHT

Juliet Regina Sanchez entered the world the following morning at 7:28 on Friday, February 14. The wrinkled cherub was healthy and slept in the crook of her mother's arm.

In the exhausted glow that followed the miracle of creation, Coralina felt a nearness to God that humbled and amazed her. For the first time she fully understood what her parish priest had referred to as a state of grace.

PART 2
The Missing Bride

CHAPTER NINE

The letter that would solve one mystery and cause a second was delivered on February 20 to the Merle Norman Cosmetic Studio. This explains the delay in reaching its intended destination: the Vega Detective Agency

The businesses were two blocks apart in downtown Cathedral City. Yet, the misdelivered letter took the better part of three weeks to eventually reach the agency, having been returned to the U.S. Postal Service for redelivery rather than hand-walked to the correct address as neighbors once did without a second thought.

But this was 1969, not 1959. Neighbors weren't as neighborly as before. No longer sharing cocktails or watching out for each other. No friendly conversations on the front lawn or sidewalk. If asked, many residents couldn't even summon the name of the family across the way. Being neighborly was something of a lost art.

Television carried most of the blame. Why spend time outside when indoors was more entertaining? Lucy and Desi tickled the funny bone far more than the couple next door. Any episode of The *Twilight Zone* was more thought-provoking than any yarn spun over the back fence.

National politics also was at fault. Roiled by war, race riots, and assassinations, people braced for another year unparalleled for its ability to shock and madden. The cultural landscape, meanwhile, was transforming the arts, sex, religion, and politics, creating moral ulcers in the heartland.

And so it was... that on a late morning in March of 1969, a morning of abundant sunshine and relaxed temperatures in the Southern California desert, a letter of unknown origin finally arrived at the Vega Detective Agency.

Nancy Randall inspected the smudged envelope that advertised its protracted journey. The envelope was addressed to A. Vega, 68675 D Street, Cathedral City, CA. The return address included an abbreviated name – L. Löwenstein – a city and state – Steilacoom, Washington – and two numbers. The first, 98388, was the postal code, a method designed six years earlier to simplify and speed delivery of the mail.

"Fat good it did with this letter."

Nancy's attention was drawn to the second number: 24171-157. Its eight digits meant it was not another postal code. Phone numbers were eliminated quickly. They were either five digits following two letters for the exchange prefix – AL1-8175 – or seven digits in all.

Perplexed, she considered other possibilities. The first three numbers could refer to the Dewey Decimal System arrangement for books about Christian Moral and Devotional Theology. But the five other numbers did not correspond with that classification's subsections on Hope, Love, and Sex. Aviation squawk codes use eight figures: zero to seven. And the now-extinct Yuli Indians of Northern California once counted the eight spaces between their fingers rather than the fingers themselves.

The answer, Nancy knew, fell outside the base of knowledge she had collected in her nineteen years. As a research librarian at the Welwood Murray Library in downtown Palm Springs, Nancy astonished patrons with her skill in locating hard-to-find information and her ability to remember every piece of information she ran across, from the name of Napoleon's horse to the opening date of baseball season.

In that capacity she once assisted Vega, helping the detective crack a local homicide case. Shy and pale, and skinny as an Ocotillo cactus, the teenager reminded Vega of the girls in gym class who were last to be picked. Except for her eyes. Behind black-framed cat-eye glasses, intensity coiled.

With Coralina at home with her baby, Nancy accepted Vega's offer to fill in at the agency. She quickly grasped the daily responsibilities, including opening the mail.

Still holding the envelope with the mysterious number, Nancy walked it to the coffeemaker where steam levitated above the spout. The office door squeaked open as she silently counted off twenty seconds.

"I usually take my coffee black, but I'm open to a dollop of glue now and then. I hear it cures amnesia."

"I didn't hear you come in, Mr. Vega. This will take a few more seconds, plus or minus. I can stop if you want that cup of coffee now."

"Please continue. I'm certain your chemistry experiment is more important. I'll be at my desk."

Vega hung his sports jacket on the Bauman coat rack before checking phone slips from the prior afternoon. Problems with his eyesight – at times double vision or vertigo – would come and go, usually attacking in the late afternoon. Rather than fight through the episodes, Vega would call a cab and head home until the symptoms abated, usually by five o'clock when the siren song of happy hour would lead him to Jilly's or the Purple Room.

Names on the phone slips piled on his desk were familiar: Scott Jarvis from the *Desert Post*, Lily Navarro from LAPD, Erika, and Vivian Dy for her weekly check-in. Nothing of note that might help pay the overhead. The initial flurry of interest that followed the Tooth Fairy Case three years ago had evaporated as fast as winnings at a blackjack table. The cases that followed – a missing crackpot, insurance fraud, adultery, and a triple homicide – kept the agency open.

Until now.

Vega was paying the salaries of two employees. Nancy was covering for Coralina, who needed a paycheck to care for the baby. Vega would have to shutter the agency without a sudden influx of cash. Start-up costs, travel, and overhead had sapped his initial grubstake. Without Erika footing his hospital bills and rehabilitation, he would be under water.

Amid the gloom, Nancy arrived holding a steaming cup of Folgers in one hand and the unsealed envelope in the other.

"Thanks. Plan to tell me why you were using the percolator to steam open an official piece of U.S. mail?"

"May I sit?"

"Help yourself."

"This letter took quite some time to be delivered. Three weeks. It was postmarked on February 13."

"Does it have a stamp?"

"Two. Each three cents. Each from the Liberty series."

"Maybe it got lost. It happens. Who's it from?"

"L. Löwenstein in Steilacoom, Washington."

"Never heard of him or the town. What's inside?"

"I haven't looked.

"Hand it over."

Vega examined the envelope before removing its contents, a yellowed magazine article. On it, drawn in pencil, were two words: "She's Alive."

Vega handed Nancy the clipping.

"Read it. My eyesight's not great this morning."

"Diplopia?"

"What?"

"The term for seeing two images of one object."

"No. I think the medical term is hangover. The article?"

After adjusting her glasses up the bridge of her nose, Nancy began reading.

Mary Showalter was not a celebrity. Nor was she known in Palm Springs social circles, where names like Sinatra, Hope and Crosby appear routinely in the local newspaper. There was nothing about her life that stood out. That is, until she disappeared in 1952, two days after becoming Mrs. Arthur Quail.

The missing bride did not simply vanish into thin air. Left behind were several tantalizing clues: her blood-smeared car that seemingly was moved in broad daylight, flowers left by a secret admirer, and a credit card receipt.

An army of investigators from Palm Springs and Riverside County, joined by police in other states as well as the FBI, sifted through the evidence for an entire year but were unable to find a body or coherent theory of what happened. Their principal suspect, her new husband Arthur, had a seemingly iron-clad alibi. Others – friends, colleagues, relatives – were investigated and eventually cleared.

A decade later, the whereabouts of Mary Showalter Quail remains a whodunnit worthy of an Agatha Christie novel.

"Go on."

"The article ends there. The rest continues on a different page that wasn't included. On the back is an advertisement for Chevrolet. Look at the envelope. There's an unusual number on the return address."

Vega examined the envelope.

"Eight digits. I suppose you're going to tell me what it means."

"I saw the number only minutes ago. I haven't had time to determine its meaning."

"And here I thought that encyclopedia of a brain of yours was infallible."

"If I see it, I remember it. It's a condition, Mr. Vega. Not a gift. I can't turn it off, except when I sleep."

"This condition, it bother you?"

"It did."

Nancy's curt answer didn't surprise the detective. He found her reluctance to talk about herself or her personal life similar to those who refused to reveal their religious beliefs or political views. It was a matter of privacy, a personal trait that seemed old-fashioned in an age of tell-all magazines and *Candid Camera*.

"How does it work? Once you see something, does it stay with you? Can you retrieve it anytime you want?"

"My memory works like a slide projector. When somebody gives me a date or a year or an event I witnessed, I see all these little slides. I scroll through to find the one I want."

"Amazing. Will this ability remain through your lifetime?"

"Doctors say it should, as long as I don't abuse my brain with alcohol or stimulants, suffer a brain injury or…sorry, Mr. Vega."

"Fall into a coma?"

"Yes."

"Don't worry. Stay off the booze and out of the line of fire. You'll be fine."

"You'll do the same, Mr. Vega? I enjoy working with you. It's more challenging than researching Napolean's horse."

"I'll work on staying out of the line of fire. But a good saloon at the end of the day is my promised land."

Without announcing why, Nancy went to Coralina's desk in the outer office where she retrieved a National Geographic atlas and a postal code directory.

"I purchased these the other day. We need more reference materials in the office."

"We call it the agency, Nancy. Office is too stuffy."

Nancy thumbed through the atlas until she found the page for Washington state.

"Steilacoom is in Pierce County, south of Seattle, near Tacoma. Know anyone from that area?"

"A few Eskimos."

Switching to the postal guide, Nancy found the page for Pierce County.

"Tacoma is the largest city, but it has several zip codes of its own. The area we're looking at, 98388, includes the town of Steilacoom and two islands: Ketron and McNeil."

Vega looked up from the phone slip he was considering.

"McNeil Island? I'll be damned."

"You know someone there?"

"Strangely, I do. There's a guy I know who lives on that island. You could say he's stuck there."

"Is he the one who sent the article?"

"Not his style. The guy I know avoids putting down anything in writing."

"This island, McNeil, does he own property there?"

"His uncle does. Uncle Sam."

Nancy's eyes flickered like the fleeting images on a casino slot machine calculating the winning line.

"There's a prison on McNeil Island."

"Not just any prison. A federal pen."

"You know a federal prisoner?"

"A few. And a few guys who ought to be behind bars. Call the prison administration at McNeil. See if I can speak to an inmate named John Roselli."

— • —

Scott Jarvis answered Vega's call on the third ring. The veteran police reporter and Vega had established a symbiotic relationship, trading information and corroborating leads on criminal cases.

"Is this Scott Jarvis, the celebrated journalist?"

"Flatter me or insult me, Vega. Each raises the same question: What do you want?"

"What do I want? You left a message for me."

"If I did, I forget why I called."

"You sound busy. I'll cut to the chase. Do you recall the disappearance of a woman here in 1952? Name's Mary Showalter. Married a guy name Quail only to disappear two days later."

"Sure do. Happened my first year at the *Post*. I was a copy boy at the time. The guys on the news desk dubbed it The Case of the Missing Bride. It scared the shit out of half the town. Never found a body. No ransom note. Just a shitload of conspiracy theories. The cops couldn't figure it out. The mayor at the time was pissed and embarrassed. Our paper got a lot of mileage out of that crime. Still does."

"How's that?"

"Every five years we roll out a story on the anniversary of her vanishing act. We claim to do it as a public service, but it's really just a means to boost single-copy sales before ABC."

"ABC cares about the story?"

"Not the network. ABC is the Audit Bureau of Circulation. Each fall newspapers like ours report our numbers: subscribers and rack sales. Advertisers use it to determine their spend levels for the coming year. Big bucks are on the line. What's your interest in a seventeen-year-old case?"

"Was there a reward offered?"

"I think it stands at twenty grand. Not as much as Sinatra offered for the return of his snotty son. But it'll buy you a decent three-bedroom home around town."

"I got a nice home. Who put up the reward, family?"

"Nah. Mom and Dad died when Mary was a teen. She had one sibling, a sister on the East Coast. The bank Mary worked at made the offer. You gonna tell me why you're interested?"

"Not yet. I don't know if it's worth chasing but I could use the payday. Can you have someone pull together all the stories? From the get-go to your last anniversary special. Can you do that for me, Jarvis?"

"It'll cost you. A Sherman pastrami for starters."

"You got it."
"And you keep me in the loop if you find anything."
"That too. Thanks."

— • —

The news from McNeil Island wasn't promising. Inmates aren't allowed to receive incoming phone calls. Nor could they make telephone calls except to names on an approved call list, a process that can take up to 15 days – assuming the inmate wanted you added.

After delivering that information, Nancy was dispatched to the *Desert Post* to pick up copies of the articles Jarvis had promised. She had a rapport with the newsroom librarian and was certain copies of the articles would be quickly forthcoming.

"I'll also see what I can find about the prison. Shouldn't take me long."

"No rush. The phone hasn't made a sound since I arrived."

CHAPTER TEN

Vega was snoring on the office couch when Nancy returned from her errands. She set the stack of papers on his desk and was about to find her own when he stirred.

"Whaddya find? Was only resting my eyes."

"Coffee? I can make a fresh pot."

"No. Have you read the articles?"

"Yes. But first, that eight-digit number on the return address? It's the number assigned a federal prisoner. Likely Mr. Löwenstein. The first five digits are unique to the inmate and the last three identify the federal court where he was sentenced."

"Good to know. Now, about the crime?"

For the next half-hour, Nancy provided a concise summary of the baffling disappearance of Mary Showalter and the mystery that still surrounds the case.

Mary was twenty-five when she disappeared. An account manager at CV Savings & Loan on North Palm Canyon Drive, she was described by her colleagues as hard-working and quiet. Her friends said Mary was somewhat shy. She lived alone in a one-bedroom apartment not far from the airport. Mary met her future husband a year earlier. He was a bank examiner for the Federal Deposit Insurance Corporation working out of a field office in

Riverside where he had an apartment. They met during one of his twice-annual stops at CV Savings. Arthur Quail was thirty-two at the time. According to Mary's friends, it was one of those love-at-first-sight moments.

Colleagues at the bank said Mary was in good spirits before she disappeared. Although Arthur was out of town, he was due back the following day. They planned to catch a movie, *Singin' in the Rain*, after dinner at Mary's apartment. For the short term, the couple agreed to keep two apartments until they found a house where they could start a family. A honeymoon trip would have to wait.

The evening she disappeared, Mary shopped for groceries at Mayfair Market on South Palm Canyon. She then met a coworker from the bank for dinner at Keedy's Fountain and Grill in Palm Desert. The colleague, Dorothy Conner, told police that Mary was giddy after spotting Lucille Ball at the grocery store. There was nothing in the conversation the two women shared that indicated to Dorothy that Mary was fearful or had any premonition of what was to come.

The two finished dinner around eight. Mary's parting words before heading to her car were "see you."

"When she didn't show up for work the next morning, Dorothy informed her boss, the bank manager. Mary was usually punctual, had not called in sick, and was not answering her phone."

"That's when police were called in?"

"There was no delay. The bank manager made the call. Police went to her apartment and found nothing amiss. No indication of foul play, no suicide note, no car, nothing. Remember the groceries she bought? They vanished too."

"The case of the hungry kidnapper?"

"Not only did Mary and the groceries disappear, so did her car... that is, before it turned up."

"Go on."

"Remember that she was last seen in the parking lot after dinner at Keedy's? When police arrived at Keedy's the next morning, the car was gone. A bulletin for her car was issued. A fifty-two Mercury Monterey. Blue."

"Hardtop or..."

"Convertible."

"Where was it found?"

"At Keedy's, the very next day. Almost in the same spot."

Pausing to allow the bizarre news to sink in, Nancy adjusted her skirt before continuing.

"Inside were three bags of groceries – undisturbed. Police later compared the items with the register receipt. Nothing had been taken. There's more."

"Let's have it."

"There were bloodstains. In the front seat. And her clothes..."

"Yeah?"

"Her clothes were found in the front seat...neatly folded on the passenger side."

"Were they bloodstained too? Torn?"

Staring at her hands, Nancy shook her head.

"Were they the same clothes she had worn at dinner the night before?"

An affirmative nod.

"All of them? Nothing missing? Bra, underwear?"

"Nothing."

Realizing his temporary assistant was uncomfortable with the topic, Vega pared his questions to a final few before deciding to take the clippings home.

"What about her purse and car keys?"

"Missing."

"You said earlier that the husband was out of town? Where?"

"He was in Redlands. Had an appointment with Bank of America."

"Redlands is less than an hour away. Why didn't he come to Palm Springs that night? The night Mary disappeared."

"He told police he stayed at his apartment in Riverside. It was closer and he wanted to pick up extra clothes for the weekend with Mary."

"Doesn't hold much water. Not too many guys would pass on a night with their new bride. The article said he had an iron-clad alibi. What was it?"

"His neighbor saw him that evening entering the Riverside apartment. Said they exchanged in small talk."

"Only a few more questions. I need to get home to rest. I'll take the clips."

"I have printouts about McNeil Island and the penitentiary."

"Save those for the morning. Now, uh, when did the husband find out his bride went missing?"

"After Mary failed to show up at work, the bank manager reached Mr. Quail at his apartment."

"Does it seem curious to you that the branch manager would have the bank examiner's home telephone number handy?"

"He got it from a Rolodex on Mary's desk. Mr. Quail told police he raced to Palm Springs after the call. He met officers at Mary's apartment. Maintained his innocence from the start. And, as I said, he had an alibi that held up."

"Convenient."

— • —

That evening, after a two-hour nap and a half-hour swim, Vega fixed a Beefeater martini and then settled at the kitchen table with the batch of clippings. The case of Mary Showalter Quail was as beguiling as it was bizarre. The more he read, the further the case disappeared down a rabbit hole.

Staff at Keedy's confirmed to police that Mary's car was not in the parking lot when they arrived for work the morning after her dinner with Dorothy. Yet, there it was later that day, parked in the same area where it had been the night before.

A layer of sand and dust coated the exterior as if the car had been driven in remote areas of the desert. Blood was found on the passenger seat. Testing later proved the blood type belonged to Mary. There were unidentified fingerprints, mostly smeared, on the back seat.

A growing sense of frustration was evident in the early days of the investigation, judging from the newspaper clips. Investigators were at a loss to explain the picture the evidence was painting. How could Mary have been overpowered, injured, and forced to strip naked in the parking lot without attracting attention? Keedy's remained open until 10 p.m. and receipts showed a steady stream of customers that evening.

Two days after Mary's disappearance, Arthur Quail made a brief public statement. He asked for help from "the good citizens of greater Palm Springs" in locating his "beloved Mary." He repeated what he had told police. He was at his apartment in Riverside the night the abduction took place. When asked if he feared for Mary's life, Arthur answered: "What husband wouldn't be concerned?"

The following day, CV Savings & Loan offered a $15,000 reward for information leading to Mary's whereabouts. The branch manager, Tobias Blackpool, said he would increase the amount each week until Mary was found. Vega shook his head at the stupidity of the statement, certain that police had explained to Blackpool that such a stipulation would only encourage those with information to delay coming forward until the reward had grown considerably.

A recent photo of Mary was circulated with the reward information. Vega studied the photo displayed on the front page of the Post. The pleasant-faced brunette gazed off the page with a relaxed, almost wistful smile. The description that followed – hairstyle, dress, height and weight – could have matched half the female population of 1952.

Contrary to public statements by the mayor and chief of police, the newspaper disclosed that investigators feared the worst. Mary had been abducted not for ransom, but by someone intent on harming his victim. Someone fearless enough to return Mary's car to the same parking lot a day later. In daylight no less. What type of person would risk being seen merely to taunt or confuse police?

Investigators were insistent that Mary was abducted by a lone wolf, not a criminal gang, though their reasoning was not fully explained. Vega jotted another note. See if Jarvis knew where those Post reporters were today.

By the end of the second week, with no new information on Mary's disappearance, national and international news took over the front page.

MORE THAN 7,000 ENEMY SOLDIERS WERE KILLED IN ONE WEEK OF FIGHTING IN KOREA.

THE U.S. DETONATED A THERMONUCLEAR BOMB IN THE MARSHALL ISLANDS.

WORKERS COMPLETED CONSTRUCTION OF THE UNITED NATIONS BUILDING IN NEW YORK CITY.

THE CALIFORNIA SUPREME COURT UPHELD THE CONSTITUTIONALITY OF A LAW REQUIRING STATE, COUNTY AND LOCAL GOVERNMENT WORKERS TO PLEDGE LOYALTY OATHS.

RESIDENTS AND BUSINESSES IN THE PACIFIC NORTHWEST WERE ORDERED TO REDUCED ENERGY CONSUMPTION BECAUSE OF THE WATER SHORTAGE AFFECTING HYDROELECTRIC DAMS.

DARKNESS GETS THERE FIRST

— • —

Mary's abduction returned to the front page of the *Post* weeks later when a bank colleague belatedly told the newspaper that Mary had received a dozen red roses from a secret admirer shortly before her disappearance. Investigators, confronted with the news, traced an order of flowers to the bank from a floral shop on Ramon Road. Details about the person who placed the order were lacking, police claimed.

Further leaks from the investigation followed as reporters dug for leads that would keep their bylines on the front page. An old school chum revealed that Mary had been receiving phone calls at work that had left her shaken. This was subsequently confirmed by co-workers at the bank who recalled Mary hanging up abruptly on several calls to her desk. On one such call, Mary declared, "I told you. I'm getting married," before banging down the receiver.

No information on the mysterious caller was uncovered. Arthur Quail said he was unaware of any past boyfriends that Mary had mentioned. Schoolmates recalled one boy who took Mary to their senior prom. But, as investigators found, the young man in question had joined the Navy after high school and was currently serving aboard the USS Essex off the Korean coast.

As was his usual custom, Vega made a list of questions and topics to pursue in his notebook. High on the list were subjects to interview: Arthur Quail, his neighbor, *Post* reporters, and the manager of the savings & loan. That is assuming, all or some were still around.

Armed with a second martini, Vega left the kitchen table for the hammock in the back yard to consider what he had learned. Mary's body had never been recovered. No one had been brought to trial. Seventeen years later, an inmate reaches out to Vega from McNeil Island, sending a partial magazine clipping about the crime with a statement that Mary Showalter was alive.

Vega had been mailed a jigsaw puzzle with pieces that, if they ever could be found and assembled, could net him a healthy grubstake that could keep the agency open and offer him a reason to carry on.

Warmed by the vodka, Vega drifted onto the cusp of sleep. A wayward breeze carried a whiff of rosemary and sage – a scent that retrieved a memory, faint and ghostly, of a floral perfume. As the air stilled, the breeze took with it his fleeting recollection.

CHAPTER ELEVEN

"**Did you know that** handwriting and dreams are similar?"

Vega was at his desk the next morning, barely into his first cup of coffee, when Nancy raised the question.

"I'm sure you're about to tell me."

"Both provide insight into the psyche and personality of a person."

"You're interrupting my morning coffee to tell me this why?

Brushing off Vega's surliness, Nancy pulled over a chair.

"I spent yesterday afternoon at the library researching graphology – the study of handwriting. Had to check the Dewey Decimal catalogue, even with my background. Handwriting analysis is lumped in with tarot cards, fortune telling, phrenology, of all things. I made a note to write the Library of Congress. Graphology is a serious field of study, not a Ouija gimmick. That error ought to be rectified."

"Of course. Why are you telling me this?"

"I thought it important to understand the traits of the persons who sent us the magazine article."

"You said persons, as in two."

"I'm convinced that one person wrote 'She's Alive' and another addressed the envelope. If both writers are inmates, the handwriting should help us identify Mr. Löwenstein's writing companion."

"Us?"

"Yes, Mr. Vega. Us. You and me. You need an assistant on this case and, well, here I am."

"I need assistance? And who said this was a case? A case is an investigation that pays."

"You suffer vertigo and migraines, Mr. Vega. You have difficulty driving and need to get to McNeil Island. I have a car, valid license, and an unblemished driving record. To your second point, the reward. Before I went to the library, I stopped at CV Savings & Loan. I spoke to Mr. Blackpool, the branch manager. He's still there. He said the reward now stands at $20,000. He was surprised we were re-opening the investigation."

"There you go again. Using we."

"I meant the agency. I told Mr. Blackpool the case may be of interest to the Vega Detective Agency."

"Did he ask why?"

"He did. I said Mary's disappearance came up in a conversation. He pressed me for more but I said I had to run. Do you want to know more about the handwriting?"

"Sure. Go ahead. You seem to be one step ahead of me."

Nancy brightened, like a child hearing applause after a first piano recital.

"Human beings are complex, often confusing creatures. It can be difficult to understand our own behaviors and motivations, let alone somebody else's, so we look for clues anywhere we can, including in handwriting. Jotting down words or images, a seemingly small action, can reveal more about your personality than you might think. That's why I found graphology so interesting. It's akin to body language. You can attempt to gain a deeper understanding of a person's motivations or personality."

"Cut to the chase."

"Unlike nonverbal gestures or dreams, handwriting leaves a trace. When handwriting analysis is done properly, it can provide insights into someone's personality style, level of intelligence, even character."

"The chase?"

"I'm not a handwriting expert, however... The person who wrote 'She's Alive' on the article scribbled in pencil. He likely has a limited education or has difficulty holding a pencil, perhaps from an injury or deformity. Whoever addressed the envelope, in pen, is highly educated or highly trained. A perfectionist. If the two are working together, one is the leader, the other a lackey or disciple."

"Well, this perfectionist is now squatting like other minions behind bars on a rusty metal toilet in a cramped cell that stinks to high heaven."

Vega stood and made his way to the couch, where he stretched out, leaving Nancy sitting by his desk.

"Headache?"

"Yeah. I'll be fine. Tell me this, Nancy, why would two inmates send such a cryptic note? Why not set it down in a letter? Make their intentions clear."

"Rules allow guards or the warden to open and inspect mail, coming or going, as long as the mail is not privileged, like correspondence to and from an attorney. The sender knew his envelope would be opened before it was mailed."

Impressed with Nancy's ability to use evidence to form a theory, he asked how they could confirm the identity of both inmates.

Adjusting her chair so she once again faced Vega, the prim teenager didn't hesitate.

"We already know that L. Löwenstein's name was on the envelope, likely with his prisoner identification number."

"And the other one?"

"John Roselli. You said you know each other. He knows where you work."

"If John Roselli wanted to reach me, he certainly wouldn't resort to a cryptic note. Roselli's an in-your-face type."

Rather than crestfallen, Nancy responded quickly.

"Mr. Roselli is the one who addressed the envelope. The perfectionist."

"Nancy, I appreciate your due diligence in this matter, but you don't know John Roselli. I do. You don't make your way in the family business like he did by helping others. You move up the ranks by making things happen. Stir things up. Take action. Break some eggs. If Roselli is involved in this note, there is only one reason. To help himself. What about this other guy, the disciple? You have a theory about him and Mary? Of course you do."

Nancy ran her thumb and index finger in opposite directions across her lip as if she were stroking an invisible mustache.

"The only way this inmate, or any other, would know that Mary Showalter is alive is to have seen her. There, at the prison. Likely visiting an inmate. We have no way of knowing whom she was visiting. But she was recognized by someone who once knew her. Who knew her well enough to remember what she looked like seventeen years ago."

"Go on."

"Seeing her must have driven him rather nuts, I would think. From what we've learned, Mary Showalter was either kidnapped or killed."

"Or both. Or neither."

"Or both or neither. Either way she vanished. Suddenly, Mary appears out of the blue. The odds of her being recognized after all this time are minuscule, but someone is so certain that it's her that he reaches outside the prison walls to find proof. He reaches out to you, Mr. Vega."

"I told you, John Roselli is the only guy I know holed up there. Sending me a magazine article is not his style. Definitely not."

"But he may have helped this other inmate. Remember, two people sent that mail judging by the handwriting."

"I know, the leader and the disciple. Listen, you have a good imagination, but…"

"You need to talk to him."

"Who."

"Mr. Roselli."

"I can't. Remember? Prisoners can't take calls. And I very much doubt I'm on his guest list."

"Do you know someone who might be?"

CHAPTER TWELVE

Unlike most women who inhabit Palm Springs' highest social circles, Erika Lake was neither a blueblood nor among the top echelon of Hollywood entertainers. After fleeing the Midwest as a teenager, she took the sorts of jobs a pretty girl could get in Tinsel Town, working in retail and modeling while nibbling at the edges of filmdom. Most roles as a featured extra ended on the cutting room floor. Her few appearances that made it to theater screens were dubbed. Erika couldn't sing and her dialogues were marred by a stammer that elicited chuckles from co-stars and stage crews.

Still, Erika persevered, using her looks and business acumen to remain on the payroll of several studios and in photoshoots for *Movieland, Modern Screen*, and other fan magazines. Audiences were kind, until Louella Parsons went public with news about Erika's speech impediment, the voice-overs, and an alleged illicit relationship with studio mogul Harry Cohen.

The gossip column, which appeared in more than 700 newspapers, devastated Erika. She left Hollywood and aborted her career as an actress, escaping to Las Vegas on the arm of John Roselli. At the time, the one-time saloon town was undergoing a transformation that would make it the mecca of gambling and entertainment. Hotels and casinos were going up along The Strip in quick succession: the Sahara, the Riviera, the Dunes, the Tropicana, and the Stardust.

Erika used her time there to great advantage. She found her way easily among the Jewish and Italian mobsters who trusted Roselli to keep a watchful eye on their investments. Men such as Bugsy Siegel, Moe Dalitz, and Tony Accardo.

"The boys were gentlemen at all times to me and treated me like a queen," Erika once told Vega. "It was like a family. You could go to any of the hotels, and you didn't pay for anything. If you wanted to go to the bar and get a couple of drinks, there would be no check."

As for the relationships she formed during her time in Sin City, Erika told friends she would rather die than surrender those secrets. The exception she made was Sinatra.

"Of course, we had a romantic relationship. I would have been crazy not to have had one with him. To just be friends with Frank Sinatra? I'd have been a fool!"

Her time in Las Vegas ended when she met and then married Eugene Vanderpol, a shipping magnate worth nearly as much as Aristotle Onassis. They made their home in Palm Springs where Erika remade herself into one of the desert's great benefactors and a flamboyant party hostess. Surgery and a speech therapist took care of the nagging stutter. The couple adopted a daughter, a Hungarian orphan.

Erika's life in Palm Springs became a whirlwind of parties at the Racquet Club with the likes of Marlene Dietrich, Robert Taylor, Ginger Rogers, and Spencer Tracy, and dinners at the Chi Chi, Melvyn's, and Johnny Costa's.

Not one to hobnob with movie stars, Eugene instead introduced Erika to industry moguls and political leaders like Jack and Robert Kennedy. The couple were present at Bing Crosby's home when the president invited Marilyn Monroe to perform at his birthday fundraiser at Madison Square Garden. They attended the event, entertained by Ella Fitzgerald, Marie Callas, Peggy Lee and, of course, Marilyn's sultry rendition of *Happy Birthday*.

Those heady days seemed to draw to an end with a series of unimaginable tragedies. Less than three months after the party, Monroe was found dead in her Brentwood home. A year later Jack Kennedy was assassinated. Then, in 1966, Erika's adopted daughter died when her sports car careened off a cliff above Palm Desert.

Erika retreated from the world following the funeral, remaining hidden in her mansion much like Miss Havisham, the wealthy spinster in *Great Expectations*. She emerged months later, appearing like pale afternoon sunlight, muted and colorless. A divorce from Eugene soon followed. Eventually, Erika resumed her philanthropy with a singular focus on raising funds for a new hospital, an effort spearheaded by Bob and Dolores Hope.

Vega owed Erika far more than he could ever repay. Yet here he was, like a trust fund baby, needing to tap her generosity once again.

— • —

"**Aloysius, how nice of you** to call. I thought you had forgotten me."

"Never. You're my lifeline."

"I'm not sure I know how to handle such advanced flirtation. You must want something."

"I need to reach Roselli."

"You do know that John is in jail."

"Prison is the correct term. And, yes, I do know where he is. I was hoping you could get me in to see him."

"You could rob a bank."

"The thought has crossed my mind. I was thinking more along the lines of a visitor's pass. I thought you might contact him to put me on the list."

"What is this all about, Aloysius?"

"I'm trying to locate a missing girl. Roselli might know a thing or two about it."

"John has his weaknesses, but kidnapping girls is not one of them. You're leaving me in the dark. I don't like that."

Vega summarized the puzzle of the missing bride and that Roselli might know the inmate who wrote Vega.

"Seems like a stretch, Aloysius. Are you that desperate? Running after reward money from so long ago? If keeping the agency afloat is your concern, I could loan you the money."

"You bankrolled my hospitalization, Erika. Seeing that I intend to pay you back at some point, it makes no sense to take out a loan from the same piggy bank."

"Aloysius, I've told you more than once that you do not need to repay me. It was not a loan. More like a wise investment in my sense of security. However, if you must see John and go on this madcap adventure, I know someone who can arrange a meeting."

CHAPTER THIRTEEN

Accompanied by his acting assistant, Vega arrived at Palm Springs Airport at 5:30 Friday morning. Erika had offered her private aircraft for the trip north, avoiding the long drive up Interstate 5. Nancy was excited. She had never left terra firma.

Inside the hangar, standing between them and the Piaggio 808 jet, was a tall man in his early fifties. Big eared with an ample nose and a receding line of graying hair, he was dressed well in the manner of a businessman who scores. Vega knew the look. The type of tough guy who enjoys good bourbon and likely has Chagalls and Renoirs adorning the walls of his principal home.

"I take it you're not the pilot."

"You're late."

"If you're not the pilot, and you don't dress the part of a mechanic, I have to assume you're a friend of Erika."

A smile flickered before disappearing like a serpent's tongue.

"I represent John Roselli. Miss Lake contacted me, asking that I arrange for you to meet with my client. I assume you are Aloysius Vega."

"I am."

"Who's this?"

"This? This is Nancy Randall, my assistant who will accompany me. I didn't catch your name."

The two exchanged a brief handshake.

"Sidney Korshak. I understood only you would be meeting with my client."

"Miss Randall will remain outside when I meet with your client."

"Fair enough. My reason for greeting you here is to go over the restrictions the prison system and I are placing on your visit."

"Don't worry, I forgot to bring the bottle of scotch I wanted to give your client."

The pilot, who had been inspecting the sleek Italian jet, worked his way around the tail. Tipping his cap, he moved to escort Nancy to the steps and into the aircraft. After the two boarded, Korshak briefed Vega. The detective would be allowed no more than fifteen minutes with Roselli. No conversation about Roselli's own case could occur.

"His conviction is being appealed. I don't want anything that might endanger that effort. Understand? As for why you want to meet with my client, I have no knowledge. As far as I'm concerned, it's a private matter. However, to get you proper access on such short notice, I left word with prison administration that you are working for me in the capacity of an investigator. As such, I'm sure you will understand that, for that purpose, you are acting on my behalf and are expected to conduct yourself accordingly."

"Understood. But if I'm working on your behalf I expect to be paid."

"You'll find an envelope on your seat. Any questions, Mr. Vega?"

"None."

"Safe travels to you and Miss Randall."

— • —

Vega spent most of the two-hour flight in silent reflection, avoiding any opportunity to view the California coastline from 41,000 feet.

Instead, he stared ahead to the cockpit where the pilot and Nancy were engaged in a lively conversation about the intricacies of the control panel of the tiny turbojet, certain that his young assistant could earn her pilot's license by the time they landed.

Closing his eyes, the detective turned his attention to John Roselli. The two had locked horns not long after Vega arrived in Palm Springs. Both had done favors for Erika and remained in her debt. They made nice for her benefit.

As a young man, Roselli cut his teeth in Al Capone's outfit before being dispatched to Los Angeles where he oversaw the mob's business interests, including the horse-racing betting wire and Hollywood's film studios. Known around town as Handsome Johnny, Roselli dated starlets including Jean Harlow and Marilyn Monroe and arranged liaisons for bigshots like Jack Kennedy. His success in Los Angeles earned him a ticket to Las Vegas where he kept watch on various casino operations for the bosses in Chicago and the East Coast.

Law enforcement officers believed Roselli was responsible for more than thirteen murders, including a role in the assassination of Benjamin "Bugsy" Siegel at his Beverly Hills home in 1947. Still, Roselli was usually able to escape conviction. Now 64 and in ill health, the law had finally put him away. Roselli had been convicted the prior year of racketeering for his role in scamming card players at the Friars Club in Beverly Hills. He was sentenced to serve five years at McNeil.

Any clues the mobster was holding about Mary Showalter would remain unknown until the two met at the island prison. Was Nancy right? Did Roselli encounter a fellow inmate who claimed to have seen a woman who vanished seventeen years ago? Perhaps Roselli had something else in mind.

After a brief glance out the window at the carpet of gray clouds, Vega considered Mary's disappearance and the oddest turn in that cold case. One month after she vanished, Mary's credit card statement arrived in the mail. The card had been used at an all-night gas station in Twentynine Palms just hours after she disappeared. The former supply town for gold miners rests at the southern edge of the Mojave Desert, some fifty miles north of Palm Springs. Certain this lead would break open the case, investigators found it instead to be a bizarre dead end.

With the credit card statement in hand, police made the hour-plus drive to the high desert town to interview the gas station attendants. The two men who ran the business claimed they were unaware of the woman's disappearance. They lived nearby in a decaying trailer park with no television set. Newspapers sold in a rack outside their gas station provided the men additional income, but they insisted they never follow the news. They told detectives they played cards when not working.

According to an article in the *Desert Post*, the two men identified Mary from photos police provided. They told detectives the woman who entered the store to pay for gas appeared to be hiding her face with a scarf. Her forehead displayed a minor injury, as if she had been badly scratched. The men told police the woman was unaccompanied when she came in. It did appear, they said, that someone was waiting in the car. Neither could offer a description or whether the person was male or female.

The newspaper article left Vega with a host of questions. Was the companion sitting in the passenger seat or behind the wheel? Why couldn't the two attendants offer a description of the companion? Why were the two men both working at that late hour? The receipt for the gas purchase bore what appeared to be Mary's signature, police later told reporters. Comparisons had been made between the receipt and documents Mary had signed as part of her responsibilities at the savings and loan.

On their way to the airport, Nancy raised a question that never would have occurred to Vega. How did Mary obtain the credit card?

As a single woman, she would typically be denied credit – even if she had an income that could demonstrate she would be able to make monthly payments. A male family member would have to act as co-signer. If Mary obtained the credit card after she married Arthur, the card would be under his name.

Those answers, Vega told Nancy, could only be found in the case file. Gaining access to those police documents would occur on their return trip to Palm Springs.

— • —

Blindly cutting its way through the dull overcast that hung over their destination, the Italian-made jet descended rapidly, eventually revealing emerald green farmland 2,000 feet below. Wipers did their best to repel the drizzle that sprayed the cockpit window. From the co-pilot's seat Nancy shouted to Vega to tighten his seatbelt. Heading into the prevailing wind, the jet banked slowly left, bucking like a rodeo horse before leveling off then gliding as it found the runway.

Seeing farmland rather than a downtown on either side of the plane, Vega shouted a question over the whine of the twin engines now throttling down.

"I thought Seattle was a major city. This looks like Podunk, USA."

The pilot replied that they landed at Thun Field in Pierce County where a driver was waiting.

"It's closer to McNeil than Seattle's airport."

The jet stopped in front of two vanilla-colored hangars. A black sedan parked nearby would take them to the ferry terminal in Steilacoom, according to the brief note Korshak left with the money.

Rain, cold and bleak, smeared their vision as Vega and Nancy dashed from the plane to their ride. Once inside, they were handed a towel to share. The driver was a middle-aged man in an ill-fitted coat and a demeanor as raw as the surrounding sky.

"How long until we reach the ferry at Steilacoom?"

Nancy's question was met with a grunt.

"Not long."

— • —

Still damp and chilled by the time they arrived at the Steilacoom ferry landing, the duo waited in silence with their sullen driver for a signal to board what looked like a glorified tugboat. The sixty-foot wooden vessel knocked against the tired wooden pier, buffeted by a sullen wind and waves the shade of blue smoke. Fifteen minutes later, a dockhand who Vega likened to a union bus driver with a bad attitude waved them forward. Walking briskly but carefully along the wooden dock, the pair joined five men huddled inside.

The two found solace on a wooden bench beneath the pilothouse as the ferry cast off into the salted arteries of Puget Sound. The smell of diesel oil, sink drains, and wet rags promised eventual asphyxiation. Sensing a spell of vertigo, Vega closed his eyes as the boat bounced and swayed, praying the nausea wouldn't worsen. Nancy sat next to him shivering as she grasped the handrail to her right. Her soggy hair dangled to her shoulders like strands of overcooked spaghetti.

His eyes still shut, Vega draped an arm around Nancy's shoulders, pulling her close for Neanderthal warmth. An uneasy moment passed before she scooched closer. Fifteen minutes later, the curtain of rain parted slowly, revealing their first glimpse of McNeil Island.

CHAPTER FOURTEEN

A **cluster of white-washed buildings** appeared above a shoreline of rock and bony driftwood, surfacing out of the gloom like a ghost ship run aground. Behind, a wall of towering Douglas firs lined the hillside, their tips hidden by low gray clouds. The choppy ride eased as the ferry's engine slowed to a low churn. The water's surface flattened into a dark, glassy calm, disturbed only by the slow wake trailing behind. Within a hundred yards of the shore wooden signs staked in the water appeared, warning unauthorized vessels to "KEEP OUT!"

Government owns every inch of the island, Nancy told Vega as the boat drifted the last few feet, guided by the tide and memory.

"The prison's been home to bandits, sociopaths, con artists, and killers since 1875. It predates not only Alcatraz and the entire federal penitentiary system, but even the State of Washington itself. In addition to your Mr. Roselli, prisoners have included Robert Stroud and..."

"The Birdman of Alcatraz?"

"That's him. He was here from 1909 to 1912 for killing a bartender. Before he was sent to Leavenworth and Alcatraz."

"Who else?"

"Well, there's Roy Gardner, a train robber. And Mickey Cohen, the gangster. Samuel Bowers, he's here now, was the imperial wizard of the Klan. He was convicted two years ago for killing three civil rights activists."

"Lovely company."

"Alvin Karpis was paroled just last month."

"Karpis? The heavy in the Ma Barker Gang?"

"That's him. I looked up his history. When he was ten years old, he was smashing shop windows to steal. Before he was twenty, he was sentenced to ten years at a reformatory. He escaped, and after a few months of adding to his record, he ended up at the state prison of Kansas. This was 1930. He met Fred Barker there, formed a gang, and robbed banks, kidnapped, and murdered. You know what Mr. Karpis was quoted as saying?"

"Tell me."

"When asked how many men he had killed, he answered: 'Well, I did try to count them once.'"

"And he just got out?"

"Freed in January after thirty-three years behind bars."

"What did your research find about Mr. Roselli?"

Nancy re-combed her damp dark hair with her fingers, her attention turned to the men looping ropes over thick, splintered posts along the long pier that creaked with their footsteps. She waited until they boarded a small bus that wheezed and rocked its way up the road bank leading to the prison.

"He is a dangerous man, Mr. Vega. He's imprisoned for fraud, but he started his career in Chicago with Al Capone before working for the Mafia in Los Angeles and Las Vegas. This man you say you know that you are going to see, is a gangster."

"So I'm told."

Her eyes, never flinching, burned with questions much like a daughter facing her wayward father. Questions Nancy decided would have to wait.

The bus slowed to a stop at a security gate outside a chained fence topped with reels of razor wire. On the other side were a half-dozen buildings, each no higher than three stories. Guard towers marked the corners of the compound. The bus driver signaled for his passengers to disembark and to enter the building to the right.

"You'll get your visitor passes there after filling out the required forms. When your visitation ends, the bus will be waiting here. I won't. This is my last shuttle of the day. Next shift is Andy's."

— • —

After each filled out the three-page visitor information form, Vega and Nancy quietly waited with the others for escorts to arrive. Per his agreement with Korshak, only Vega would meet with Roselli.

"I get fifteen minutes. You gonna wait here? At least it's dry."

"Only if I can't talk my way into seeing the library. I read that it's large. Over 15,000 volumes. Other prisons were modeled after it."

"Good luck with that."

Outside the smudged windows, rain resumed its steady assault, filling the island with monotony and dreariness like a hopeless disease.

CHAPTER FIFTEEN

John Roselli embraced the ideal of the gentleman soldier, a man of honor and dignity, who commanded respect as well as fear. To his friends he was loyal, charming, and generous. They obeyed him without question. Mafia leaders, dons of national stature like Meyer Lansky and Frank Costello, considered him a rare asset. They sent him to Las Vegas where he orchestrated deals and kept a watchful eye on the mob's money. Smooth as silk, he carried business cards that labeled his occupation as "Strategist." Another, under an assumed name, identified him as "World Traveler, International Lover" and "Last of the Big Spenders."

Yet, here he was, sitting across from Vega in the basement of the prison's administration building wearing the striped uniform of a federal inmate instead of his custom-tailored, two-piece Italian suits. Roselli's jauntiness and characteristic dark sunglasses were gone along with his perpetual suntan, replaced by a pudgy, pallid face and a hacking cough that sounded like a wounded hound.

"You look like shit."

"Emphysema. Bronchitis too. This fuckin' place ain't helping. Fuckin' damp and cold can put down a younger man. For me, it's a death sentence. What did Korshak tell you?"

"Nothing. Except not to discuss your Friars Club rap. This lung shit you got, contagious?"

"Nah. Had it as a kid. It comes and goes. Right now, I can't shake it. Been in the ward. Gave me oxygen and pills. Helped. I hear you lost a lung gettin' shot."

"Didn't lose it. Deflated then fixed. You got something to tell me, John? We got all of fifteen minutes."

Roselli surveyed the other inmates, visitors, and two bored guards positioned at each end of the table that spanned the width of the room.

"I want you to get me the fuck out of here."

Vega's laugh was loud enough to draw the attention of the few others in the room, including the two guards.

"How am I to do that? This place is like Alcatraz if you hadn't noticed."

For the next several minutes, Vega listened to Roselli cough up phlegm and outline a deal the mobster thought would get his sentenced reduced. He was getting his hair cut in the prison barbershop where an inmate rattled on about how he was certain that a girl who disappeared for seventeen years was alive.

"This is a guy named Löwenstein?"

"Yeah. He kept saying he was sure he saw this broad. Said everyone assumed she was dead. But here she was, visiting an inmate. Says she was having a nice chat with Karpis."

"Karpis?"

"Yeah. That guy. Public enemy number one, if you can believe it."

"This guy, he saw them together? Here? When was this?"

"Around Christmas."

"I heard Karpis got paroled."

"He did. Can you believe it? Guy's been in the can for thirty fucking years! I'm going out of my mind thinking I'm doing five, but this guy, he does three decades in this hell hole. Get this. The last five he's out of the cell block. Living in Summit House as a trustee. He does work for the guards. Warden calls him a model prisoner. They even taught him how to drive a car with an automatic transmission. Never had those when he was first sent up. He even drove the school bus for kids here on the island. Model prisoner, my ass. Bank robberies, kidnapping, they say ten killings in all. He goes free as a fuckin' bird and I'm sitting here for allegedly cheating big shots who were dealing cards. Where's the fairness in that?"

"You meet him? Karpis?"

"By the time I got here he was already out of the block as a trustee."

"What about this other guy, Löwenstein? The inmate who claimed he saw this missing girl with Karpis and sent me the magazine article. What were the circumstances?"

Roselli's answer was aborted by another foul coughing jag.

"He swears he saw the two inside the guards' quarters. That's the story he told over and over. He was certain it was her. Said they worked together at one point in Palm Springs. At a savings and loan."

The connection to Mary was now obvious to Vega.

Roselli told Vega he made a point of sitting next to Löwenstein later at mealtime, chumming him up. Rather than get all the details in front of other inmates in the dining hall, Roselli waited until later when the two were on break in the prison yard. They struck up another conversation and the topic of "the missing broad" was broached. Roselli learned about her disappearance and the resulting police investigation that went nowhere fast.

"He mention her by name?"

"Mary Showalter."

"He say anything that would lead you to think he had anything to do with her disappearance?"

Roselli spat a glob of phlegm on the floor before answering.

"Don't think so, but it don't matter.

"What's he in for?"

"Bank fraud. Now let's get to why I wanted to see your ugly mug. Guards are about to end visiting hours. Listen up, here's my deal."

For the waning minutes of their visit, Roselli outlined what he wanted. Intrigued by Mary's case, he told Löwenstein he knew someone on the outside, in Palm Springs, who could track down Mary.

"I told my buddy I knew a famous detective who not only could solve the case but was such the gentleman that he would park half the reward money in a bank account for your eventual release."

"He knew about the reward?"

"No shit."

"Why all the subterfuge? The magazine clipping, the two-word note?"

"My idea. I told my friend he needed to bait the hook to get this famous detective interested. Sure took you a long time to bite."

Roselli was not telling the whole story. A piece of the puzzle was missing. A big piece.

"What's your play, John? You want the reward money? Is that it?"

"You kidding me, right? I'll do fine when I get out. But not if I die in this rathole. What I want, Vega, is for you to tell the parole board that I helped solve your case. That I was the one who saw Mary. I remembered her picture from the magazine and reached out to you. We both become heroes."

"You want to cut Löwenstein out and take the credit."

"That's it in a nutshell. Help me get out early, Vega, and I can do for you what only I can do for you."

"And what's that, John?"

"Make you rich. That reward money? It's all yours. A small down payment for your assistance. Capisce?"

Vega pressed ahead. He needed more answers.

"I need to hear directly from Löwenstein. I need you to ..."

"Nope. You go through me. Understand? You go through me."

"It might speed the investigation."

One of the two guards in the room barked that visitors had one minute remaining.

"I guess you don't understand my offer, Vega."

"John, this guy wrote me directly. The letter was addressed to me. It had my name and the agency's address on the envelope. I need to speak to him."

"I never gave him your identity. He got the magazine from the library. I told him to scribble 'She's Alive' on it to get your attention. I addressed the envelope and mailed it. Got your address from Erika. She and I talk from time to time."

"She knows what's going on? Is she in on this deal of yours?"

Roselli smiled. It was the only time he did.

"Time's up! Visiting hours are over."

Vega and the aging mobster stood.

"So, detective, we got a deal?"

"What if I don't find Mary? What if she's been dead all these years? What if your buddy was mistaken about her?"

"I hope that's not the case, Vega. For your sake…and mine."

CHAPTER SIXTEEN

The return flight to Palm Springs was uneventful...except for the menacing shadows that produced a clammy sweat that ran from Vega's neck to the arch of his back. He waved off Nancy's concern for his welfare, asking only to be left alone.

"I'll be fine."

He knew better. The peculiar smell of decayed flowers had returned. With it, a warm metallic taste and the fear of suffocation. As he did on the earlier flight, he kept his eyes closed, this time fearing if he turned his head to glance out the jet's window a sinister presence would appear, riding weightless on the wing.

The haunting spells he encountered in the ICU had returned, morphing and changing shape. An old woman smiled as her weary face melted like wax. He found himself on a grimy floor. Blood seeped through cracks in his skin. He was at the very brink of an abyss, a vast pit, looking down, unable to move. An invisible force pinned his body to the edge of the chasm. Scared he was about to die, he cried. His tears drizzled into the emptiness. Hours passed until they reached the bottom, echoing back like faint heartbeats.

— • —

Unable to recall how he made his way home, Vega surveyed the post-and-beam ceiling from his bed. Where the edges met the walls. At the abandoned spider's web still clutching a dusty and tattered corner. At the space between canister lights that remained off. Mostly, he measured the distance between then and now. Who he once was and the relic inhabiting this house and this bed.

Sitting up, he removed his shoes and unbuttoned his shirt, feeling the raised scars along his left shoulder and beneath his right armpit. The shoulder scar was smooth. As his fingertips traced its length, memories of the crazed dentist who fired the bullets were as vivid as the seams on the first baseball he held as a boy.

His fingers moved across to the lumpy circle marking the recent wound, the one that left him comatose. The skin felt raw and tender, like a burn. Yet, the cause, the circumstances surrounding the wound, remained hidden behind an impenetrable fog, refusing to lift. Newspaper accounts of the shooting were out there, of course, but Vega refused to read them. He also avoided those who had witnessed and survived the shooting: Coralina and Lily Navarro, the LAPD officer and friend. He found his caution as mystifying and alarming as his nightmares.

The world where Vega once felt comfortable no longer existed. He was wandering on the other side of darkness, not where light exists, but rather where the unknown waits.

— • —

Until the fourth jingle, the telephone in the kitchen failed to invade Vega's thoughts. He took his time getting there, hoping the jarring noise would stop. No such luck.

"Yeah?"

"Not the greeting I expected. How was your visit with John?"

Erika Lake was not Vega's priority at the minute. A cold martini and more ceiling time was.

"Brief."

Her exhale was loud and stiff with impatience.

"Aloysius, if you hadn't noticed, I provided my jet to get you and that pimple-faced assistant there and back safely and quickly. I expect a little more than a one-word explanation."

"I understand. By the way, the pimples are pretty much gone."

"Delightful. Now, did you agree to John's proposal?"

"The one to help spring your favorite gangster?"

"Yes. Please don't refer to John in that manner."

"Hoodlum? Racketeer? Card cheat?"

"John Roselli is a friend of mine. That is enough for you to know. Now, did you agree to his proposal?"

"I did."

"Good. Have you started looking for this girl?"

"I haven't even had time to shower. I intend to start in the morning, if that's okay with you. One more thing. The missing person Roselli wants me to locate? She's not a girl. She was twenty-five when she disappeared in 1952. That makes her a lady of about forty-two or so. Your age."

"How do you intend to locate her?"

"Well, that's the rub, assuming she's alive."

"But I understood from John that she was seen on that... that island."

"It's a prison, Erika. More like a bastille. Roselli gave me information, second-hand information that Mary Showalter was seen visiting another inmate. That does not mean it was Mary. It could be someone who resembles her."

"How do you intend to get to the bottom of this?"

"Before I answer that question, I have one of my own. Why are you interested in this old case? Girls disappear all the time. Why do you want to help Roselli find Mary Showalter?"

"I've told you several times. John did favors for me when I was in Hollywood. I owe him. Getting him released early is important to me. He's quite ill."

"I saw that firsthand."

"Then you know that he needs medical care, certainly more than he can obtain in custody."

"Roselli offered me a lot of money. I'm not sure I want his money."

"I've never known you to be concerned about how you got paid."

"Maybe I've developed scruples in my old age."

"I believe you're thirty-five. That's still young. Young enough that scruples aren't in play."

"Thirty-five is only young if you live to be thirty-six. And my odds have gone down considerably."

"My dear Aloysius. I understand you've been through an ordeal. Several, in fact. If I didn't care for you, for your well-being, I wouldn't have paid for your hospital bills, now would I?"

"I wondered how long you'd hold that trump card. Is that what this is? Springing Roselli pays off the debt I owe you?"

"Pays it off? No. Reduces the principal? Certainly. And don't worry about getting your fingers dirty with John's money. Mine is acceptable, I suspect."

"It is."

"Good night, Aloysius."

"Wait. You didn't…"

The line went dead.

"…tell me why you care about…"

CHAPTER SEVENTEEN

Arriving at the agency after nine, underpowered by a six-martini headache, Vega found company waiting. Nancy cradled a tiny baby in her arms next to a beaming Coralina. Seated on the visitor's couch were two men dressed in white shirts, dark suits and matching single-colored ties. Their appearance screamed FBI.

"My lucky day. Hello, Coralina."

Nancy returned the infant to her mother.

"Aloysius, I'd like you to meet Juliet."

After setting down his briefcase, Vega approached the mother and child, ignoring the two crewcuts who stood when he arrived. Bending slightly, Vega caressed the infant's appled cheeks.

"Would you like to hold her, Aloysius?"

"Never done that. Best not. I'm..."

"Here, take her. She will not bite. Just keep her head raised."

The detective took the cherub with the carefulness of a bomb technician.

The FBI agents remained standing.

"When you're done playing pawpaw, we need to talk."

"At ease, gentlemen. Whatever you're here for, it can wait."

Vega continued to gently rock Juliet.

"She's bald."

Coralina and Nancy shook their heads in tandem.

"Most babies are born without hair, Aloysius."

Vega returned Juliet to her mother.

"I better see what these federales want. Thanks for stopping by. Nancy, grab a notebook and join us in my office."

— • —

Familiar with the two federal agents from the Liar's Paradox case, Vega was not in the least surprised when they raised the name of John Roselli.

"You paid a visit on March 7 to your old chum, now cooling his heels on McNeil Island."

"Wasn't a conjugal visit if that's what you're implying."

"What did you two discuss?"

"None of your business."

"We can subpoena your testimony."

"Go ahead. But I think your subpoena can't breach attorney-client privilege."

"I don't recall you having a license to practice law, Vega. You have no protection. Answer the question."

"Your memory is good as always. I don't practice law. However, I visited John Roselli on behalf of his attorney, Sid Korshak. You'll need to get his okay before I answer any further questions."

The quick glance between the two wasn't lost on Vega or Nancy, who looked up from her notes.

"Korshak? How do you know Korshak?"

"He employed me as a consultant to meet with Roselli on his behalf."

"Korshak doesn't deal with pissants like you, Vega."

"Would you like to see a copy of the check he wrote, made out in my name? Or maybe we can call Mr. Korshak. Ask if it's okay that one of his consultants is free to talk with the FBI. Whaddya think? Nancy? We have his number on speed dial, right?"

Nancy nodded slightly.

"You and Roselli seem to be close buddies, Vega. First, you go to work for him in Las Vegas, doing side gigs and stuff. Now, here you are, fresh from a trip to Seattle to check on your buddy. You working for the mob now, Vega? Using this 'private detective' agency as a front?"

"Prove it or I'll sue your starched ass for slander. Nancy, ring up Mr. Korshak."

Uncertain at first, Nancy stood clutching her notebook and pen.

"I'm sorry. I forgot to put him on your speed dial. I will need to get his card from my file. Just a second."

The three men waited in silence for Nancy to return. Vega's hangover had morphed to a five-alarm fire in his gut.

"Here it is. Area code 312. Shall I dial it now?"

The two agents stood.

"We'll be back."

"Empty-handed as usual."

— • —

It wasn't until the car doors slammed that Vega noticed his agency's business card trembling in Nancy's hands. He immediately moved to close his office door before asking her to sit.

"I'm sorry. You're not used to your boss getting braced by the FBI. Probably didn't happen at the library."

"It didn't."

"You did good. Don't worry about Mutt and Jeff."

"I know the law, Mr. Vega. Lying to a federal law enforcement officer is a crime, a felony."

"Did you lie? I didn't hear anything close to one."

"I nodded when you stated we had Mr. Korshak on speed dial."

"Looked like a nervous tic to me."

"I said we had his business card on file. I didn't. I was never given one."

"An oversight. Long day for both of us."

"Mr. Vega? I agreed to help you out while Coralina is taking care of Juliet. I did not agree to assist in criminal activity. I am not willing to go to jail for you or anyone else."

Getting up from behind his desk, Vega sat in the chair next to his temporary assistant.

"Look at me, Nancy. Look me directly in the eyes. I will never ask nor encourage you to commit a crime on my behalf for the agency. Never. At times it may appear that I am crossing a line. I know where those lines are drawn. I will not cross them and I certainly would never put you in a situation where you find yourself on the other side of that line. We deal with troubled people in this business. Crooks, adulterers, perverts, to name a few. As clients, my job is to get to the bottom of whatever they are paying me to investigate. I gather facts, evidence, and present it to them. And I do so above the board. I may steer close to the legal shoals, but I won't break the law. I'd lose my license, for one thing. For Christ sakes, Nancy, I'm a former cop!"

"As if there is no history of crooked police."

"Right you are. But if you know anything about my history, Nancy…"

"I do."

"Well? Then tell me, Miss Research Librarian, was I a crooked cop?"

"No. You said you quit rather than accept bribes."

"I rest my case."

"That wasn't the entire story, though."

"The case rests. No further evidence can be introduced. The jury's out!"

His last word, shouted, echoed off the walls of the Cathedral City office. Nancy waited before speaking again.

"You never told me what you and Mr. Roselli talked about. I need to know if I can continue to work for you."

"I will tell you what I can and protect you from the rest. If that is not acceptable, so be it."

Another uneasy silence followed, broken only by the sound of the occasional car on D Street. Nancy nodded her agreement.

"Okay then. Here's the scoop."

For the next ten minutes Nancy learned about Roselli's deal and how Löwenstein claimed to have seen Mary Showalter at the prison visiting Alvin Karpis, the Depression-era gangster.

"Your instincts were dead on, Nancy. Roselli used this guy and the magazine clip for his own purposes. Roselli doesn't want us to involve Löwenstein."

Vega explained how earning the reward money and Roselli's offer was essential to the detective agency remaining in business. Left out of the conversation was Erika's offer to funnel Roselli's money.

"Got it? Are we good? Okay. Now, onto our next steps. I need you to find out a cuppla things. First, find out what you can about Löwenstein. If he was convicted of bank fraud, there must be a newspaper account. Second, where has Karpis landed? A famous guy like him must have made the evening news when he got paroled. If that was Mary who showed up at McNeil, Karpis is the only guy who can tell us why and lead us to her. It's a long shot for sure, but it's the only opening we have. Got it?"

"I do. What else?"

"Third, I want you to use that research nose of yours to track down Arthur Quail. See if he still works for FDIC and lives in Riverside. While you're doing your thing, I'm going to look at the police file on Mary's disappearing act. We got newspaper clips, but they're likely incomplete and maybe flat-out wrong. Detectives might have fed the press false information to mislead the suspect. Or they were just bullshitting the public because they came up goose eggs. I need to see those files. Read the logs, see the crime scene evidence, go over notes from the interviews with the gas station attendants. That kind of stuff. Let's meet back here in the morning and compare notes. Capisce?"

"I understand."

Nancy remained seated.

"Something is nagging me."

"Shoot."

"You may get angry for me asking. I know you will."

"So don't ask. C'mon, we don't have time to fool around."

"It has nothing to do with Mary Showalter. But it…it involves the agency."

"Spit it out."

"Why were you so cold to Coralina? She loves you. Don't you know that?"

CHAPTER EIGHTEEN

Nancy's question and a lingering hangover put Vega in a fine mood as he arrived at the Tahquitz Canyon headquarters of the Palm Springs Police Department. Even better, behind the reception desk was none other than Gary Turner, a ham-fisted patrol officer who kept his day job by marrying into the family of one of the city's long-standing counselors. Vega and Turner had exchanged pleasantries in the past.

"What the fuck do you want, Vega?"

"Top of the day to you too, Officer Turnover."

"I said what the fuck do you want?"

"I'm sorry, I thought the sign on the desk said receptionist. I was expecting a fresh-faced boot, not Barney Fife. I want to see the case file for a missing person case from 1952. Name: Mary Showalter."

"You know the drill. Fill out the PRF. Forms are on the table. Over there."

Snapping a crisp salute, Vega made his way to the public desk. As he filled out the records request, a woman entered the foyer dragging along a disoriented teenager unable to control his giggling. Wearing a paisley shirt and blue jeans, the kid looked to Vega like most teenaged boys in town. Blond hair worn surfer-style, a perpetual Southern California tan, and a desire to be anywhere else in the world.

"Morning, ma'am. How can I be of help?"

"Aaron, he's my son. I caught him smoking marijuana. I want him arrested."

In a show of authority, Officer Turner stood to his full six-foot-three height, glowering at the kid as he did.

"Is that correct, Aaron? Your mother found you with a Schedule One substance in your possession?"

The kid's laughter dialed up another notch. Turner faced the mother.

"Ma'am, please have a seat. Where did this alleged incident occur?"

"In his bedroom. The door was closed. There was smoke coming from underneath. I thought there was a fire."

The kid laughed himself into a coughing fit.

"Sit down, young man. You need to understand the seriousness of the situation."

Aaron sat but was still doubled over. Overhearing all this, Vega offered to get the kid a cup from the nearby water fountain.

"Mind your own business, Vega. Finish your paperwork and get out of here."

"Just trying to be of assistance, officer. Ma'am."

Turner sat behind his desk, puffing up his chest to maintain the pose of authority.

"Possession of marijuana is a Class One felony. The minimum mandatory penalty is one to ten years in state prison. How's that, son? Still strike you as funny?"

The boy's face, bruised red from coughing, was now smudged with tears.

"M-mom, can we go home? I don't feel good."

Faced with the choice of leaving her son at the hoosegow or returning him to the family roost, maternal instincts prevailed.

"I should get him home. He should be home. Can we leave? I'm sorry to bother you, officer. I-I- I just wanted to scare him. These drugs..."

"In a minute. Where is the marijuana cigarette that was in his possession?"

"I swallowed it. Mom, I'm gonna puke."

Turner stood again.

"Fine. Take him home. Aaron, next time will have a different outcome. Understand?"

"Yes."

As soon as the two left, Vega slapped the records request form on Turner's desk.

"Nice work. Now can I see the file?"

"We'll get back to you in ten business days."

"What?"

"You heard me, Vega. The law gives us time to find these documents for public inspection. You play detectives don't get special treatment. Now, get out of my sight."

"You know something, Turner? You're the reason the rest of us drink."

— • —

Rather than return to the agency empty-handed, Vega walked the short distance to the offices of the *Desert Post*. The receptionist pointed him to a window-encased meeting room down a hallway. Inside, Nancy was surrounded by several stacks of large green books.

"Studying for final exams?"

"Hardly. Renee, the librarian, is off today and the microfiche reader is down. I've located only two articles on László Löwenstein. Both are brief. Apparently, editors here didn't see it as much of a story. Mr. Löwenstein lived in Cathedral City, not too far from our office. I might be able to find more in the *Press-Enterprise*. That's the local newspaper in Riverside where the trial was held."

Sitting across the conference table from Nancy, Vega asked his assistant what she had found. She reached for one of the volumes where a page marker stood out.

A federal grand jury recently returned a four-count indictment charging László Löwenstein, age 33, of Cathedral City with embezzlement and bank fraud. Löwenstein appeared for his arraignment and pled not guilty to the pending charges.

According to court documents, Löwenstein was employed at Coachella Valley Savings & Loan from 1948 to 1953 as a loan manager overseeing business transactions and practices at the bank. In that capacity, Löwenstein had the authority to access customer accounts, instruct others to open and close accounts, issue cashier's checks, and transfer funds in and out of bank customers' accounts.

Beginning in 1950, and continuing through in or about April 1953, Löwenstein exploited his position of trust at the bank to embezzle funds from customer accounts and deposit the money into different accounts, court documents say. Löwenstein also falsified documents to conceal his scheme, prosecutors allege.

Löwenstein used some of the traceable fraudulent funds to make loan payments on personal items such as a car, according to charging papers. Through his scheme, Löwenstein caused a loss to CV Savings & Loan of more than $190,000, they allege.

The embezzlement and bank fraud indictment counts are punishable by a maximum penalty of 30 years in prison and a maximum $1 million fine.

Löwenstein's attorney, R. Phillip Mankiewicz, vowed to contest the charges.

"That's it? Nothing more? Like how the fraud was uncovered?"

"That's all I've been able to find. The later article, about his sentencing, just repeated information from this article. Sorry. Like I said, there's probably more in the Riverside newspaper archives."

Standing up, Vega looked out the conference room window to an expansive open area he knew housed all the *Post's* functions: news, advertising, circulation, and accounting. Everything but the pressroom and storage for dozens of rolls of newsprint and large tanks of ink.

"One would think the *Post* would have reported more. The bank is located almost on their doorstep. Does it strike you that coincidences are starting to pile up?"

"You mean the fact that Quail and Löwenstein both knew Mary?"

"That's one. When you go to Riverside, to the newspaper, I need you to check if Quail still lives there. If you happen to run into the guy, do not attempt to question him. That's my job."

"You're assuming Mary's husband is still living in Riverside, in the same apartment from seventeen years ago. Highly improbable."

"Unlikely, but not impossible. What else strikes you about our jailed bank employee?"

"That he likely also knew Mary's husband, the bank examiner?"

"Which raises the question…"

"Of whether Mary was aware of the fraudulent activity?"

"Which could be one reason behind her disappearance."

Vega turned from the window.

"We have a theory, Nancy. One theory that lacks any evidence of value."

"True. What did the police file reveal?"

"Nothing yet. They're making me wait ten days."

Vega returned to his chair, clasping his hands together.

"There's a lot of work that needs to get done. Some of it will require us to split up."

Nancy indicated she understood.

"I can drive to Riverside in the morning."

"Good. We need a strategy. Let's grab lunch."

"I have one more item before we leave, Mr. Vega. While going through the archives, I looked for and found a brief notice about Mary and Arthur's marriage. Pretty typical notice. Quite brief. Location of ceremony. A bit of background on the couple. Two things that stood out. One, there's no mention of family members attending. That's typically included along with the backgrounds of the bride and groom."

Vega reminded Nancy that newspaper articles said Mary's parents died when she was a teenager. Her one sister lived on the East Coast.

"Perhaps it was a quick engagement and the couple wanted to keep the ceremony private. What's the second item?"

Nancy shoved the bound newspaper volume across the table.

"There's a picture of the couple above the article. It's small but take a look. There's Mary, Arthur, and one other person off to the side who's not mentioned in the article. I think you'll recognize her."

Indeed he did. Standing in the background of the black-and-white photograph was a young woman who looked to be Mary's age. Her dark wavy hair was swept to one side, giving her a sexy peekaboo look. There was no mistaking who it was.

Erika Lake.

CHAPTER NINETEEN

Over a lunch of almond beef (his) and chow gai pan (hers) at Don the Beachcomber, Vega and Nancy divvied up their tasks. He would interview the manager of the savings and loan and attempt to locate Löwenstein's attorney.

"If Mankiewicz remains his legal counsel perhaps he could provide us access to his client. We have Roselli's interpretation of what went down. I'd like to hear it directly from the source."

Vega also intended to see if the reporters who wrote about Mary's case in 1952 were still working at the *Post* or at least remained in the area.

"They may give up stuff they couldn't report at the time."

Nancy's to-do list included researching Karpis and finding out more about Löwenstein at the Riverside library. Verifying the original addresses of both was essential. If she located Quail, she was to call Vega.

"I don't want you knocking on any doors, understand? This Quail guy isn't right. Too many coincidences in his alibi."

Vega signaled to the waiter for a second martini and asked Nancy if she wanted
something to wash down her chow mien.

"Gai pan."

"Whatever. Look at this drink list. There's got to be over two dozen specialty cocktails. Barbados Punch, Daiquiri, Hot Rum Grog, Pearl Diver."

"All too sweet for my tastes. I'll stick with my iced tea for now. It's lunchtime. Plus I'm underage. I'll have an occasional glass of sherry in the evening with Mom. Sometimes I'll break down and have her purchase for me a bottle of champagne."

"The picture you just painted. The demure research librarian at home enjoying a flute of champagne."

Nancy's cheeks flushed.

"Sorry, didn't mean to embarrass you."

"I'm fine."

Eager to switch subjects, Nancy asked about the woman in the wedding picture.

"You didn't have on your list to ask Miss Lake about her connection to Mary. And why she attended their wedding."

Vega thanked the waiter for the martini, which he sipped before responding.

"I'm saving Erika for last. Like a good attorney, I want to know the answer before I ask a question of a witness. Same with Karpis. If we find him, we'll need something to keep him on the phone line."

Nancy nodded her agreement between sips of iced tea and glances at the hippie couple across the room. Like the trap door under a hangman's noose, her jaw dropped when she recognized Sonny and Cher. Vega reminded his understudy not to gawk.

"These Hollywood folks? They come to the desert to escape the limelight. Some come to party, most just to unwind before their next assignment. You'll meet your share – mostly at restaurants, on the tennis court, even shopping."

"I hardly eat out and I don't play tennis."

Not surprising given what Nancy had revealed to Vega about her personal life. Born to Thomas and Georgia Randall in 1951, Nancy was a sickly child, prone to catching colds and the latest virus. When she was six Nancy contracted the Asian Flu that was sweeping across the world after emerging in Hong Kong and Singapore. The virus killed over a million people. Nancy was spared, though the chills and fever had left her terribly weakened. She missed an entire quarter of school that year. She spent that time reading hundreds of books, capturing to memory information about science, arts, and history.

"Is that when you first discovered your gift, this ability to remember everything?"

"No. I knew, and my parents knew, that my ability to retain information seemed innate from a very early age."

"What's your earliest memory?"

"Being baptized. I remember the water. I remember the white garments."

Nancy's unusual gift set her apart from her schoolmates as she progressed through the public school system in Salem, Oregon. She fell further behind her peers in socialization as she devoured information night and day. She was teased at school by the girls as being odd and by boys for her scrawny appearance.

After her father died of cancer when she was thirteen, Nancy moved with her mother to Palm Springs where a distant aunt lived. Attending public school in California further isolated Nancy. Her mother worked two jobs to stay afloat. Fellow students were cruel. Nancy wore mid-length skirts while her classmates were parading about in miniskirts. Where they wore colorful bras to tame their breasts, Nancy still wore white tee-shirts underneath her modest blouses. Boys nick-named her after the undergarment.

Encouraged to help out with household finances, Nancy began part-time work at Welwood Murray Library. The chief librarian saw the girl's potential and put her to work as a part-time researcher. Library patrons were enamored and donors took notice of her capabilities. After senior year, she worked full time. Now, at age nineteen, she was assisting Vega on a cold case that began when Nancy was a year old.

"What does your mother think of your new profession?"

"She holds out hope that I'll come to my senses and attend college. Find a profession that pays well."

"Why don't you?"

"The thought of sitting in a room with dozens of over-sexed, under-educated classmates is nightmarish. I like working for you. It's challenging to be sure, but also somewhat exciting."

Looking around at the elaborate interior of the restaurant, its thatched roof, bamboo furniture and Polynesian artwork, Vega shook his head. The gesture was noticed by his lunchmate.

"Don't like this place, Mr. Vega?"

"Nah. I prefer old school. Dark wood paneling, plush red booths. Mahogany bar. Behind it a skilled bartender with silver hair and a snappy vest. The food here is okay, but this place ain't for me. Reminds me too much of the time we're living in. A garish veneer over a world growing darker by the minute. Underneath the colorful clothes and proclamations of free love, is a dark environment. I can sense it. It's like that pirate tale, *Treasure Island*. A grand adventure that becomes poisoned by greed and excess."

Nancy's concerned expression splintered his train of thought.

"I was talking about restaurants, wasn't I? Good bars and restaurants are like a third place to go. There's home, your job, and your bar."

"What about church?"

"I was an altar boy. Got married in the church. That's enough for this life."

Vega downed the remainder of the martini, staring at the stem.

"I like a place completely removed from the current era. A bar that feels like a relic from an old version of the world that I've seen on television or in the movies. A saloon and a dining establishment that somehow feels like an old suit from the first moment I slide onto a bar stool. Or the baseball glove that still holds memories in its pocket. I like places like that."

Looking across the table at her employer, Nancy asked why he had chosen the Beachcomber for lunch.

"I thought you might like it. It's young, like you. Full of energy and promise."

"Promise me this, Mr. Vega. Should we solve this case, find out what became of Mary Showalter, take me to one of your favorite spots. One that feels to you like that old baseball glove."

CHAPTER TWENTY

Vega's interview with Tobias Blackpool added little to the investigation. The branch manager of CV Savings & Loan confirmed the basic facts of Mary's disappearance that day in 1952 and the subsequent police investigation. His description of Mary – professional, private, and sweet – was already known. Instead, Vega turned his attention to the crime that put Blackpool's employee, László Löwenstein, in the slammer.

Initially reluctant to discuss the crime that occurred under his nose, Blackpool ultimately opened up when Vega asked about the young man's unusual name.

"Löwenstein's not a name that one would expect to find here in Palm Springs. Maybe New York or New Jersey. How did he come to your attention and land a job here?"

"László came to America from Hungary. The mother and father were devout Jews. The father, I was told, made plans to get his wife and only child out of the country during the German occupation. Apparently, they were among the few to escape. Most were murdered on the banks of the Danube or deported to Auschwitz-Birkenau. Somehow, László and his mother made it to Switzerland and then to France, where they remained hidden in a remote village near Dijon until the Allied victory."

"What happened to the father?"

"They never learned."

"How old was László at the time?"

"Late teens."

"Old enough to have worked with the Resistance at the time."

"If he did, he never offered that part of his history. László and his mother arrived in America after the war and eventually settled in Chicago."

"What brought them all the way out here?"

"Only László came. His mother died of a stroke before he left Chicago. He told me his dream was to find work in Hollywood. Make it big, his exact words."

"You were about to tell me how he came to be employed here."

"László told me he ran out of money by the time he reached Arizona. He worked odd jobs there before resuming his journey west. He ran out of money again by the time he reached the Coachella Valley. He walked into our office and asked to speak to the person in charge. That was me. He struck me as quite an ambitious young man, so I agreed to meet. His English language skills were strong despite his pronounced accent."

"What skills did he possess?"

"The ones that impressed me most were his grasp of mathematical operations and cash handling. His mother was a bookkeeper in the old country and, for a limited time, in Chicago. She was very much nineteenth century in her responsibilities. She was used to recording all transactions in the daybook, managing the cashbook, and keeping inventory. László learned all this at his mother's side."

"Did László have valid references when he applied for work?"

"No. He gave me two contacts in Chicago who, he said, would vouch for his mother's work."

"He didn't hold a job? Unusual."

"It was. I called both contacts as László sat right where you are. The references raved about Mrs. Löwenstein and her bookkeeping skills."

"So you took a chance on her son?"

"I did. I gave him two dummy accounts to analyze, a test I typically give for account managers rather than the opening for a teller I had at the time."

"He aced it?"

"In record time. He found the disparities in both, reconciling one and pointing out the error in prepaid insurance expenses in the other, a small business account. I was sold on the young man. I hired him that very day. Within three months I promoted László from one of three tellers to one of two account managers. Customers loved him. He had the personality, particularly with our female customers, both young and elderly."

By now, Vega had the background he needed on the man behind bars at McNeil Island. The inmate who told Roselli that Mary Showalter was very much alive. It was time to press the bank manager for information on the crime itself and any connection to Mary.

"Mr. Blackpool, you've been very helpful in providing the background on Löwenstein. I have a few more questions, if you have a little more time."

"You said you were investigating Mary's disappearance, but you appear more interested in László. Do you believe he was involved in her disappearance?"

"At this point I'm not ruling anything in or out. Was there any relationship between the two, Mary and László? Romantic or otherwise? You said the ladies were quite taken by him."

"They acted quite professional in the office. To your question, I didn't detect anything between them. Nor did their names appear in any office scuttlebutt. The only spark I witnessed was between

Mary and Arthur Quail. It was obvious the two were attracted to each other. I believe it was on one of Arthur's regular stops here that he asked her out to lunch. After that, Mary – always professional and reserved – seemed more, I don't know the right term ... maybe inspired? Always a hard worker, Mary kept to herself. After meeting Arthur, we all noticed the change. Mary became more talkative with her co-workers. Like a flower, she seemed to open up."

"How was the criminal activity of László uncovered?"

Blackpool startled at the sudden shift in topics.

"Mr. Vega, your line of questioning is interesting to say the least. I agreed to speak with you about Mary."

Fearing that Blackpool was about to end the interview, Vega abandoned subtlety.

"Löwenstein claims that he saw Mary earlier this year."

Blackpool's head jerked as if someone had slipped a garrote around his neck.

"Good lord! What did you say?"

"I said Löwenstein claims to have seen Mary very much alive."

"After all these years? How could that be? I don't understand. He's still in prison, isn't he?"

"Until 1984, if he serves the full term. Listen, I don't know if Löwenstein has all his marbles. Prison can do that to even the best. Especially a place like McNeil. It's a dark hellhole on an isolated island near Seattle."

"You spoke to László?"

"No. I was at the prison but didn't speak to him. I heard this through another inmate."

"Do you believe him?"

"I don't know, but I intend to find out. Mary is either dead or alive. Those are the only two possibilities."

"I cannot, under any circumstance, believe that Mary faked her own death. It's impossible!"

"That trick has been tried many times, Mr. Blackpool. Most have financial motives. Theft. Life insurance. Other times, it's an attempt to avoid danger, such as escaping an abusive relationship."

"Mary was in love with Arthur. They just got married."

"There's also something thrilling about the idea of disappearing and starting over, leaving all your problems behind."

"What problems? Mary seemed to have it all. A well-paying job, a new husband. A bright future, if you ask me. Why would she throw that away? I don't see it."

"Let me draw a picture. A possible motive for Mary to vanish. What if she was aware of what Löwenstein was doing and got involved? What if they were working together colluding, embezzling customer funds from your institution?"

"I don't buy it. Even if it were a possibility, it would have come out in the investigation."

"An investigation that began with the bank examiner, the man Mary was in love with. Don't you think it's possible that Arthur Quail uncovered the fraud that Löwenstein and Mary were committing, then manipulated his findings to protect her?"

"Far-fetched, Mr. Vega. Even if Arthur was clever enough to cover up her role in the embezzlement, other investigators were involved. Investigators from the FDIC and the FBI. I sincerely doubt Mary's role would have slipped past them. All my employees cooperated in the investigation. They were questioned together and individually. Several times, in fact."

"My theory is a stretch, I'll give you that. But what if Mary was not directly involved? Maybe she discovered what Löwenstein was doing and demanded something in exchange for keeping quiet."

"In exchange for what?"

"Money. Sex. Maybe both."

"Then why would she marry another man?"

"Makes for a great cover. Also, pillow talk with the bank examiner. Mary would be able to learn if her secret lover was about to be busted."

Blackpool's brain was about to explode. That was clear by his perplexed appearance. Vega continued down the path he deliberately chose.

"Let's look at the timetable. According to the press reports, Löwenstein began to embezzle funds from customer accounts in 1950. Mary was already working here at the time, correct?"

"Yes."

"In what capacity? As an account manager?"

"Yes. She first worked as a teller."

"Mary disappeared two years later, two days after marrying Arthur Quail, who would later report to authorities that a co-worker had stolen some two-hundred grand. Coincidence, Mr. Blackpool?"

"Far-fetched, Mr. Vega. What about the blood they found in the car? It was Mary's blood. She obviously was badly hurt before she disappeared."

"Self-inflicted to send police in the wrong direction."

Vega stood, stretching his legs and looking out the windows of the branch manager's spacious office as he considered his final questions.

"The money that Löwenstein took from your customers? What happened to it?"

"A small amount was recovered."

"Knowing the FBI, their search for the missing dough would be thorough. But they never found all of it?

"According to police and the FBI, the money was transferred in bits from the accounts of others to dummy accounts Mr. Löwenstein had set up. He withdrew funds from them over time."

Vega was now pacing. Blackpool remained arrested behind his ornate desk.

"So, most of the money had been withdrawn from those dummy accounts by the time Quail, the bank examiner, called the scheme to your attention and to his superiors at FDIC. Is that correct?"

"Yes."

"You've reviewed the records of those accounts?"

"Of course."

"Let me ask you this. Was the money withdrawn before Mary disappeared or afterward?"

The answer came after considerable thought and in a voice low and resigned.

"The FBI said László spent a portion of it over the years on personal items, but the balance remained in the accounts he had established. That is, until seventy-five thousand dollars was withdrawn from four different accounts in varying amounts over a two-month period in 1952."

"I'll ask you again. Before or after Mary disappeared?"

"Before. Two months before she disappeared."

Vega picked up the notebook he had placed on Blackpool's desk. "Thank you for your time. That's all I have for now."

Vega stopped at the office door.

"I forgot. That reward money? It's still there, right?"

"It is."

"And I would be entitled to it, should I provide convincing evidence that Mary Showalter is alive. Right?"

"Correct."

"And if I provide convincing evidence that Mary Showalter is dead, the twenty grand is mine? Either scenario, right?"

"That is correct. However, the balance of the reward account is now fifty-thousand dollars."

Vega stared at Blackpool. Had he heard right? Fifty thousand. Not twenty.

"The extra thirty? Where did that come from? You?"

"Goodness no."

"Who?"

"I can't say."

"Can't or won't?"

"Both, I'm afraid. The donor wants to remain anonymous. That's all I can tell you."

Vega left CV Savings with renewed interest. Fifty grand changed the equation. Someone out there wanted the investigation finished bad enough to open the wallet wide. And there were only two people interested enough to raise the stakes.

CHAPTER TWENTY-ONE

Over a lunch of hot pastrami sandwiches with sides of creamy coleslaw and sliced tomatoes, Scott Jarvis delivered the bad news. The two reporters who initially covered Mary's disappearance for the *Post* were no longer alive.

"Charley died from liver disease around fifty-nine. Gaylord in sixty-five. Suicide. He was in bad health as well. No one else burrowed into the case like they did. Our anniversary stories are based entirely on the clips you already have. All rewrites from the original reporting. Sorry."

Vega asked about notebooks.

"These were old-school newspapermen, Vega. They protected their notes like the gold in Fort Knox. Probably buried with them. You would have liked Charley and Gay. Blood and booze hounds. True newsmen. They knew the history of Palm Springs cold but never got lost in it. They wrote all the big stories for the *Post* in the forties and fifties. Got fired and rehired close to a half-dozen times. Fought with editors, mayors, business leaders, and a few drunkards at Chi-Chi's. Charley and Gay weren't college guys. Strictly blue collar. When I was learning the basics of reporting I learned from two of the best. Always spell a person's name correctly. Never assume. Ask for the spelling. How to gather facts and report with truth, accuracy, and integrity."

"Sound like a couple of good eggs. Fired and rehired?"

"Mostly over the vulgarities they hurled at the copy desk for changing a word here and there. The biggest blow-up was over Section Fourteen. Heard of it?"

"Do I need to?"

"Yeah. If you're going to live here, you ought to know some history."

Jarvis explained that when the Coachella Valley was initially surveyed, the federal government divided and numbered the land into square-mile sections. In the 1870s, the federal government deeded the odd-numbered sections of land for ten miles along either side of railroad routes to railroad companies across the West to encourage rail expansion. This created a "checkerboard" of one-mile-square sections with odd numbers owned by the railroad and even numbers owned by the federal government.

"In 1876, President Grant issued an executive order setting aside a parcel, Section Fourteen, as the Agua Caliente Indian Reservation. They lived there. Mexican laborers and domestics too. Some Negroes, Chinese, and Filipinos. Rental opportunities off the reservation were not offered to these workers, most of whom had jobs in the resorts that were being built. Restrictions on this deeded land prevented them from purchasing property. What you had, Vega, was de facto segregation."

Jarvis swallowed another bite of sandwich before continuing.

"The houses on Section Fourteen were pretty run down. Mostly old wooden trailers. Gotta say it was a shitty-looking area. The roads were dirt and kicked up a lot of dust. No water. No sewers. Those who lived there had to burn their trash and dig septic tanks. Know why? Cause it was sovereign Indian land. The city wasn't obligated to provide any services, so it didn't."

Vega asked where the land is located.

"The heart of the downtown, buddy. We're sittin' in it as we eat. Bordered streets are Alejo and Ramon and East Palm Canyon and

Sunrise. Most of the bad stuff came down between here and Sunrise. So, here was this hellhole in the middle of Hollywood of the desert. Not the picture the city fathers wanted *Life* magazine to see. So they claimed Section Fourteen was a health hazard and seized the land to make room for new hotels and restaurants for all the tourists. The feds gave them permission."

"Somehow, I'm not surprised."

"You gotta understand a town's history to see its future. Palm Springs ain't much different than Las Vegas. There's just a lot more money up there. Anyhow, the city didn't provide any funds to relocate residents. Negroes were encouraged to move to north Palm Springs. Latinos and Filipinos migrated to the east. So after the city evicted all these folks it quickly demolished the shacks and trailers. Most were burned to the ground. Residents – mostly farm workers, hotel maids, day laborers – lost their life possessions in the flames. Charley and Gay did most of the reporting on this. When an editor deleted a quote in one of their articles, they both quit."

"What was the quote?"

"Burning Section Fourteen was a city-engineered holocaust."

— • —

After finishing lunch, Vega returned to the agency where he sat at Coralina's desk rifling through the *Yellow Pages* for local attorneys. Mankiewicz Law was found on page 293. The small advertisement proclaimed, "Aggressive Representation of Criminal & Drunken Driving in the Courts of Riverside County."

Vega's phone call was answered by a pleasant female voice who, after inquiring about the reason for his call, placed him on a brief hold.

"William Mankiewicz. How may I help you?"

Vega explained he was attempting to reach Phillip Mankiewicz regarding a client he represented in 1954.

"That's my father. He's semi-retired. Who was the client and what is your interest, if I may ask?"

"Client was László Löwenstein. Convicted of bank fraud. My interest is getting access to Mr. Löwenstein regarding a different case I'm investigating. I'm told he has information that could be helpful. He's still locked up in a federal pen, so I need to speak with his attorney, your father, to see if I can arrange a visit."

"I'm familiar with your work, Mr. Vega. You tend to end up on the front page. You say that Mr. Löwenstein has information you need? Can you share?"

"I'm investigating the disappearance of a young woman, Mary Showalter. You may be familiar with that case too."

"I'm familiar with the circumstances. Has her body been found?"

"Not to my knowledge."

"I'm rather confused, Mr. Vega. Are you saying the two cases are connected?"

"Again, not to my knowledge. How can I reach your father?"

"When he's not on the golf course he's playing cards with friends. How about I call him and see if he's interested in speaking with you?"

"Or you could give me his number."

"Dad's rather vigilant about his privacy."

"As is his right. Here's my number."

— • —

It was two o'clock. Vega headed to the couch across from his desk at the agency. Nights were punishing. Sleepless, he would sit in the living room drinking, staring absently at the surface of the pool. All he saw was an unremittingly bleak landscape. Vivian Dy had cautioned that his depression may appear worse at night, when he was tired and there were fewer activities and friends to orient his thoughts.

By the time Phillip Mankiewicz called, it was nearly four o'clock. Disoriented from his nap, Vega made it to his desk with the speed of an old man up in the middle of the night, shuffling to the bathroom in brown slippers scuffed by age. The caller's dried-out voice was loud and impatient.

"I have nothing to tell you about László Löwenstein."

Vega recovered his bearings in time to prevent the call from ending on that sour note.

"If you have nothing to say, Mr. Mankiewicz, why did you bother to call? You must have something you want to tell me."

"Are you hard of hearing, Mr. Vega? I have nothing to tell you. My son harangued me. I had to get him off my back."

"Your client..."

"I no longer represent Mr. Löwenstein. After the appeal was dismissed, he fired me."

"Got it. Your former client says he saw Mary Showalter, a girl who vanished here in the valley seventeen years ago."

The pause informed Vega the hook was baited.

"I remember Mary. She worked at the savings and loan. Nice girl. Sad, perplexing event. You say my former client claims he saw her? How could that be? He remains incarcerated."

The fish had the bait and was now wiggling on the line.

"According to information I received, Mary was visiting another inmate at McNeil Island when Mr. Löwenstein saw her. I learned this from a fellow inmate. Someone I came across in a previous case."

"You believe this second-hand account? That Mary Showalter is alive after all? And was visiting a federal prisoner? It stretches plausibility, Mr. Vega."

"Was Mr. Löwenstein given to such flights of fancy?"

"Sure was. Thought he could get rich by stealing other people's money. Learned the hard way it rarely pays off."

"As his attorney at the time, you had to mount a defense. What..."

"There was little room to work with. The act in question occurred and his fingerprints were all over the transferred money. My job was to challenge whether the prosecutors could prove intent. A conviction required that the acts were done knowingly. And that the amount was material to the savings and loan. Prosecutors didn't have a difficult time proving both to the jury. I had to rely on first criminal offense and his difficult childhood. Jury didn't buy it. I sought a plea deal to reduce the sentence he faced. I got nowhere. Fresh-faced prosecutor out to prove his bones. No deal."

"And the appeal?"

"As you must know, an appeal in a federal case is not a retrial. I attacked on the grounds that the prosecution violated Rule Twenty-Six regarding the bank examiner's written notes to the branch manager. The Court of Appeals deferred to the trial judge's ruling that the notes in question, while delayed in discovery, were not material. The examiner's formal reports had been properly presented."

"Did you call any defense witnesses?"

"There were none. No family. No friends to speak of. I did, on cross examination, elicit a good deal of positive character testimony from his colleagues at the savings and loan, including the branch manager. That was about the best I could do. I don't like losing, Mr. Vega. But in this case, I had little to work with."

"Did Löwenstein have anything further to say after the jury found him guilty?"

"Not much. He asked me 'what happens now?' I told him I'm going to go home and have a bourbon. And you're going to prison."

"Were you aware at the time that the bank examiner, Arthur Quail, was in a romantic relationship with Mary Showalter?"

"I was not."

"Would it have made a difference?"

"Doubtful. I certainly would have raised the issue, but to your question, there was no evidence or indication that Mr. Löwenstein had an accomplice."

"How were you paid?"

"That's none of your business."

"But you were paid for your services."

"I was indeed. Now, you've taken up more of my time than was my intent."

"I appreciate your time and patience. I have only one or two more questions."

"Make it quick."

"Although you no longer represent Mr. Löwenstein, would you be able to help me obtain access to him at McNeil Island? If your name is still on the visitor's list, could you call them and add me to the list as a consultant?"

"That is a very unusual request. Care to tell me what this is really about?"

For the next several minutes, Vega presented his case to the aging lawyer. He explained that if Löwenstein was truthful, that could lead Vega to Mary Showalter. That information could eventually help Löwenstein to seek an earlier release from the parole board.

"Far-fetched, Mr. Vega. I am not inclined to help. He's no longer my client. But I am curious more about how you learned of this information about the Showalter girl. Who is this other inmate, the one Löwenstein spoke with?"

Initially reluctant to offer up Roselli's name, Vega found he had little choice.

"Roselli! That bum?"

"You're aware of John Roselli, I take it."

"Aware? He fleeced one of my clients in the Friars Club case. That's the reason the bum is behind bars."

"Your client?"

"Herbert Marx. The brother known as Zeppo. I represented him in that case. Mr. Vega, I want you to listen to me carefully. There is nothing on God's green earth that I will do to help John Roselli or, in this case, you. Goodbye."

— • —

Nancy's phone call from Riverside arrived at four-forty as Vega was about out the door. Not pleased to be held up from the first martini of the day, he barked.

"About time. Whaja find?"

"Not as much as I hoped. The library here had nothing more on the trial and conviction of László Löwenstein. His case was denied on appeal."

"I know that. What else?"

"Karpis is in Montreal. Told reporters when he was released that he was going to work at an accounting firm there."

"Name of the firm?"

"Didn't say, but the newspaper report said a prominent figure in the city, Frank Roberts, would help him get the job. If we can locate Roberts we'll find Karpis."

"Good. What else?"

"About Karpis? Told reporters in Seattle that he intends to lay low. Said all the attention isn't good. Here's a quote: 'I'm going to try to stay down on a level where I belong.' He also refused to answer a question as to whether he really was arrested by Hoover. He said it would be in bad taste to comment on that now."

"A real gentleman."

"That's the way the press wrote it. They quoted guards and prison administrators as saying Karpis was – quote – a great guy. They said he coached other inmates how to stay out of trouble, on the outside and in prison. He also taught inmates how to play guitar."

"Anything else?"

"Karpis said he was disappointed in the Seattle Space Needle. Thought it would be taller."

"What about an attorney? Who's his legal counsel?"

"James E. Carty. In private practice in Woodland, Washington. Want me to contact him?"

"I'll do it. Easier than finding this Roberts guy in Montreal. What about Quail?"

"Arthur still works as a bank examiner. Was promoted and is now working out of the FDIC's field office in Mission Viejo."

"Where's that?"

"Orange County, south of Long Beach. I'll head there in the morning."

"No way. I want you back here. We can ride together, if need be. I don't want you out there on your own. Got it?"

"I do. I also spoke with the landlord at Quail's former apartment here. Said Arthur Quail was a model renter. Quiet. No parties or disturbances. Gave notice back in fifty-two. Said he was getting married and moving to Palm Springs. Seems to match what Quail told police at the time."

"That was seventeen years ago. Convenient memory."

"He's still the landlord there. Also, remember the neighbor who corroborated Quail's whereabouts the night Mary disappeared? He still lives in the same apartment. Landlord says he works swing shift at a packing house. I'm going to try to catch him in the morning before I head home."

Vega said he was uneasy with her remaining in Riverside overnight and questioning an important witness.

"I'm not a child, Mr. Vega."

"You're nineteen, Nancy. Not far removed from diapers."

"I understand you don't follow the news, Mr. Vega. I do. Are you aware there is a war underway in Vietnam?"

"Of …"

"And there are thousands of young women serving in combat zones. Most are nurses dealing with amputations and death. I think I can handle…"

"Calm down. I understand…"

"As of today, at least five of those young women have died. Not from disease or illness or accidents. They were killed in the line of duty."

"Okay. Okay. You can stay there overnight and question this guy in the morning, but I need to go over the questions before you meet with him. Fair enough?"

"Sure. I sense you're late for your cocktail."

"How's that?"

"You're awfully grouchy."

CHAPTER TWENTY-TWO

Arriving shortly after sunrise at the intersection of Mission and Vine, Nancy parked in front a building that on one side bore a striking resemblance to the Alamo. Inside, she informed the cinnamon-haired receptionist she wished to speak to Abraham Barnheiser about ... well, it was a private matter. Told his break would begin promptly at seven, Nancy spent the time browsing black-and-white photographs framing two walls – pictures that told the history of the 1912 building and California's second gold rush. It was her way of distracting from her growing anxiety about interviewing a witness without the presence of her boss.

The caption beneath the first photograph explained that the Mission-style building was constructed eight years after the railroad opened a stop in Riverside. Leased to the Sutherland Fruit Company, it served as one of two-dozen packing houses serving the orange groves that filled the valleys of Southern California in the decades that followed the Gold Rush that began in 1848.

The soil and climate in Riverside were ideally suited for Brazilian navel oranges, a variety that failed to take hold in Florida. They were even sweeter and more bountiful than oranges grown in the Los Angeles basin. Seedless too. As a result of its commercial success, the navel orange fueled the economic and social development of

Riverside, making the city at the turn of the century the wealthiest per capita in the entire nation.

"You wanted to see me?"

Standing behind her was an elderly man in blowsy jeans and a tan sweatshirt stained with a day's work. He was blowing his nose as he looked her over. His face was weathered and puffy. His weedy hair neither gray nor white.

"Mr. Barnheiser?"

"Uh-huh."

Nancy offered a hand that was not taken. His fingers were busy folding the soiled kerchief.

"I'm Nancy Randall, an associate with the Vega Detective Agency in Palm Springs. I would like a minute of your time to ask a few questions about…"

"I have nothing to say to the police."

"I work for a private detective, not the police."

"Still got nothing to say."

"You don't know what the topic is."

"Don't matter."

With that, Abraham Barnheiser turned away, past the bored receptionist, toward a wooden swinging door that sported injuries from years of abuse. Metal hand trucks. Tougher workers.

"It's about Mary Showalter, a woman who vanished in 1952. You knew her husband, Arthur Quail!"

Nancy's shout was ignored except for a brief pause as Barnheiser pushed through the door marked Employees Only.

— • —

Loitering behind the steering wheel of her Toyota Corolla, Nancy reprimanded herself. First, she failed to call Vega to review the questions for Barnheiser. Second, she was unable to obtain any information about Arthur Quail from his one-time neighbor, someone who had provided police with the alibi on the night his bride disappeared.

Checking her watch, Nancy drove from the packing house toward downtown Riverside, determined to call the agency before eight. Leaving a phone message for her boss was preferable to explaining.

It took an inordinate amount of time to find a pay phone. The area was clogged with cars and walkers making their way to the blocks of federal, state, county, and local government offices that were the heartbeat of the city's downtown. Finding a phone booth outside Chan's Chinese Restaurant, Nancy deposited a dime and prayed Vega hadn't arrived.

He hadn't. He remained in bed, unaware of the crippling hangover that would greet his return from the half dead.

Nancy's announcement to the answering machine was brief.

"I'm on my way to Mission Viejo. Will call after I locate Quail."

Her message joined two others waiting for Vega's arrival. The first was from Vivian Dy who wanted to know why he had missed his scheduled check-in call. The second was from Coralina, inviting him to dinner that evening.

CHAPTER TWENTY-THREE

Dressed in charcoal capris pants with a blue chambray shirt left untucked, Coralina nervously checked the clock in the kitchen where she put the finishing touches on a meal of pork enchiladas, Spanish rice, and grilled corn salad. Her small dinette table was set with red and white floral dinner plates, a wedding gift she never was able to share with her husband.

The doorbell sounded at twelve minutes past the appointed hour. Checking her image in the mirror, Coralina pinched the loose-fitting shirt to shield her remaining post-partum tummy bulge. At the door was not the man she had invited. Instead of the dashing Spaniard, the impersonator was masked in dark eye circles, bloodshot eyes, and a face as puffed as a budgie. Even his clothes looked unhappy.

"Come in, Aloysius."

"I was going to bring a bottle of sangria but I was running late."

"It is not a problem. Please make yourself comfortable. Dinner is almost ready."

Vega paced before sitting at the dinette as Coralina touched up the fixings.

"Where is..."

"Juliet? She is sleeping. I expect she will wake us before dessert. Would you like a glass of water?"

"Uh, sure."

"You appear to need hydration. And in need of a home-cooked meal."

"I haven't been eating well, that's for certain."

"And sleep?"

"Could use more."

Their conversation meandered over dinner.

Juliet.

The challenge and joys of motherhood.

Juliet.

The agency.

Mostly Juliet.

The baby was healthy, slept well, and was constantly hungry.

When the topic turned to the agency and Nancy's trip to Riverside, Coralina bolted out of her chair, shouting at Vega.

"¿Estás demente? ¡Permitiste que Nancy, que tiene diecinueve años, se fuera por su cuenta! ¡Enfrentarse a un hombre que puede ser un asesino! Yo... No puedo expresar con palabras lo irresponsable que es. Deberías estar avergonzado. ¿Su madre es consciente de cómo pones en riesgo la vida de su hija?"

"Dammit, Coralina! Nancy's doing this on her own. I can't control her. And, no, I did not inform her mother. Not my position."

"Why did you not accompany her?"

"I had my own calls to make."

"Eres imprudente!"

"Reckless?"

"Yes! You are reckless with your own life and the lives of those who are close to you!"

Coralina threw her napkin on the table before marching out of the kitchen to comfort Juliet, whose cries began as they argued. While she was out of the room, Vega fidgeted. He needed something stronger than ice water. Something to calm his nerves. When

Coralina eventually returned, the combatants silently picked at the cold remains of their meal. It was left to Coralina to break the uneasy quiet.

"It is not like Nancy to keep you in the dark."

"I know that. The brief message this morning is all I've gotten. I checked the answering machine again before I came over. Nothing. I don't know if she's contacted Quail's neighbor or found Quail."

"Nancy is very smart. There is a reason for her not to check in. I am certain of that."

After clearing the dishes, Vega followed Coralina to the living room where they sat on her modest sofa. He felt awkward in her presence, almost disoriented. He stared ahead, his eyes absent and empty.

"What is the matter, Aloysius?"

"Fix me a drink."

"I will. But only one. You will need to drive home. You cannot stay here tonight."

The two sat quietly after Coralina returned. A nod of the head was all the thanks she received. She waited to speak until he had reduced the martini by half.

"Is it Nancy that has you so troubled, Aloysius?"

"That too."

"What else, then. You may confide in me."

His eyes forecast the apprehension of the words that would follow.

"Each morning I look in the mirror. I recognize my face. I know my arms and legs belong to me. When I look around, I recognize my home. But then I notice the couch in the living room is blue and I wonder why I picked blue."

"I helped you choose that couch. Blue is your favorite color."

"Why do I like blue? I feel like a child again. I'm being told that my favorite color is blue."

Reaching out to place her hand on his, Coralina reassured Vega that his memories would return.

"Doctor Gargery said it would take time. You are missing memories of your past. You can still form new memories."

Vega turned to face his host, measuring the kindness in her eyes.

"Were we more than colleagues, Coralina? I mean, there was something more between us, right?"

Coralina stared at her guest, wondering if it would be rude to tell him the truth.

"Yes, Aloysius. You loved me, and I loved you."

Still fixed on her round brown eyes, he asked if that were the case, why did she marry someone else and have another man's child?

"Because you would not marry me. You would not profess your love for me, a feeling you held within your heart but would not reveal. A feeling obvious to me."

"Your husband, he died. I know that. And Juliet is his daughter."

"Juliet will never know her father. She will be the daughter of the man who loves me and embraces Juliet as his own."

Vega stood, releasing her hand, downing the last of his drink.

"You were there when I was shot."

"I was. We were waiting in line to see Johnny Rivers, in the cold, outside the Whisky a Go Go. You are remembering this?"

"I was told this. I have no memory of being shot. Not even a vague recollection. Just heartbeats. I heard heartbeats. That's it. To be honest, I don't want to know. I don't ever want to remember."

His tone in telling her this was terrifying.

"Sit back down, Aloysius. You are tired."

He did, and was soon resting his head on her lap, inhaling her floral perfume as he wandered into sleep. She combed his hair, certain the flecks of gray were new and multiplying. And considered how difficult it must be for a man who cannot remember to work alongside a young woman like Nancy, someone born never to forget.

CHAPTER TWENTY-FOUR

Vega called directory assistance from home the following morning after waking up disoriented on the couch in Coralina's living room. He slept through Juliet's two cries for breast-feedings. Jotting a note of thanks for the dinner, he was quickly out Coralina's door before five a.m.

After a shower, shave and a breakfast of Cheerios and a tall screwdriver, he waited until a minute after eight to telephone James Carty, the attorney representing Alvin Karpis. After identifying himself, he told Carty his client may have information on a woman who mysteriously vanished seventeen years earlier. He explained how a McNeil Island inmate claimed to have seen Mary Showalter with Karpis.

"That's quite an interesting case you're pursuing, Mr. Vega. My client never mentioned this Mary Showalter by name but he attracted many pen pals during his incarceration. Especially after that movie came out about Bonnie Parker and Clyde Barrow. They started reaching out, seeking a connection to those bygone days, wanting to contact the last survivor, my client. Many were writing school papers. Others, mostly young women, were seeking some kind of relationship. I know that seems peculiar, even deviant behavior given the hardships."

Vega admitted he didn't understand such attraction. Carty agreed.

"These relationships are a mystery for the average person. Many of these women are drawn to inmates because they are lonely or have experienced abuse and trauma in their lives. Their self-esteem is low. For the prisoner, he has little else to do. The two can be a potent mix."

"Getting back to my case, you don't recall Mr. Karpis mentioning Mary Showalter?"

"As I said, there were many female pen pals. My client did not share correspondence with me, and I do not recall that name on any of the visitor logs."

"You have access to those logs? The information I received said Mary met with Mr. Karpis just prior to his release. Checking the log may reveal the name of his visitor."

"I do have access, but I'm afraid I cannot provide those names to you without my client's permission."

Unsure such a request would be honored and knowing that visitor logs were not available to the public, Vega was determined to keep Carty on the line.

"I appreciate your time. May I ask how you came to represent Mr. Karpis?"

"Of course."

For the next ten minutes, Carty explained how he came to meet Old Creepy, as the tommy-gun ringleader of the Barker gang was nicknamed. One of Carty's other clients began serving time at McNeil. He took guitar lessons from Karpis, who taught other inmates. Carty's client began sharing information about the gangster's case.

"I was aware of Karpis and his Depression Era gang, but I was surprised to learn he was alive and remained behind bars."

Carty said he met Karpis at McNeil Island in 1967. The gangster had been up for parole since 1951 but was repeatedly refused release despite good behavior and glowing references from prison staff, including the warden. The next parole hearing would be the following year. By this point Karpis had been mostly abandoned by his legal counsel. He had no money for an attorney and, at age sixty, had little hope for release.

"After our meeting, I was determined to represent him. I was confident he was a reformed prisoner. I believed he was being denied a fair parole hearing. I offered to provide my services for free. I was certain I could secure his release."

Carty explained that when Hoover personally arrested Karpis in New Orleans in 1936, the confrontation drew front-page headlines across the nation – publicity sought by the FBI director. Hoover was determined to send a message that crime did not pay. Gangsters such as John Dillinger, Pretty Boy Floyd, and Baby Face Nelson were to be presented as low-life criminals, not sympathetic Robin Hoods. By the time Karpis was arrested, the others had been killed in shootouts.

"The main obstacle to obtaining parole for my client was Hoover himself."

Carty said the young FBI director had attended the initial interrogation of Karpis and had refused to allow an attorney to be present. The questioning continued for 108 hours. Karpis was soon charged in the kidnapping of William Hamm, a wealthy Minnesota brewer. Hamm was freed after the Barker gang was paid a $100,000 ransom.

"I established that, under Hoover's direction, the FBI coerced Karpis to sign an extradition waiver on the promise of legal counsel. That, and the lack of such counsel during the extensive questioning were grounds for a new trial."

For the next year Carty said he undertook a determined campaign of requests for records from the Department of Justice and the FBI. Using political connections in Washington, D.C., Carty made it known that he was eager for a new trial and intended to put

Hoover, then seventy-three, on the stand should Karpis once again be denied parole.

The strategy worked. Hoover declined all requests and the parole board unanimously approved the release of Karpis. State and federal officials moved quickly to release and deport the former gangster to his native Canada.

"Nice work."

"Thank you. But Hoover remains behind his desk. He'll never retire and members of Congress are gutless to remove him. He'll have to die before a new director is named. Now, Mr. Vega, you know the story of my client. Do you still wish to speak with him?"

CHAPTER TWENTY-FIVE

Mr. Vega, please don't be angry with me. I've located Arthur Quail."

Hearing Nancy's voice and her plea for mercy released some of the anger that had roiled Vega's gut, but gnawing discomfort remained.

"Dammit, Nancy. You can't run off like that and not keep me informed."

"You sound like my mother."

"I'm your boss. That carries more weight. Where are you?"

"I'm at the Hillsdale Inn in San Mateo, which is..."

"I know where San Mateo is. What-the-fuck are you doing there? You said..."

"I said I was driving to Mission Viejo and I did. That's where Quail works. However, he's here, in this very hotel, for an FDIC conference. I decided I better keep on his tail."

"You decided? You work for me, remember? And quit trying to act like a private eye. You're not Sam Spade or even Nancy Drew. 'I better keep on his tail.' For Christ sake."

"Okay, perhaps I didn't follow your instructions to a tee. But I did leave a message that I would call again *after* I found Quail. I did speak with Quail's neighbor, Abraham Barnheiser, yesterday before I drove up the 101."

The girl has chops, Vega said to nobody.

"Keep talkin'."

"He didn't have much to say. Nothing, really. Refused to talk. But he paused as he stepped away when I mentioned Mary Showalter by name. That's a tell, isn't it?"

"Could be. Or it might just be a reaction to hearing her name after all these years. Mary's vanishing act was big news back then. Anything else to report? Did you learn anything about Quail aside from he's in the Bay Area on business?"

"I found his address in the telephone directory. He lives in a nice home near Trabuco Canyon. I mean a really nice house. It's up on a hill overlooking the mountains. He's married now. I checked with the county recorder. Married Marjorie Ford in 1957, five years after Mary disappeared. They have at least two children. I spotted the missus and two kids leaving the house. The kids go to Fairmont, a private school for all ages. Both likely in the middle grades. Boy and a girl. Might be twins."

"Good work."

Vega considered the options before responding. The choice he made wasn't smart, wasn't clean, but felt inevitable.

"If I'm going to let this happen and have you talk to Quail, I need you to be prepared."

The plan they discussed was purposely simple. Nancy would cull Quail from the flock of conventioneering bank examiners by calling the hotel's front desk asking them to page him for an important telephone call. Nancy would call from her hotel room.

"There's a bank of telephone booths off the lobby. I can place the call from there. It would give me a good view of the courtesy phone without being too obvious, and I wouldn't have to dash down to the lobby from my room."

"Smart girl. I like it. Go down there now and call me from the booth you pick out."

When the two reconnected, Vega had Nancy describe the distance and line of sight.

"Good. Do you think you could see the courtesy phone if the lobby was crowded?"

"If need be, I could stand on the seat. It's wooden."

"I hope that's not necessary. Now, don't hang up. I want you to go find the hotel's listing of events. Find out when the day's FDIC seminar concludes."

A minute later, Nancy informed Vega that the afternoon's session on "Legal Elements in Financial Fraud Investigations" would end at four o'clock.

"It's scheduled to begin at one."

"Like his colleagues, our Mr. Quail will be anxious to get to the bar after three hours of indoctrination. Be in the phone booth by 3:30 in case they wrap up earlier. Once you see these guys start flowing through the lobby – to the bar or their rooms – place the call. If Quail decides to head to his room, you won't be able to identify him. Now, let's talk about the phone call."

Vega proceeded to script the call Nancy would make. After identifying herself as working for the Vega Detective Agency, she would tell Quail she had information on Mary Showalter. She then would begin to ask a series of questions Vega had prepared.

"After the call, our man Quail may to go to the reception desk to see if they have a description of the woman who placed the call. They won't. He also may look in your direction. If he does, pretend you're on a phone call. Act it up. Like you're gabbing with a girlfriend. Under no circumstances do I want you asking questions other than the ones I'm giving you. Or doing something stupid like leaving the phone booth to get a closer look at our guy. I don't want you trying to be a hero. A voice on the phone, that's all I want you to be. Understand?"

"Yes, Mr. Vega. I'll stay on script."

Following her call with Vega, Nancy returned to the stillness of her spare hotel room. She checked her watch. The seminar would begin shortly. With almost three hours to kill, she turned on the television set that rested unevenly on a wooden stand tilted to one side because of a broken caster. Rotating the dial past *Jeopardy* and *The Guiding Light*, she settled on an old Spencer Tracy movie. Portraying a priest, the actor was conversing with a convict on a faraway volcanic island.

> "I was a pretty good thief in my time."
> "I believe that. It's never too late to change."
> "My mother, that's what she used to say, It's never too late."
> "She was right."
> "She kept after me – kept tellin' me – there was another thief once dyin' on the cross right next to Christ."
> "The Good Thief."
> "That's what she called him."
> "He didn't chicken out. He just got smart and at the very last moment, he stole Heaven."
> "That's pretty good stealin', huh, Father?"

Unable to concentrate, Nancy stood, studying her mirrored reflection on the sliding closet door across from the bed. She looked much as she did years ago. Dark hair long and straight. Her figure tailored as narrowly as a pencil skirt. Her face still displaying the shyness that condemned her to home on two prom nights. The open side of the closet revealed the few clothes she had put on hangers after arriving. A dark pair of slacks. A camel-colored sweater. A navy-colored shift with ivory cuffs and collar.

Her part in the Showalter investigation was insignificant, like the convict's bit part in the old film. Walk on, utter a line or two of dialogue, then disappear. Not even a mention when the end credits roll.

Nancy understood that any moves off Vega's careful script would further jeopardize her already shaky standing. Still, she considered his options. If he were to fire her, Coralina wasn't ready to return to the agency. Unless he found another assistant, Vega would have to close the agency, precisely the situation he was trying to avoid with this desperate gamble to locate Mary Showalter.

After reviewing her reflection a final time, Nancy switched off the television set before closing the door to her room behind her.

— • —

The Persimmon Shop in downtown San Mateo was the destination for young women who wouldn't be caught dead shopping for clothes at Macy's or the Emporium at the city's nearby mall along El Camino Real. With curated outfits from the designs of Mary Quant to styles of art nouveau, Hollywood, and Villager, the shop had been recommended to Nancy by the hotel's concierge. Finding an outfit that would make her appear older than her nineteen years was imperative should a chance meeting with Arthur Quail occur.

After trying on several styles, including miniskirts she found too revealing and pantsuits that were garishly colored, Nancy left the store with a light floral maxi dress with wedged open-toe boots that laced midway up the calf. Three doors away, Nancy entered a local hairdresser where she obtained an immediate seating. Ninety minutes later, half of her elbow-length dark hair littered the tiled floor. The remainder, now with caramel highlights, flowed in lazy waves to just above her shoulders.

The waning hour of Nancy's afternoon was spent back in the hotel room experimenting with her mother's jewelry to see which went best with the new outfit. Working two jobs and without a husband, Georgia Randall had little use for the necklaces, pendants, and bracelets she wore dining out or at the theater as a married woman. They remained in dusty jewelry boxes until presented to her daughter on her sixteenth birthday. At the time Nancy declared she had no use or desire for jewelry. Her mother thought otherwise.

"You won't always be a tomboy, Nancy. You are an intelligent, perceptive child with a very special gift. But you were born a girl and will soon become a woman. You will have a lady's perspective on the world and become the kind of lady that society expects."

Nancy recalled the admonition as she fingered the gold locket hanging above her breastbone. Her mother's comments had been made only three years earlier but seemed from another era, a gray time of stability before young people began kicking hard against the status quo. She had observed society's wild eroding from the sideline, in the safety and quiet of a library rather than in the streets or universities like many of her generation.

From an early age Nancy used her library card as a passport to inhabit worlds other than her own. She traveled the road with Sal Paradise and lingered with Anna. She inhaled the novels of Fitzgerald, Lawrence, Flaubert, and Marquez. Her memory fastened on the lessons of humanity stumbling over itself in pursuit of lasting fulfillment only to be swallowed by mortality.

Yet, it was Scout who remained for Nancy the honest compass. Jean Louise Finch was most like the girl in the mirror. Unusually intelligent and confident, uncomfortable with the portrayal family and society was imposing on her, Scout nonetheless slowly shed the chrysalis of childhood.

Nancy set the locket and chain on the six-drawer wooden dresser, instead picking up her mother's akoya pearl necklace, admiring the perfectly round beads held against her carelessly freckled skin.

"This one."

CHAPTER TWENTY-SIX

Tired of sitting in the stillness of the Vega Detective Agency waiting for a call from Alvin Karpis, Vega made his way to the headquarters of Palm Springs Police Department. Ten days had passed since he requested the investigation files on the Showalter case. That was the allowance given government agencies to produce documents under the state's new Public Records Act.

"Where are my files, Turner?"

Vega's nemesis was scanning that day's *Desert Post*, not even looking up when the detective arrived.

"My files? Time's up."

The uniformed officer took a leisurely swig from a coffee cup before closing the day's edition and looking up at his customer.

"Don't have 'em."

"What the fuck? The law says..."

"The law says the public is entitled to see certain records ... unless there is a specific reason not to do so."

"You telling me the department is claiming the files relating to a seventeen-year-old missing person case are exempt? That there's a need to keep the files from the public? Is that what you're telling me?"

"Not at all. And keep your voice down or..."

"Or what? You'll have me arrested?"

"That would please me to no end, Vega. Escorted out of the building is likely all I can do at the moment. Now, as to the records you requested, I'm told they no longer exist."

"What did you say?"

"I said the records department says those files no longer exist."

"They were destroyed? The case is still open, for Christ sake. Mary Showalter has never been found."

"I didn't say they were destroyed, Vega. I said they no longer exist in our custody."

"Who has them?"

Turner shrugged.

"DOJ? FBI?"

Another shrug.

"So, what you're telling me is that the Palm Springs Police Department has no idea the whereabouts of their own case files related to the disappearance of one of your own citizens?"

"We don't have them. That's what I'm telling you."

"Jesus! Did you guys even bother looking?"

"We followed the letter of the law. I have work to get back to."

"Must take you forever to get through the funny pages."

— • —

Vega's next stop was the *Desert Post* where he relayed his encounter to Jarvis.

"We don't have them, that was Turner's response?"

"Yep. You gonna do a story?"

"Needs more digging. I'd rather write a story that says where these files ended up and why before I convict Turner and the other Keystone Cops. Like you said, they could have been turned over to other agencies that were involved in the original investigation."

"Or they were deliberately hidden or even destroyed to cover up shoddy police work."

"Either way, their disappearance is worth pursuing. But I gotta have more or it won't get through my editor. You wanna tell me now why you're pursuing the Showalter case? Got to be more than the reward money. Do you know what happened to her?"

"I wish. Would make my life a lot easier. You work on the missing files. Get to the bottom of that and I'll spill what I've found on the missing girl. Deal?"

"Throw in a Sherman's and we'll shake on it."

— • —

Returning to his Cathedral City office, Vega checked his watch and the answering machine – no messages. It was nearly three o'clock. Rather than pace as he waited for calls from Nancy or Karpis, Vega placed a call to Erika.

"Miss Lake's residence."

"Afternoon, Calvin. Is the lady of the house available?"

"She's out back, Mr. Vega. I'll see if she'll take your call."

"Graci."

Vega nibbled on a fingernail, another bad habit that had suddenly made its way into his psyche. The nail was notched by the time she answered.

"Aloysius, you must be a mind-reader. I was about to call you. Two things. First, anything to report on your search for the Showalter girl? Second, I am extending an invitation to a party. The theme is Aquarius. Guests are to come dressed as flower children, hippies, what have you. You will come won't you, Aloysius?"

"Sure. First, I need to understand why the Showalter case is important to you. Important enough for you to arrange airfare for me to talk with your favorite convict."

"I wish you wouldn't speak of Johnny that way. It hurts my feelings."

"What's in it for you, Erika? Your interest in Mary Showalter goes beyond helping Roselli get a reduced sentenced. The reward money? Somebody bumped it up thirty grand. You? Be straight with me now."

A hand muffled the phone on the other end. Vega could hear two voices but was unable to make out what they were saying.

"Erika? You there?"

"Yes. I was just asking Calvin to fix me a martini that I can enjoy on the patio. I can have him make two?"

"I'm waiting here for two important phone calls. Now, about your interest in Showalter."

"What do you want to know, Aloysius?"

"Let's start with the reward. Did you ante it up? There's always purpose to what you do, Erika. Did you know the Showalter girl?"

"I knew her from the bank. She was quite an accomplished girl. Reserved, but very smart. She handled our accounts, so I got to know her quite well. Pardon my pause, but Calvin has arrived with my cocktail."

Vega kept an eye on the answering machine light as he waited. It remained unlit.

"There, I'm back. Sure you don't want to join me?"

"Love to, but as I said..."

"When did you become all business, Aloysius? I recall a time when you were a lot of fun."

"That was before I took bullet to the chest. Being the target of an angry husband can do that to a person."

"But your chest has healed, hasn't it?"

"It has. I'd like to get back to..."

"Come now, detective. At one time you wanted to seduce me. I recall a late-evening attempt to get between my legs."

Erika Lake was like that, especially with alcohol. One minute pseudo-nobility, the next a hungry predator.

"I was toasted."

"You were dashing. You arrived like Errol Flynn, with a bottle of champagne in one hand and roses in the other. How was I to resist?"

"You did resist."

"As charming as you were, you were, as you say, quite inebriated. I doubted you could fulfill your promise"

"Can we get back to the reason I called?"

"If you must."

"You knew Mary Showalter only through the savings-and-loan, is that correct?"

"I feel like I'm being interrogated. Am I?"

"On the day Mary and Arthur Quail were married, you were there for the wedding. Why?"

"I don't know what you are talking about."

"Your picture was in the newspaper. Standing with the two newly-weds. I saw the picture, Erika."

"That photograph? It was taken at the courthouse. After their marriage ceremony. They needed a witness and I was there."

"You just happened to be at the courthouse when they got married? Quite the coincidence."

"I know how you feel about that word. You told me the universe is rarely that lazy. I was at the courthouse that day, if you need to know. Eugene and I met with Judge Lawson about his re-election campaign. Eugene was a major contributor. I had not met the judge, so we went to the courthouse that day. As we were leaving his private chambers I saw Mary in the hallway. She was in tears. She and Arthur had just been named husband and wife by Judge... oh, I don't remember the name ... when the person who was to witness the ceremony abruptly left the before she signed the marriage certificate. I volunteered to sign the certificate even if I hadn't witnessed the ceremony. I checked with the judge and he said to go ahead. Mary had to pull herself together, fix her makeup before the photographer they hired took the post-ceremony photos. Mary asked for me to join her and Arthur for one. I did. That's the one that was published in the Post, the photograph you saw."

The story was a stretch and Vega guessed there was more to Erika's relationship with Mary Showalter but pressing her now seemed futile. Instead, he asked about Mary's husband.

"Arthur Quail, what was he like?"

"Movie star good looks and charming. I understood why Mary was attracted, but I couldn't figure out what he saw in her. I know it sounds catty but Mary was cute in her way, polite as could be, but she didn't strike me as Arthur's type. Golden boys don't usually go for Plain Janes. Look, I'm tired of talking. If you don't want to join me for a cocktail, I'll have to find someone else."

"Final question, Erika. Just one."

A gulp and the sound of glass on metal told Vega that Erika had finished her martini and was about to have Calvin serve a second.

"Who was the witness who left without signing the marriage certificate?"

"That was Mary's sister."

CHAPTER TWENTY-SEVEN

Reaching the bank of hotel phones, Nancy was relieved to see the other booths were empty. Twenty minutes remained before the scheduled end of the FDIC conference taking place down the hallway to her left. She passed the time practicing her questions and taking deep breaths, worried her rapid heartbeat would find its way to her voice.

A crowd of men in white shirts and gray suits emerged from the ballroom at 3:45. Nancy sent a dime clicking its way into the telephone's internal mechanisms and dialed the hotel's main number. Across the lobby, a young woman paused from registering a well-dressed couple with one suitcase to answer the call.

"Hillsdale Inn, can you hold?"

Before Nancy could respond, Vivaldi's Violin Concerto in E Major came on, an enchanting piece from 1725 now used to comfort those on hold. She waited helplessly as the crowd began to split like an ameba in different directions. Some toward elevators, others for the bar. Several headed her direction, taking seats in the phone booths on either side.

"Thank you for holding, how can I help you?"

After explaining the urgency that required paging a guest during such a busy time for hotel staff, Nancy again was placed on hold.

The audible page for Arthur Quail came quickly. It was broadcast twice, asking its target to come to the white courtesy phone near reception.

From a small, animated group to Nancy's right, a tall, curly-haired man made his way toward the phone in question. He moved with an unhurried pace that suggested both detachment and swagger.

"Arthur Quail."

His name only. No hello. No "this is." Just two words, spoken in a voice confident and somewhat hoarse.

"Mr. Quail. My name is Nancy Randall. I work for the Vega Detective Agency in Palm Springs."

A slight pause, but no change in pitch or confidence.

"How can I help you, Miss…"

"Randall. I'm calling you regarding Mary Showalter."

A brief pause.

"Yes?"

"Your first wife."

A longer pause. Perhaps reflecting that Miss Randall is aware of more personal background than first thought.

"I'm aware of whom I married. What is this about?"

No trace of confusion or astonishment. No question as to whether Mary were alive or that her body had been found. Nancy waited for Quail to continue. He didn't. Nancy moved to her next practiced statement.

"Our agency is looking into her disappearance. We would like to…"

"After seventeen years? You're looking into her disappearance seventeen years later?"

"We would like to speak with you about that time. We…"

"Miss Randall, as you apparently have learned, I have moved on with my life. I remarried. I have a family. I have no desire to resurrect the past. I told police and FBI at the time everything I knew. Repeatedly. I'm certainly not willing to speak with you, your agency or anyone else about that. Especially not to someone who doesn't have the courtesy to reach me beyond a telephone call from Palm Springs."

Arthur Quail looked neither right nor left after hanging up the courtesy phone. He returned to his pals, apparently picking up the conversation he had been called away from. Nancy watched all this from the phone booth, pretending to be on another call. Several minutes of laughter and chit-chat passed before the group headed toward a hallway that led to the hotel bar.

— • —

Back in her room, Nancy briefed Vega on her short conversation with Quail. The responses, they agreed, provided little useful information. Nancy was troubled by how cold he seemed.

"He never even mentioned her name. How can someone move away from love so completely? Even after seventeen years, shouldn't a piece of his heart belong to Mary?"

"You assume he loved her. We don't know if he did. Only that he married her."

Vega withheld from Nancy his conversation with Erika.

"Did you get a good look at him?"

"I wasn't close and I left my glasses back in the room. But he was tall, had an athletic build, curly brown hair. Dressed well. Better than the others. More of a moneyed look – executive – than bank examiner. I can try to get a better look, if you'd like."

"No way. We know where he lives. You know what he looks like. We can always track him down later. Get something to eat then a good night's sleep. You got a long drive back in the morning. I expect you back in the office by…"

"I'll be there by three. It's an eight-hour drive and I'm stopping for lunch."

"See you then. Safe travels."

After a call to reassure her mother, Nancy modeled her new outfit before returning to the lobby. Her change in appearance – new clothes, new hairdo – had changed her. She was certain of it, aware of the glances from the men in the lobby. She felt as different as she looked. Like her first period, a transformation was underway. Another stage in her journey from child to adult, from girl to woman.

CHAPTER TWENTY-EIGHT

Three taxis meandered through a grove of eucalyptus trees along Coyote Point Drive until they stopped in front of the Castaway Restaurant. The first two unloaded their passengers, five men in one, four in the other. One man stumbled as the group climbed the few wooden stairs at the entrance, provoking snorts and chuckles from his buddies.

As the lone passenger in the third taxi dug into her purse, a TWA jetliner screamed overhead as it approached San Francisco's international airport across the saltwater bay.

It's quieter inside, the driver told Nancy as she paid the five-dollar fare.

"I sure hope so. Thanks so much for the history lesson!"

Inside the Polynesian-style restaurant, Nancy asked for and was seated at a table just outside the bar. She told the hostess she was not expecting anyone, looking instead for a quiet meal before a long drive the following day.

Across the main dining area, a wide swath of windows offered a stunning view of another jetliner about to touch down less than a mile ahead.

"Amazing view, isn't it?"

The waitress delivered the menu and asked if Nancy wanted something to drink before ordering. Despite her new outfit and hairdo, the waitress wasn't fooled.

"Honey, you don't look old enough for a cocktail, but I can have them mix up a special Mai Tai or Passionate Virgin without the booze."

"Sure. The Mai Tai sounds good. Thanks."

In one corner of the dining room, the band of merry bank examiners were loudly teasing another waitress as she took their drink orders. Nancy's table allowed her to watch the group without being obvious. A menagerie of float lamps, fishing nets, hanging strings of seashells, and other flotsam-and-jetsam decorations provided coverage.

Her plan to confront Quail had not been entirely thought through. She kept a low profile in the hotel lobby, waiting for the group to leave the bar. They did, forty minutes later, reassembling outside as the valet signaled for two taxis. Nancy took a third, asking the driver to follow the others at a reasonable pace behind.

Her first sip of the Mai Tai announced it was not a virgin. Rum and orange liqueur were prominent. A quick glance toward the bar disclosed the reason. Busily cleaning a log-stemmed wine glass was a handsome young bartender. He flashed a toothy smile her way, signaling the secret was to be kept between them.

Left alone, with no companion to occupy her, Nancy inspected the expansive restaurant, now rapidly filling with customers. In the far corner, where windows looked both east to the cities across the bay and north toward the airport, Quail seemed to be holding court with his boisterous male companions. Sipping more of her cocktail, Nancy considered her gamble. This was her one chance to encounter Quail. In the morning she would have to leave for Palm Springs. Too long a drive to return empty-handed. The game, she smiled, is afoot.

"How's the Mai Tai, darling? Too sweet?"

"It's fine, thank you. I'm ready to order. I'd like the Breast of Capon Castaway. However, please ask the chef to leave out the nutmeg. I'm allergic. The reactions aren't severe, just irritating."

"No problem, honey. Any other allergies we should be aware of?"

"None. Thank you for asking."

Already light-headed, Nancy sipped more of her Mai Tai, altering her focus between Quail's boisterous table and the constant trail of jetliners landing across the bay at twilight. She designed two scenarios for confronting Quail. Should he head for the men's room, she would approach him before he returned to his table. If he made it through their meal and additional rounds of cocktails without getting up, she would confront him as his group left the restaurant.

— • —

Later, as she picked at her dessert of pineapple cheesecake, stretching out her time at the Castaway, Nancy considered her foolishness. What exactly was she hoping to achieve? If Quail had murdered his first wife, he certainly wasn't going to confess to someone he didn't know, a young woman acting like Mata Hari. If he had nothing to do with her disappearance, what other information could be gained beyond their brief phone call? It was all a dumb dress-up game. Vega had been right. Get a good night's sleep and head home in the morning.

But as a Scottish poem loved by Nancy as a child foretold: "The best laid plans of mice and men go oft awry."

"Well, hi there! Are you here alone?"

It was one of the men from Quail's group. He was quite inebriated.

"No woman should eat alone. Why don't you join us? The table in the corner. We can pull up another chair."

"I appreciate the invitation, but I'm about to leave."

"Can I buy you an after-dinner drink?"

"No thank you. If you would…"

She was lifted from her chair by the elbow, knocking her dessert fork to the floor.

"Staff will pick it up. Don't worry. I gotta introduce you to the guys. I told them about the pretty girl in the hotel lobby. C'mon."

Rather than resist, Nancy allowed herself to be ushered across the dining room toward the table of bank examiners.

"Guys! This is the gal I told you about. At the hotel? Didn't I tell you she was pretty?"

The group fumbled their way to their feet, introducing themselves in a cacophony of clattering plates and first names, many of them slurred beyond recognition. The commotion continued as they fought to make room for another chair.

"Guys, please sit down. I can't stay. I have a long drive ahead of me in the morning. Back to Palm Springs."

A chorus of "aw c'mon" and "how 'bout a nightcap" eventually quieted as they returned to their seats.

"Really, tomorrow's a long day. And it sounds like you're having a good time without my company...or that of your wives."

"Alvin over there, he's not married. Neither is Marvin."

Nancy glanced at the two men who had been singled out.

"Sorry, guys, I'm not looking for a husband."

"How about a boyfriend?"

"Not one of those either."

"Well then, what brings you to here from Palm Springs? You must be looking for something...or someone."

The comment was made by Arthur Quail. His emerald eyes inspected Nancy as she turned to face him.

"I came here on business, actually. Looking for a missing person."

From the far end of the table came two questions.

"An ex-husband who owes you a lot of dough?"

"You a lady cop?"

Nancy looked away from Quail and surveyed each member of the party.

"Nope. Neither. It's a woman I'm searching for."

"See? I told you she was a dyke."

The crass insult was whispered, but it was heard by Nancy and ignored by the other men at the table.

"No. Not that either. The woman I'm looking for has been missing for seventeen years. I intend to find out what happened to her."

One of the men asked if the woman had been murdered. It was Quail who answered.

"It's only murder if they find a body. Otherwise, it's just a missing person."

CHAPTER TWENTY-NINE

The sun had already retired behind the coastal mountains by the time Quail and Nancy set off along one of the lightly graveled trails along the peninsula of Coyote Point. A waning crescent moon cast just enough light to guide the way along the bluffs of serpentine bedrock. A prevailing wind from the east, bitter and unrelenting, buffeted the pair and slapped murky waves against the shoreline sixty-four feet below. Overhead, jetliners arrived at a pace that seemed to match Nancy's stumbles on the scree beneath her new boots.

"I'm afraid I didn't pick the right shoes for this."

Quail was waiting for her outside the ladies' room at the restaurant where she stopped after paying her bill. When she emerged, Quail said he would answer her questions as best he could. He offered to share a taxi back to the hotel.

"We can talk on the ride. Or at the hotel. My room or yours."

"Sorry, that's an unacceptable offer, Mr. Quail."

"The bar here then?"

"I'm not twenty-one."

"It doesn't matter."

"It matters to me."

The decision to talk outside was mutual but they found little privacy. Patrons were arriving non-stop. Smokers took up the corners beside the entrance. The parking lot offered some relief until deserting diners found their cars. An entrance to a trail through the eucalyptus trees was spotted. Nancy hadn't balked. Getting Quail to talk pushed aside any concerns she had about safety.

"What is it you want to know, Miss Randall? I haven't seen my former wife since she disappeared. You surely must have read the newspaper accounts."

"I have."

Quail assessed Nancy briefly before continuing.

"So then, how can I help you?"

"Did you search for Mary?"

"Search for her? No. There was an army looking for her. Police. FBI. Eagle Scouts. Friends. Neighbors. I had no clue where she could be. Turns out no one did."

"So, what did you do? Just sit at home?"

"I gathered everything I could – letters, her book of phone numbers, bills, credit card statements, diary, her clothes, makeup, all..."

"She kept a diary?"

"That's what I just said. I turned it over to police."

"Did you open it? Read the entries?"

"She told me it was private. I respected that."

As the trail bent left, they could see Pacific fog curling over San Bruno Mountain, inching its way toward the airport.

"We should head back. The fog will wash away the little light we're getting from the moon."

Retracing their steps, the lights along the East Bay caught Nancy's attention. She stopped, pointing her finger toward a single light that shimmered above all the others.

"See that point of light?"

Quail stopped and nodded, unsure for the first time where Nancy's line of questioning was going.

"It's called The Eye of Mount Diablo. My cab driver said it's a beacon at the summit of the mountain, and that it was first ignited by Charles Lindbergh in 1928 as an aid to early transcontinental aviation."

Quail tucked his hands into the pockets of his tailored suit, rocking on his heals.

"This is what you wanted to tell me?"

Nancy resumed walking, once more glimpsing the Eye of Diablo twenty-one miles to the east. Quail followed a short distance behind.

"How long did you wait to divorce Mary?"

"Five years. That's what it took for the state to consider her legally dead. You get one more question, Miss Randall. After that I'm going back to the hotel, with or without you. You'll need to subpoena me for any further statements."

"Fair enough. What do you believe happened to Mary?"

Quail stopped. The restaurant and its lights were visible ahead.

"What do I believe? I haven't the foggiest. There were indications of violence, her blood, but no body was discovered. No reports of someone matching her description showing up in an emergency room. No further contact except for that identification at the service station. And even that wasn't entirely reliable. Hell, I don't have an answer and, frankly, after all this time, nearly twenty years, I don't care. Life goes on ... including mine."

With that, Arthur Quail walked away, toward the first in a line of taxis waiting outside the Castaway.

"Mary's alive, Mr. Quail! She was seen!"

CHAPTER THIRTY

The voice on the telephone line was clipped. Fatigued rather than annoyed.

"Am I talking with Mr. Aloysius Vega?"

"You are."

"Mr. Carty tells me you think I have information concerning a missing person case from 1952. That I'm not a suspect, being that I was incarcerated at the time. That your interest in interviewing me, and what we discuss, is not being recorded, and will not end up in a newspaper, magazine or in some future book. Am I understanding the rules correctly?"

"You are."

"Fine. What is it you want to know?"

"Mr. Karpis, thank you for your call. I am indeed wanting to talk with you about a woman who vanished from Palm Springs back in fifty-two. The circumstances are rather complex. I'll give you the short version."

The former gangster listened quietly as Vega summarized the case – the brief marriage, the bloodstained car, the victim's neatly folded clothes, the credit card used to purchase a tank of gas, the lack of evidence, the magazine article that was mailed to the agency.

"And this girl, Mary Showalter, you believe visited me at McNeil Island shortly before I was paroled?"

"That is what I have been told. I have no evidence other than what was told to me by an inmate."

"And this other inmate, you trust him to be honest?"

"Short answer: no."

"Then why do you believe him and his account?"

"I need the reward money."

A raspy cough followed. A smoker's cough.

"Jim told me you appeared to be a straight shooter. This inmate, can you tell me his name?"

"John Roselli."

Another phlegmy hack.

"A big cheese in Vegas at one time. Now, just a dime-store con caught cheating at cards. How did he say he came to see me with this woman?"

"He didn't. He related what he was told by another inmate, László Löwenstein. Know him?"

"I do. Taught him to play the guitar. Or tried to. Wasn't as driven as my other pupils, especially Charlie. But László was gifted. In financial entries and law. I would have liked to have him at my side, back in the days."

On the other end of the wires that connect Cathedral City with Montreal, the voice suspended. Thinking.

"Getting back to the reason you called, Mr. Vega – or that I called you – I can now understand how this tangled mess of a case came alive after so long. László had earned privileges to Summit House, which is where I bunked. He was among the handful of inmates allowed out of the main campus to help maintain equipment and ensure staff quarters were properly cleaned."

"So, you can confirm that Mr. Löwenstein saw you with Mary Showalter?"

"Not at all. He did see me with a woman at Summit House. Caught me with my pants down, in fact, enjoying a visit from a correspondent, a delightful dick-licker. But it wasn't your Mary."

"How do you know?"

"After he spoke to you, Jim faxed me a newspaper article with the photograph. I can assure you, the woman practiced in the art of fellatio, the one László saw, was not Mary Showalter. I can see how he was mistaken. There is somewhat of a resemblance. Dark hair up. Maybe in the eyes. But the two were not anywhere close in age. According to the newspapers, Mary was twenty-five when she disappeared. That would put her at forty-two now. My visitor was much younger. In her twenties. About the age of Miss Showalter when she disappeared."

The room darkened around Vega, prelude to an onset of vertigo. The Showalter case had collapsed. With it, the reward and any hope of keeping the agency afloat.

"Mr. Vega? Are you still there?"

"Yeah. You certain the woman you were with was not Mary Showalter?"

"I have no reason to lie to you."

— • —

Nancy found her boss dead to the world on the sofa in his office when she arrived later that afternoon. Rather than interrupt his sleep, she busied herself around the office. The place was filthy. Papers were scattered across his desk and on the floor as if someone had brushed them aside in a fit of anger. The coffee pot would need to be replaced. The bottom was baked with melted grounds.

There were no phone messages to check, so she pulled from her desk drawer a cotton cloth and a bottle of Old English furniture polish and began to clean the dust off her desk. When she finished, she covered Vega with a blanket before locking up the office and returning to her car, now crusted with blotches of bugs she had killed on her drive down the 101.

She returned to the agency the following morning after a long bubble bath, a longer night's sleep, and a new coffee pot. Vega was at his desk looking as if he had never gone home. He hadn't.

"I'll put on some coffee. I bought a new pot. You killed the old one."

"Bring anything to eat?"

"No. Want me to run over to Elmer's?"

"Yes."

"Anything special?"

"Food."

"I hope you have more to say when I return."

— • —

After chowing down a plate of eggs, bacon, ham, sausage links, hash browns, and a buttermilk biscuit, Vega asked when Nancy got back into town.

"Yesterday, around four. Had to change a flat in Gilroy."

"Anything else to report?"

Not surprised that Vega hadn't noticed her new hairstyle, Nancy took his greasy plate to the sink.

"What about you? Any new information to share?"

"The case files are missing. Erika was a last-minute witness to Mary's marriage. Karpis said the woman he was with at McNeil wasn't Mary. Any money left over from your escapade to the Bay Area?"

"What? The files?"

"The money, Nancy. How much is left from the two hundred from petty cash?"

"I...I haven't counted it. I have the receipts for everything. Gas, hotel..."

"I don't care how much you spent. I want to know what's left."

From her desk drawer, she returned with her purse. The wallet contained forty-four dollars and sixteen cents, which she handed to Vega.

"What's wrong, Mr. Vega? I know you're mad at me for…"

"We're broke, Nancy. The agency's kitty has less than a hundred bucks including what you just handed over. My personal accounts are almost dry. I cannot continue to afford you or Coralina. We're shutting down. I'm sorry."

Vega's pronouncement was dismissed by his temporary assistant. Her attention lingered on his statement that Erika was a stand-in witness at the wedding of Arthur Quail and Mary Showalter seventeen years ago.

"Why?"

"Why? Because we're outta money."

"Not that. Why was Erika the witness at Mary's wedding? Did the original witness not show up?"

Itching for a Bloody Mary or some other early-morning fortification, Vega shrugged.

"Who the fuck knows. Erika said she happened to be at the courthouse to meet with a judge she and Eugene were helping get re-elected. Said Mary was in tears. The ceremony was over, but they needed a witness to sign the certificate to make it legal."

"What happened to the person who was supposed to be the witness?"

"Who knows?"

"Erika didn't say?"

"She said Mary's sister abruptly left."

"Her sister?"

"Yeah."

Nancy stared at Vega. His faculties were not firing on all cylinders. Whether from the booze, the fallout from his coma or his depression, his mental state was off. His investigative instincts had been dulled. She re-entered their conversation cautiously.

"Her sister lived on the East Coast, if I recall correctly. She was the only remaining member of Mary's family."

Vega played with his empty coffee cup as she continued.

"So this sister comes across country to attend Mary's wedding and abruptly departs before signing the marriage certificate. Seems odd, don't you think?"

"Maybe they didn't get along."

"Then why would she make the effort to come thousands of miles in the first place?"

"Who knows? Women are a strange breed."

Ignoring the dig, Nancy pursued her questioning.

"Something happened after the sister arrived. Some disagreement."

"Maybe the sister was making googly eyes at the groom."

"Perhaps. Arthur Quail is quite handsome."

Vega looked up from the coffee cup.

"You got that good of a look?"

With a deep breath, Nancy forged ahead.

"We took a walk together."

"You did what?"

"We took a walk together, outside the ..."

What remained of the coffee cup lay shattered on the floor. A brown stain and the hole marked where it smacked the wall. Vega was out from behind his desk in a flash, his face flushed with anger.

"What the fuck did I tell you! Dammit, you agreed to my rules! Rules I made to protect you. This guy you go walkin' with, he could be the guy who killed Mary. What the fuck were you thinking! I ought to fire your ass!"

Nancy waited for her boss to sit down before answering.

"I thought you already did. Said you couldn't afford me anymore. Right? So either I walk out the door now as an ex-employee of the Vega Detective Agency or you listen to what I have to say."

Vega glared.

"When did you suddenly get a mouth on you? I hired this polite little librarian as a temp and she goes rogue on me. Fuck!"

"Your choice?"

"My what?"

"Do I finish my train of thought or do I walk? Your choice."

Vega unballed his fists.

"Go ahead."

"Okay. Hear me out. So Mary's sister comes to the valley to be at the wedding. Something goes sideways and she leaves before signing the document. Erika happens to be there, which seems a bit of a stretch. The presiding judge could have signed the certificate. Anyway, Erika signs for her. The newlyweds leave the courthouse on their way to a happy life together...until, two days later, Mary vanishes."

"Until death do we part came somewhat early."

"Glad to see your sense of humor has returned. Now, tell me what Public Enemy Number One said. About the woman at the prison not being Mary."

Vega summarized the conversation, sanitizing what Karpis had said about the pen pal. The age difference, he said, was the kicker.

"Unless Mary was frozen in time, it wasn't her. This woman sent Karpis a love letter and decided to visit him after she heard he was about to be paroled."

"Mr. Vega, doesn't it seem strange that she didn't wait until he was out? That she only sent one letter? Did Karpis say where this pen pal lived?"

"He didn't say."

Another lapse by the one-time Sherlock Holmes. Something to share with Doctor Dy.

"What else did Old Creepy tell you?"

"Said he was taking inventory as a free man. That he had no apologies to make for his past. He intends to settle down in Montreal, where he was born. Wanted to fit in. Said freedom took some getting used to. He used the example of a simple dinner date. Taking a woman to a restaurant. Does he still help her into a chair? Take her coat? Light her cigarette?"

"I can imagine the shock after thirty-three years of confinement. Going back to the woman at the prison. She was too young to be Mary, right?"

"Yep."

"About how old did he say she was?"

"In her twenties."

"So, it seems that our friend László Löwenstein thought this young woman was the spitting image of Mary ... at least the way he remembered Mary seventeen years ago."

"Carty had sent his client pictures of Mary so Karpis knew what Mary looked like."

"Did Karpis see any resemblance between the two women?"

"Said the hair color was similar. Maybe the eyes."

Vega's inability to make the connection was frightening Nancy. Shouldn't his intellectual faculties be improving as the impact of the coma recedes? Shouldn't the path be in the direction of improvement? What if his spiral was like the descent of a screw, turning slowly at first before disappearing downward – somewhere – until the final twist.

"Mr. Vega?"

"Yeah?"

"We don't know the age of Mary's sister. But if she were younger than Mary, perhaps the woman who László saw with Karpis, the pen pal, was the sister?"

Vega was unmoved by the possibility.

"Highly unlikely. Just the arithmetic is problematic. Mary was twenty-five when she got married. If her sister was now, say, the same age, she would have been, what, eight at the time? Another thing. Seventeen years is a huge interval between children."

"Long, but not impossible."

"The other stretch is this sister becoming pen pals with Alvin Karpis and happening to visit him at McNeil Island on the very same day that László is working at Summit House and sees them together. It's more than a stretch, it's a span of coincidences...Hell, the odds would be up there with me making an unassisted triple play."

"There's one way to find out. We need to locate this sister."

"How?"

"Leave it to me."

"I can't pay you for your time."

"That's fine. Just don't bar door when I return. By the way, the odds of that unassisted triple play? One in 12,492."

CHAPTER THIRTY-ONE

Vega arrived at the entrance to Erika's estate on Hermosa Place where a line of cars emptied passengers dressed in the most garish outfits he could imagine. Technicolor pantsuits, hemp-colored kaftans, lilac miniskirts, blousy tops, fringed jackets. The matriarchal masterclass of Palm Springs – invariably leggy, rich, and privileged – were flagging up their groovy credentials. Their husbands and boyfriends added to the false pageantry with pastel shirts, golden necklace chains, and even a few Nehru jackets.

Vega handed his keys to the young valet who had abandoned his white shirt and pressed slacks for a collarless tunic embroidered with a floral print. From the entrance, Steppenwolf's *Born To Be Wild* could be heard over the babel of what sounded to be a hundred guests gathered out back.

Inside, he corralled a vodka martini and scanned the crowd for the hostess. Erika spotted Vega first and motioned him over to the small troop of women surrounding her. She stunned in low-rise white trousers and a sheer lace blouse that was adorned with a long silver necklace.

"Why am I not surprised that our famous private detective would ignore my directions to dress as a hippie. You do look awfully handsome in your white dinner jacket, though. I was hoping for at least blue jeans and a headband."

"James Bond was about as sixties-ish as I could manage."

"I think he looks absolutely yummy, Erika. Hello, Aloysius."

Vega met Susan Cabot two years ago. The two enjoyed a brief affair that ended in a drunken brawl.

"Susan. You look stunning, as usual."

Dressed in a low-cut peasant blouse and a blue jean miniskirt, Cabot looked ever the part of a beautiful flower child. The petite, dark-eyed actress, forever known for her film role as the *Wasp Woman*, had eased into middle age after enjoying a long-standing affair with Hussein bin Talal, the King of Jordan.

Erika introduced Vega to the other women. Viola Loewy, dressed in fringed vest and wearing a beaded headband, was married to industrial designer Raymond Loewy. Sporting a lively boho maxi dress was Nelda Linsk, wife of art collector Joseph Linsk. And Mousie Powell, who apologized for the absence of her famous husband, actor William Powell.

"Bill is not feeling well. Some type of respiratory bug. He so wanted to see you, Aloysius, and hear about your latest case."

"Give him my best and tell him to rest up."

Like most socialites in Palm Springs, these women knew each other through the Racquet Club where they drank, gossiped, drank, and played tennis. Mostly, they drank and gossiped while watching Dinah Shore or Barbara Marx compete before they all lunched and drank together.

Vega bowed out of the group when the subject turned to the protests at the University of California at Berkeley. Students there were intent creating a "people's park" instead of a soccer field planned by university administrators on vacant land near the campus. He made his way to the back lawn where partiers clustered near the pool that featured the Katni marbled mermaid.

From one group, a man defiantly proclaimed that Nixon's proposal to withdraw troops from South Vietnam was a feint, designed to give the public the appearance of peace when in truth the president was intending to bomb the North back to the stone age. Vega scoffed at the man's silly outfit, a khaki jacket that seemed inspired by the uniforms worn by the Afrika Korps. The look clashed with the man's accent, one usually heard only in a Preston Sturges film: the Palm Beach locked jaw.

Desperate for a second martini, Vega considered whether to hunt for another or just head home. He was uncomfortable among Erika's guests. Home, he could make a pitcher of martinis rather than worry about driving intoxicated. His prayer was answered when a waiter appeared with a tray full of glasses of the satiny fire and ice along with an assortment of bacon-wrapped Medjool dates and Roquefort cheese morsels rolled in crushed nuts.

"They're very tasty, very subtle," it was announced by another guest reaching for the tray. "The dry sackiness of the nuts tiptoes up against the cheese that is so nice, so subtle."

Vega told the woman she had taken the exact words from his mouth.

Careful not to spill his martini, he meandered through the various partygoers, the rich and famous who moved about with the practiced ease of people who never worried about rent or gunfire. Conversations floated past him, thick with names dropped like confetti. He was attracted to an argument about Scott Fitzgerald. The voices weren't raised. Instead, the bickering reminded Vega of a swordfight on a Hollywood sound stage. Two actors egging on the other as they parried and feinted. At stake, pride.

"So here I am. I mean, I did the screenplay for *Beat the Devil* and *The Innocents* way back. And they pay me to write the screenplay for another remake of *Gatsby*. But they didn't like it."

The voice, a man's but girlish, like a baby who had ingested helium, was unmistakable. Through a slim opening in the tight congregation, Vega saw Truman Capote's wispy blonde hair atop his large, bleached head.

"The real trouble with your script, Tru, is that it is *Gatsby*. You gave us the book again, not a new screenplay."

Vega recognized the other swordsman from Erika's previous party: Robert Evans. The producer also shirked masquerade apparel, instead favoring a coffee-colored cashmere sweater and raven slacks.

"That's what you gave us. The book. We expected something more."

Capote, cradling a martini, turned to the surrounding audience.

"All I know is after I handed in my screenplay there was silence. Total dead silence. I tried to get someone to tell me something. I mean, I wrote a brilliant screenplay and this man from Paramount is telling me that I didn't write it, I simply typed it."

With an edge to his high-pitched voice, he added: "What should I do to him?"

"Order another martini."

The wisecrack appeared to break the growing tension, but Evans wasn't finished.

"Then you admit having simply retyped a few chapters?"

"How could I improve on Fitzgerald? He's the best, so why would I rewrite him? And you will, of course, still pay me for my work."

"Of course. After all, you are a brilliant typist."

The thrust having found the heart, the swordsman from Paramount walked away, leaving the author of *In Cold Blood* and *Breakfast at Tiffany's* with the remainder of his audience.

"Someday, if I ever finish *Answered Prayers*, I'm going to tell the story of my father. He had six wives. All much younger and all much richer. He was a real charmer. Yes, he was. Fooled my mother one hundred and fifteen percent."

Capote offered a polite smile to no one in particular, the kind meant to mask disappointment but fooling no one, least of all himself.

"I like my friends because they are beautiful, bright and amusing. And I think I'm the same. You'll have to excuse me. I've been up for seventy-two hours in a photo session with Harry Benson for *People* and two dozen of the most beautiful drag queens you have ever seen."

His parting words, each syllable elongated and slurred, remained unacknowledged in the evening's air as he was ushered away like a beaten prizefighter surrounded by a tightly interlaced daisy chain of coaches and trainers.

Vega crossed the manicured grounds, ignoring the raucous cocktail chatter, making his way back to Erika, who was now with Evans. At the producer's side was a young woman dressed in a chic bohemian outfit for the party. Her long dark hair was wrapped in a silver silk scarf that fell to one side. She appeared bored with Evan's continued complaint.

"It's very difficult to take Fitzgerald and make it work as a script. We waited for a year and when Tru turned it in we couldn't find a single word on the page that wasn't lifted. It made no sense. So I encouraged Ali to make another picture."

Erika asked if he offered the screenplay to Robert Towne as well.

"I offered Townie $175,000 to write it. He said, 'I can't beat Fitzgerald.' He offered to finish his original for twenty-five. How could I turn down the top script doctor in town when he's willing to work for scale plus change?"

"You told me this before, Evans. At the Polo Lounge. An original detective story. Does it now have a name?"

"He calls it *Chinatown*. I said, this takes place in Chinatown? and he said, Oh, no, no. This Chinatown's in your mind. And I said, I didn't know what the hell he was talking about, but I paid him the twenty-five."

Noticing Vega standing nearby, Erika motioned him over.

"Aloysius Vega is a dear friend of mine and the man who single-handedly solved the murder of Al Archer. He also fingered the killer of the couple murdered last year in their home just blocks from here. Something our local police force was incapable of solving. Aloysius, is Bob Evans and Miss Ali McGraw."

The actress offered a one-word greeting before wandering over to a group of young bohemians, all handsome young men, the type usually found in tennis shorts. Blond hair, full lips, and small teeth.

After looking over his shoulder at McGraw, the studio executive returned his attention to Erika.

"Aloysius is working on a case right now, Evans. Girl goes missing two days after her wedding."

"Sounds like most Hollywood marriages. You'll have to excuse me."

Vega was anxious to bid Erika goodnight. He felt like a prop in the wrong movie. His parting words were caught somewhere between his chest and tongue when a deep male voice interrupted.

"Mr. Vega? You were hoping to find the missing girl at Miss Lake's party?"

It was Sidney Korshak. Vega felt like a buck private standing before his drill sergeant.

"The case is cold. Nothing to hang our hats on."

"Then I suggest you find a new hat."

Korshak, after kissing Erika on the cheek and thanking her for the evening, joined Evans and McGraw as they headed for the front door.

"Sidney's right, Aloysius. Much is riding on you getting to the bottom of Mary's disappearance. More than you staying in business."

"If you mean Roselli, I don't give a shit."

"You should. John is not just a friend of mine. You know that to be the case."

"I do. His interests are the family's interests."

"Which are Sidney's interests. Trust me on this, Aloysius. A nod from Sidney and the Teamsters change management. A nod from Sidney and Vegas shuts down. Am I exaggerating?"

Vega nodded he understood.

"Good. Do call me tomorrow, Aloysius. We need to talk. Not too early, though."

Making his own exit, Vega watched from the front porch as the valet hustled for his car, jogging past a crème Bentley with Korshak, Evans, and McGraw already inside. The chauffeured chariot graced Erika's lengthy driveway like a rising starlet on the red carpet.

Overhead, the cloudless night sky rolled out a carpet of amber stars, hiding only those caught behind by the looming silhouette of Mount San Jacinto. A tired breeze tousled fronds at the tips of a row of Mexican Fan Palms across the street. In the distance, Vega heard the waking growl of his fifty-eight Corvette. From behind, Jesse Colin Young's tender voice eased through the night air like a wandering spirit:

Darkness, darkness, hide my yearning
For the things that cannot be
Keep my mind from constant turning
Towards the things I cannot see now
The things I cannot see now
The things I cannot see

CHAPTER THIRTY-TWO

Less than two weeks after Erika's guests put away their headbands and necklaces, a younger generation arrived in Palm Springs to party. The town had been a destination for spring breakers since 1963 when the movie *Palm Springs Weekend* was released. Teenagers were drawn to the parties and romance in the desert oasis as portrayed by Troy Donahue, Stefanie Powers, and Connie Stevens and dozens of extras.

This year's attraction included a music festival meant as a chimerical continuation of last year's Summer of Love and Monterey Pop Festival. On the playbill were The Doors, Canned Heat, Steve Miller, Ike and Tina Turner, Eric Burden and the Animals, Jeff Beck, Moby Grape, and the Paul Butterfield Blues Band.

Carloads of students from Los Angeles and San Diego arrived hoping to score tickets for the two-day concert. Swarms of other spring breakers turned out along with the usual crowd of vacationers. A small army of Hells Angels showed up as well. Before long, bumper-to-bumper traffic tied up Palm Canyon Drive. Along Ramon Road, cars were double-parked and abandoned.

City officials – shocked by the deluge of cars and young people bathing in public fountains and lounging on sidewalks in the once-peaceful downtown – quickly determined that local police were unprepared to handle the rowdy crowd. Worse, uniformed officers reported to City Hall that thousands of "unkempt, sullen, dissipated and resentful hippie types" had set up camp in nearby Tahquitz Canyon, a sacred place for the Cahuilla Indians and a favorite of local hikers. There, they bathed naked in the sacred natural pools, smoked marijuana, drank wine, tripped out, and enjoyed carnal pleasures.

At the drive-in movie theater where the first concert got underway, hundreds without tickets crashed the gates, using bricks, two-by-fours, and bottles filled with sand to rip down the chain-link fence. Five police officers were injured in the melee. When the music ended thousands of concertgoers refused to leave. They tore down the snack bar for firewood.

The following morning, city officials decided against canceling the second night of concerts. The resulting mayhem overwhelmed a police force reinforced from Los Angeles and San Diego. Teargas grenades were lobbed back at police, along with rocks and bottles. The battle turned uglier that evening when a gas station proprietor, armed with a rifle, fatally shot a 17-year-old boy.

At Desert Hospital, doctors attended to an officer with a broken back and another who had his eye gouged out. Teenagers were treated for various injuries including a girl who had shards of a broken beer bottle removed from her vagina.

The "hippie riot" became front-page news in the *Desert Post* and in newspapers as far as Florida. The young were described as "beaded, bearded, bare and berserk" who fouled the streets of Palm Springs with filth, pot and LSD. It was left to police cadets, Boy Scouts, and volunteers to clean up the mess.

It was, said a *Post* editorial, "a weekend that had finally passed, but the bad feelings would linger for much longer.

CHAPTER THIRTY-THREE

Despite Korshak's advice, Vega shuttered the detective agency at the end of April. He returned Nancy to the library like an overdue book, and told Coralina over the phone that he no longer could mail her a monthly check. The Showalter investigation had fizzled. Little had changed since the arrival of the clipped article mailed from McNeil Island Penitentiary. Mary was still missing, her fate unknown. The police files had vanished as well. Reporters who might know more than what was reported were dead. Roselli and Löwenstein remained locked up. As for Mary's husband, Arthur Quail, nothing new had turned up.

Alvin Karpis remained in Montreal, viewed as somewhat of a Rip Van Winkle celebrity, interviewed by newspapers as well as Peter Jennings of ABC News. His attorney, meanwhile, was unable to retrieve from the government the prison visitor records. He suspected Hoover ordered them destroyed.

Vega refused Erika's offer to underwrite the agency's operation to keep the case alive. The detective preferred to spend time at home, where he could swim nude and drink all day without interruption. The bathrobe he put on each morning remained on for most of the day. Exceptions were made for the occasional trip to the grocery store or the bar at the Purple Room.

Much like his personal hygiene, the house was slowly buried under the weight of neglect. Unopened bills and letters littered the kitchen table along with barely legible notes, stained coffee mugs and empty bottles of vodka and whiskey. Soiled shirts and pants stuffed the washing machine, which was out of order. A single light remained on in the bedroom, where blankets and sheets tangled on a mattress painted with boozy sweat and littered with wrinkled newspapers.

Vega spent much of the month of May sleeping in that bed. Just getting up in the morning and grabbing something to eat took every ounce of his energy. Dinners were forgotten or half-made. The TV hadn't been turned on in weeks. It sat dead in the corner of the living room, a lifeless box gathering dust.

Vega essentially cut off all contact with the outside world. The phone no longer was answered, ignored along with the answering machine, which blinked incessantly. Only a neighbor's cat was allowed in, a gray tabby that sought refuge from a family of young children across the street. The cat would nap near Vega each morning as the detective read the *Los Angeles Times* and *Desert Post*. The relationship blossomed to the point where cat food made it to Vega's grocery list.

— • —

It was left to Erika to intervene. She reached out to Coralina who agreed to join her on a house call. Coralina suggested they also invite Nancy, as she was the last to have had actual conversations with the detective. Erika agreed, reluctantly.

The three women arrived at Vega's house on South Monte Vista on a dusty morning in early June. Wind came tearing through the Banning Pass overnight like it had a score to settle. Gusts shook windows, dumped patio furniture in pools, and stripped limbs from

Palo Verde and eucalyptus trees. The air that remained was gritty, thick with fine desert dust.

Repeated banging on his front door and Erika's shouted threat that she would call police sent the cat racing out the opened back door but got the ladies inside. Erika was the first to enter. Coralina and Nancy followed behind in single file.

Vega's appearance – bloated face, swollen belly, and in desperate need of a haircut and shave – astonished the women. The disarray inside was a close second. Dishes, pots, and pans were piled high in the kitchen where a repulsive odor of garbage germinated. Newspapers and empty bottles of vodka littered the living room. No one gave a moment's thought to checking the bedrooms or bathrooms.

"Jesus, Aloysius! You look like shit. Were you standing outside last night?"

"You wanted in, Erika."

"Your hair. It's awfully long. Going to cut it at some point?"

"Maybe."

"What would it take?"

"Scissors."

"At least your sense of humor hasn't left you."

Vega started to clear off the newspapers and paper plates to make room on the living room couch, but Erika insisted they talk outside. She led the group on a serpentine route to the back yard.

"At least you haven't let the entire place go to hell. The lawn looks freshly cut and you must've cleaned the pool before we arrived. Sit down, Aloysius, we won't stay long."

Erika confiscated the lounge chair, leaving Vega and the other women to dust off plastic lawn chairs piled against the house. They didn't exactly surround Vega as they placed their chairs. The result was more conclave than clambake. Not surprisingly, Erika opened for the prosecution.

"What an odd, lonely existence you have here."

Shrugging, Vega replied: "Some of us prefer solitude. Favoring quiet over endless attention."

"I believe Aloysius aimed that remark at me, ladies. He was once a charming rogue. A man who despite his carefree disregard for the ordinary requirements of society somehow remained so charming that people forgave him. Now our private eye has become a sort of feckless free spirit, the type you occasionally run across. A man who disconnects himself from others, from the world."

Erika waited for her soliloquy to linger in the warm air before continuing.

"You still belong to this world, Aloysius, whether you like it or not."

Vega searched the faces of his two other guests. Coralina appeared apprehensive. Nancy curious.

Erika remained fixed on her prey.

"Of course, freedom has a price. You've abandoned friends, like those of us here, to remain alone, leaving us as strangers. Your family, such as it is, now consists of the regulars at the Purple Room and the other bars you haunt. You sit on a stool, shielding yourself from the pain and complications that real relationships can bring."

A migraine was worming its way behind Vega's bloodshot eyes. Pins tattooed up his neck.

"Is that what this is all about, Erika? Giving me free psychoanalysis? Or do I get a bill in the mail? I don't need this shit. I don't need you or..."

Coralina interrupted.

"We did not come to invade your privacy or to insult you, Aloysius. We are worried. About you. We..."

Erika refused to give up the spotlight.

"Pick yourself up. If you don't want to care about the people around you or, judging by your appearance, yourself, you can at least go back to caring about finding the Showalter girl. I offered you money..."

"I don't want your money."

"Then solve the case! Earn a living again. Quit acting like... like Robinson Crusoe."

"Crusoe wasn't lonely."

Nancy's non sequitur turned attention her way.

"The word lonely is never mentioned in the novel. Crusoe complained to God about his misfortune, but the island he inhabited had certainty. It had meaning."

No one, including Vega, understood where Nancy was going.

"Sherlock Holmes, on the other hand, preferred solitude. It was a way of maintaining his independence and keeping a singular focus on his cases. He often operated in isolation, without Watson. It allowed him to think clearly and avoid the distractions and emotional entanglements that come with close relationships."

Erika said she saw no evidence that Vega was attending to a case. Nancy disagreed.

"Then you didn't observe the three notebooks on the kitchen table. Two were closed. Judging from worn edges and how the cardstock covers were slightly askew, they likely were filled with his notes. The third notebook was folded half open. That indicates additional notes are being added. A pen was left across the open page. Mr. Vega is indeed working. I suspect it involves the disappearance of Mary Showalter."

With that, Nancy left the group for the kitchen, where she began to clean the dishes that filled the sink and counter. Coralina joined her, asking how certain she was in her assessment.

"How can it be? He looks like he spends most of his day sleeping ... after drinking all night. You see the empty bottles. And Erika was right that he spends many nights at bars."

"There's a tension between his cases and his personal life. I've seen it in the short time we've worked together. He values logic and reason over emotional ties. It's not that he doesn't care, Coralina.

You should have been there when he chewed me out for contacting Mr. Quail."

"He was right to be upset. You put yourself in danger by ignoring his direction."

"Which demonstrates that he cares."

"I am not sure."

"I am. Right now, he is caring for himself."

"I do not understand what you are saying."

"He chose to disconnect from us. He closed his business. Pulled the drapes across the front window here. Locked the door. When he considered the Showalter case to be a dead end, it became another marker. Like the failure of his marriage. His early exit from police work. His missteps in the Archer case that nearly got him killed. The shooting on New Year's Eve and the resulting coma. My hunch is he finds these markers, these failures, staring him in the face."

"What you said, I worry about that. Doctor Gargery warned us that coma increases the chance of depression and apathy. That Aloysius might have a low tolerance for stressful situations. That it may increase the risk of loneliness and destructive behavior. Even suicide."

"The man you love, Coralina, nearly died. Twice. I suspect it all feels different after facing mortality."

The dishwasher was now fully loaded. Nancy turned her attention to the sticky counter tops. Coralina emptied sacks of stale garbage to bins on the side of the house. She returned to help Nancy straighten the living room mess. Erika was still berating Vega when they returned to the back yard.

"You live alone. You're out of a job. Down to your last dollar. Your level of drinking is not a pick-me-up. You're what, thirty-five? Thirty-six? You're not running out of time to turn around your life but trust me, Aloysius…you'll reach that point before you recognize it."

"Erika, it is time we leave. Juliet will be getting hungry."

"I thought your mother was watching her."

"She is. But I still breastfeed her."

Shrugging her shoulders, Erika reached one arm toward Vega to help her up from the lounge chair, which he did.

"Still a gentleman. At least you haven't lost that. Take care of yourself, Aloysius. We all love you, though some more than others."

Vega walked them to the front door, closing it without watching them drive away. He sat at the kitchen table, his eyes trained on the back door, waiting for the cat to return.

CHAPTER THIRTY-FOUR

At Erika's request, UCLA dispatched Vivian Dy to call on Vega. It was made clear this would be the final time a personal visit would be allowed. Administrators had appealed to the hospital's board, a majority of whom agreed the unusual attention to a single patient had to stop regardless of potential risk to Erika's substantial endowment.

The neuro-rehabilitation specialist arrived at Vega's home at lunchtime. They sat next to each other on the living room couch.

"I expected a bit more of a mess. Miss Lake said you lived in squalor. Looks to me like a pretty normal bachelor pad."

"Cleaned up."

"Sleeping okay?"

"Plenty."

"Appetite?"

"Comes. Goes."

"Drinking much?"

"Enough."

"How's your head?"

"Meaning?"

"Do you feel sad?"

"No."

"Happy?"

"No. Neither really."

"Three words. That's progress. I understand you closed the business."

"I did."

"Why?"

"No money."

"I may be wrong here, but doesn't a business need to be open to generate income?"

Vega looked toward the back door rather than answer. His hands, she noticed, massaged his knees continuously.

"This is my final session with you. After today, you can reach me at UCLA to schedule an appointment. You, rather than Miss Lake, will be invoiced. I cannot maintain this specialized level of treatment. You understand?"

"I do."

"Good. To start, I have a series of questions regarding your cognitive and motor functions, as well as emotional and behavioral. You're familiar with most of these questions. Asking them again will help me evaluate any residual impairments that may need further attention. Shall we begin?"

For the next hour Vega fielded questions about any ongoing difficulties with his memory and concentration, physical coordination, and other potential lingering effects of a coma. When they finished, Dy offered her assessment.

"You've made reasonable physical progress, especially given the severity of what you experienced. Coming out of a coma and regaining your physical abilities this well is a very positive sign. That said, your mental state is concerning. The signs of improvement I saw after your initial recovery have regressed. You continue to suffer from bouts of anxiety and fatigue. Your drinking is not..."

"I'm fine."

"I'm not certain you know what that means anymore. I need to be honest with you. I'm concerned about your mental state. Your energy drop. The collapse of sleep patterns. Your interest in things you used to care about has vanished."

Vega stared at the floor as Dy tried to find the right words. Non-clinical words.

"Depression can be quiet. It sits on your shoulders and makes everything feel pointless. It convinces you not to ask for help. What you're carrying, it's not something to handle alone. I don't think you can."

Vivian Dy observed Vega's decline with professional detachment, but a tightening knot of concern grew. Despite adjustments to medication and her initial therapy, his mental deterioration was unmistakable. The lapses of memory. The increasing isolation. She took aim at one target.

"You need to hear this, and don't just nod like you're humoring me. The excessive drinking that Miss Lake told me about is not just taking the edge off anymore. It's taking pieces of you with it. Every time you pour another glass, you're not coping. You're sinking. I understand how it numbs things, quiets the noise. But alcohol is a liar, relaxes you while it poisons you."

Vega glanced quickly at the back door, his jaw tight, but said nothing.

"Besides the confusion, memory problems, and all kinds of mood symptoms, alcohol damages your brain cells. People don't realize this, but alcohol is neurotoxic. It can cause structural changes to your brain, increasing the risk of strokes and memory disorders like Korsakoff syndrome or Wernicke's encephalopathy."

Still no response from the patient sitting next to her. Just the faint creak of upholstery as the detective shifted his posture.

"I've seen this spiral before. The depression feeds the drinking. The drinking deepens the depression. It's not weakness, Mr. Vega,

Aloysius, it's chemistry. Your brain is working against you. Memory, focus, emotional control – all of it starts to break down. And as it does, you'll start making mistakes you can't afford in your line of work. Dangerous mistakes."

Vega finally looked up.

"I'm managing."

"From where I sit, from my observation, you're surviving. Barely. And if something doesn't change soon, you won't be doing even that."

"Look, as much as I want you to stop altogether, limit yourself to one drink per day. You like martinis, vodka if I recall correctly. Limit yourself to one and it comes prior to dinner, not after. While alcohol might initially help you fall asleep, its effects on sleep architecture can lead to poor sleep quality. It can reduce time spent in REM sleep, which is crucial for memory consolidation. You following?"

"Yep."

"Good. Your anxiety, not surprisingly, likely stems from the physical wounds you suffered. Being shot, not once but twice, and nearly succumbing to those traumas, has left a deep impression on your psyche. Feeling disconnected, avoiding reminders of the events, anger, even guilt, are a fairly typical range of emotional and psychological effects."

Dy waited quietly for Vega to respond. This part demanded patience. When he did speak, his voice was low.

"I feel like I'm waking up from an uneasy sleep. I can't tell if I'm still dreaming or if I've forgotten how to be awake. I go through the motions. I eat. I read. I swim. But there's this delay between me and the rest of the world. Like sound traveling through water. Slow. Distorted."

A question formed, but Dy held it, waiting for him to continue.

"The nightmares? About staring down an abyss or other cruel torments? Still show up now and then. Along with a new one. I wash up on an unexpected shore. Stranded. I can see the rest of the world. The sky, the people. I'm just watching, as the island I'm on drifts farther away."

Another long pause, before Vega continued.

"The cruelest part? The spirit of the place, where I'm stranded, has its own grim charm. Like it's sinking into my soul."

Dy latched on to his last sentence. The reference to his soul.

"You were an altar boy, I seem to recall."

"Once."

"Were you good at it?"

"I guess so. Why?"

"Ever consider returning to that?"

"I doubt the fathers would have me."

"Not that."

"Then what?"

"Faith. Faith that there is more to life than this."

"This, Vivian, this is all I can handle. Right now at least. You're a doctor, a scientist. You telling me you believe in a higher power?"

"I've wrestled with it for years. Entering med school, science was certainty. Faith was wishful thinking. When I started studying the brain, I thought I was chasing certainties. Electrical patterns, neurotransmitter maps. There's astonishing order in the brain's circuitry. There's immense beauty in that precision. But after years of working with patients – some who recover against all odds, others who don't respond to anything we throw at them – I realized there's something our science doesn't fully capture."

Dy paused, glancing at the sliding door to the back yard.

"I don't believe in a higher power because I *don't* understand the brain. I believe because I *do*. There are mysteries that science can't quite explain. The resilience of the human spirit. The will to move a limb we've declared functionally lost. The moments of lucidity in someone with severe brain injury that no scan can predict. I believe there's more to a person than just the sum of their neural circuitry. And when I see the spark we can't locate on a scan, I call that the soul. And I trust that it's held by something greater than all of us."

As she waited for Vega's response, she was distracted by a visitor at the back door.

"Do you own a cat?"

CHAPTER THIRTY-FIVE

Summers arrive in the Coachella Valley in early June, beginning a forced death march of triple-digit temperatures that can last until October. The wind dies and the soft lemony sun of winter and spring turns sulfuric. A dusty haze is layered over the entire valley – a gauzy veil that can blur out the surrounding mountains and turn everyone's vision myopic. The oppressive heat loiters after sundown, when creatures of the night emerge from underground burrows. They shuffle about in concealed shadows as they go about their grisly business of survival.

For residents unable to escape, who have a paycheck to meet or are too old and poor to go somewhere – anywhere – else, summer means sweating it out at home. Sit and take it. Keep the blinds closed. Never venture out during daylight unless in desperation.

Coralina escaped to San Diego with Juliet and her mother at the invitation of the baby's paternal grandparents. Their estate in Coronado offered the family cooler temperatures and access to beaches where Juliet crawled in the sparkling gold sand and felt the first touch of ocean on her toes.

Erika fled the states altogether. She leased a private villa in Southern France that overlooked Nice and the bewitching blue Mediterranean. Her days were spent shopping the Carré d'Or and Village

Ségurane. Nights found her at the roulette tables of the Monte Carlo Casino or on the dance floors of Monaco.

Nancy toiled at the Welwood Murray Library where she assisted patrons intent on locating obscure compositions and hosted toddler story time in the afternoons. Evenings, she read academic papers on the future of computers and intelligent machinery by Alan Turing and Jay Forrester.

Vega holed up like a hermit crab, venturing out before dawn to swim in the tidal pool in his back yard before retreating into his shell. The liquor cabinet would be looted before noon, slowly blurring the remaining daylight hours.

— • —

It was from each of those locations in late July that they watched the astonishing image of a fellow human being walking on the moon. The singular event in history, broadcast live on television sets from New York to Bangkok, was witnessed by billions of human beings who looked to the moon with a new understanding of their own place in the heavens.

The following month, in upper New York state, almost a half-million young people gathered on a hillside in the Catskills to listen to four days of music from some of the biggest names in rock-and-roll. They danced, played in the mud and rain, and smoked marijuana. The feeling was summed up by the dairy farmer who owned the land.

"You've proven to the world that a half-a-million kids – and I call you kids because I have children that are older than you are – a half million young people can get together and have three days of fun and music and have nothing but fun and music, and I – God bless you for it!"

The turbulent decade of the Sixties seemed to be drawing to a promising close the summer of 1969. It was not to be.

Life magazine published "The Faces of the American Dead in Vietnam: One Week's Toll." Inside, across ten desolate pages, were picture after picture and name after name of 242 young men killed in just seven days. Turning the pages was like looking at a high school yearbook. The faces were mostly young. Some of them in civilian clothes, most in uniform. Some had voluntarily extended their tours of combat duty, the article explained, while others were desperate to come home.

A freelance journalist would later report that a company of U.S. soldiers had deliberately slaughtered more than 500 people in a small village called My Lai. The GIs also slaughtered livestock, raped and mutilated an unknown number of women and girls, and burned the village to the ground. Mothers shielding their children were shot. When their children tried to run away, they were gunned down. Not a single shot was fired against the soldiers. The lieutenant in command dragged dozens of people, including young children, into a ditch before executing them with a machine gun. He later described his actions and those of Charlie Company as a case of carrying out orders.

In Northern California, a young couple cuddled inside their car at a county park as another vehicle entered the darkened parking lot and stopped. A man holding a flashlight walked toward the car and opened fire through the passenger window. Minutes later, a police dispatcher answered a telephone call from a man who spoke in a low, monotone voice, as if he were reading from a prepared script.

"I want to report a murder. If you will go one mile east on Columbus Parkway you will find kids in a brown car. They were shot with a nine-millimeter Luger. I also killed those kids last year. Goodbye."

It was the first indication that a madman was on a killing spree. He would go on to taunt police with letters full of unintelligible cryptograms signed with a symbol resembling the crosshairs of a gunsight. He was dubbed Zodiac.

On the East Coast, a young woman newspapers identified simply as "a blond" was left to die inside a black sedan that had overturned in a Massachusetts tidal pond. The driver, a U.S. senator and the lone surviving Kennedy brother, swam to safety then huddled with aides before calling police the following morning. Nine hours elapsed before the body of Mary Jo Kopechne, a campaign worker, was recovered.

In Los Angeles, five men and women were butchered at a rugged hillside home in Benedict Canyon in manner police described as "ritualistic." The first detective who arrived would later testify the scene was the worst he had come across in fifteen years in homicide.

The first body was slumped to one side in the front seat of a car parked in the driveway, killed by several gunshots. Inside, two bodies were sprawled on the living room floor, both dead from multiple stab wounds. A rope was tied around a woman's neck and looped over a rafter near the ceiling. The other end was affixed to a man's neck. The woman, Hollywood actress Sharon Tate, was eight months pregnant. She had been stabbed more than a dozen times. More victims were found in the back yard. One man's head had been smashed like a Jack-o-lantern and his body torn by multiple stab wounds and gun shots. Officers who stayed overnight to guard the interior of the crime scene were unable to find a clean area to sit because of all the blood on the floor and walls. On the front door of the house was the word PIG, written in what appeared to be blood.

The grotesque scene was repeated two nights later, thirteen miles to the east in the wealthy neighborhood of Los Feliz. Police found the body of a middle-aged man on the floor in a huge pool of blood.

A pillow slip had been pulled over his head. Beneath it, a large knife protruded from his throat. The victim had been stabbed twelve times with a knife and fourteen times with a fork that remained stuck in his stomach. The word WAR was found etched into the man's stomach. He had been alive when it was carved, bleeding through each letter. Another body, that of a woman, was found in a bedroom. There was a pillowcase over her head as well. Around her neck was an electric cord connected to a bed lamp. She had been stabbed forty-one times.

PART 3
Shorty's Head

CHAPTER THIRTY-SIX

Boredom has a way of pushing you somewhere you didn't mean to go. For Nancy Randall, days spent organizing bookshelves, scanning microfiche, and other odd tasks at the library blurred from quiet rhythm to stifling tedium. Even the clock on the wall lacked urgency, each minute indistinguishable from the last.

She missed the challenge of the Vega Detective Agency. During lunch breaks, she would fax requests to researchers in libraries and newsrooms across New Jersey, where the initial articles said Mary was born. Her random inquiries paid off in early September with a response from the public librarian in Wyckoff, a small township across the Hudson River from New York City.

Newspaper clips that were faxed back revealed that Mary's parents died in a house fire in 1945 when she was seventeen. Mary was at school at the time the blaze broke out close to 1 p.m. The fire chief told the local newspaper the blaze started in the living room. The parents, Howard and Belinda Showalter, were apparently napping in their bedroom at the time. They died from smoke inhalation. Mary's sister Janice, four at the time, was found by firefighters hiding in a hall closet. She was rescued unharmed before flames consumed the colonial-style home built in 1931.

Additional stories in the *News* reported that neighbors took in the two girls before grandparents arrived from Michigan. The community held several fund drives to raise money for the orphans. Fire officials later identified as the cause a cigar that tumbled off an end table next to the living room couch. Howard, the father, was a heavy smoker.

— • —

The accounts, sketchy as they were, gave Nancy the impetus to contact Vega. Rather than call ahead, she turned up on his doorstep late on a Saturday morning. The detective inched aside a window shade before cinching up his robe and letting her in. Following an awkward greeting, the two sat at the kitchen table. Vega poured himself a screwdriver before sitting down to read the three newspaper articles Nancy brought along. She waited to speak until he looked up.

"I was unable to find further information about the girls in the *Wyckoff News*. The newspaper closed its doors in 1961. My contacts in Michigan were unable to locate any articles referencing Mary or her sister."

Vega studied the face of his former assistant.

"You changed your hair."

"Uh...so have you."

After glancing at the empty glass that rested next to his notebook, Vega began a conversation.

"Janice was four at the time of the fire. That puts her birth year as 1941 or so. That means she was only eleven at the time of Mary's wedding. Awfully young to be a witness."

"I checked with the state of California. There is no age requirement for witnesses. However, they must be old enough to know that they are witnessing a marriage ceremony and be able to sign their name on the official marriage license."

"And you found nothing about Janice from that point forward? No whereabouts? Nothing in high school yearbooks?"

"My contacts sampled a few high school yearbooks from 1959 when she would have been a senior in Michigan, but without knowing the town where her grandparents lived, or even their names, it was an impossible task."

"You checked phone books for Showalter?"

"Called as many as I could find. None were the grandparents. They could have been maternal grandparents under a different name. Or they could already be dead. No way of knowing."

Surprised that Vega had not made an obvious connection, Nancy pointed out that Janice would now be about twenty-eight. About the age of the woman who visited Karpis in January.

"The woman thought to be Mary was in her mid- to late twenties. You told me that Karpis said his visitor bore a resemblance to Mary. And Löwenstein, he thought it was Mary."

Vega tugged at his beard, now almost as long as the hair on his head.

"It's a stretch, but let's go with it for a moment. If Janice struck up a pen pal relationship with Karpis, is it reasonable to conclude she lived in Washington, near McNeil Island, or at least on the West Coast?"

"Reasonable? No. Possible, of course."

"So how would we..."

"Go about finding her? I already put out the word to research colleagues in Washington and Oregon. No phone book hits so far. They can only spend so much time looking while on the job."

"Are they searching for Janice Showalter or just Showalter?"

"I asked them to start with both names. Then go to any J. Showalter in the book. They're still on it. You know that, in the future, you'll be able to conduct such a search on a computer? All the phone books will be scanned like we do now to make a copy, but instead of print, the information will be on computers. Right now, government and large businesses like IBM are developing ways to link all these computers in a network, combining all the information they collect, making it available for research librarians. It's really fascinating."

"By that time I'll be dead and you'll be a gray old lady."

"Let's not bet on that, Mr. Vega. Besides, there might be another way to locate Janice Showalter."

CHAPTER THIRTY-SEVEN

Vega and Lily Navarro had not spoken since they waited on New Year's Eve in a line outside the Whisky a Go Go. There was a delay to get inside the club to see Johnny Rivers and Vega was expressing his impatience to anyone within earshot. Coralina urged him to relax. Lily was about to mouth the words "Cool your jets" when gunfire ended the conversation, seriously wounding Vega and killing Lily's companion, like her, an LAPD officer.

Once drinking buddies and occasional bedmates, Vega and Lily had not spoken since the shooting. She called the agency and his home telephone several times as he recuperated. He never answered or returned her calls. Even now, he was unsure why.

It being a Wednesday, he dialed her home. Although no longer a rookie, Lily likely was still pulling weekends and night shifts. She answered in a voice sleepy and hoarse from a night of drinking.

"What the fuck time is it? Yeah?"

"It's 9:40. Dreaming about me?"

"Who the fuck... Vega? You asshole."

"Sorry I made myself scarce, Lily. It's just that..."

"It's just that you don't give a fuck about anyone but yourself. You were always that way, but after being shot in the head, you're even worse."

"Chest. I got shot in the chest."

"May as well have been your head. That's where you're all fucked up." A phlegmy coughing jag interrupted her side of the conversation. "That sounds awful. Wanna take a minute and call me back?"

"Sure."

Vega finished his screwdriver and checked the outdoor thermometer. It was already 98 enroute to a forecasted 111. Tinged with unusual humidity for the desert, the day promised to be miserable. He emptied the remaining box of Cheerios into a bowl and ate it with milk, which smelled. He returned the jug to the refrigerator when Lily called back.

"Feel better?"

"Yeah. I still look like shit, but this is over the telephone so I don't care. So, I won't ask how you've been. Coralina, the doll she is, kept me posted on your recovery. Which is more than I ever got from you. C'mon, Vega, not even one phone call in, what, nine months?"

"Yeah, I know. I just... I don't know."

"Tell me this. Feel more yourself now than you did, say, three months ago?"

"The vertigo comes and goes, but the headaches are gone."

"That pecker of yours. Still work?"

"Been unemployed but, yeah, still works."

"Well if Coralina has no use for it, could I borrow it? Having my own dry spell. Be honest, Vega. You didn't call to ask me out. What's up?"

Lily listened carefully as he described the search for Mary Showalter.

"Jesus, Vega. That's the most fucked up cold case. That the best you can do to make a living?"

"It's the best I got right now. I closed the agency, maybe for good. My wallet's thin as paper. If I find what happened to Mary, get the reward, I can reopen the agency and maybe take you out for dinner. In the meantime, I'm staying low until we catch a break."

"We? You mean that teenager filling in for Coralina?"

"Yeah. Nancy's been a big help. She's done a lot of research and has one of those photographic memories. Remembers everything she reads or sees."

"That so? Make sure she doesn't catch you naked. So, you called. Whaddya need?"

"Calling you was Nancy's idea. Something I should have jumped on. Can you run a check on the sister? See if she's popped up somewhere for a misdemeanor or something bigger."

"I'll try, but getting access to that information is tough. The suits guard LETS like their pensions. But I know a gal who might let me near the teletype. Can't guarantee anything, but who the hell can these days."

"Thanks. And, uh…Lily? Before we hang up…sorry that Colleen didn't survive the hit. It was meant for me. She was a bystander. I'm sorry."

"Thanks. She was a good cop, better friend. They gave her a nice send-off and raised a fair amount of money for her little boy. I stop by to see him every chance I get, which isn't often these days."

"You stay safe, Lily."

"You too. Don't be a hermit."

Lily cursed Vega through the tears that came after they hung up.

"Bastard didn't even thank me for saving his life … for the second fucking time."

CHAPTER THIRTY-EIGHT

The desert began to stir from its summer slumber by the second week of October. The sun still burned from morning to late afternoon but nights cooled just enough to coax back the snowbirds. They returned to Palm Springs like clockwork. Retirees from Canada and the Midwest, vacationers from the Pacific Northwest, packing their cars and suitcases tight with Bermuda shorts and golf clubs.

The city welcomed them with a slow yawn. Shutters on boutique shops cracked open. Restaurants that had gone dark over summer flicked on their lights and rehired waitstaff. Hotel pools, empty for months except for the occasional budget-minded tourist, sloshed about with families and fresh chlorine.

Residents watched the influx with a mix of relief and resignation. Business was good again, but showing up at a good restaurant without a reservation quickly became a thing of the past.

The season had begun.

Three blocks from where breakfast platters piled with golden pancakes and thick slabs of bacon were being served to the new arrivals, Vega slumped over a bowl of Cheerios at the kitchen table reading the Associated Press account of game two of the World Series between the Mets and Orioles. His hair and beard now wild and unchecked, he looked like a castaway who failed to signal for rescue.

On the floor, next to his chair, the gray tabby swatted a string, the other end of which was wrapped around Vega's thumb. The string jumped with each spoonful of cereal. The game was a morning routine and about the only playtime the cat enjoyed when visiting the detective. Mostly, it curled up on the living room couch, napping until late in the evening when it would want out, allegedly returning to its home across the street.

Vega was studying the box scores when the phone rang. It was Lily.

"Found her, Vega. The sister you were looking for."

"Janice Showalter? Where?"

"Independence. About halfway between LA and Reno. She was among a group of hippies rounded up on suspicion of arson and a string of stolen vehicles. The locals are holding the group while they sort what else these kids were doing out pretty much in the middle of nowhere. Your gal has no priors and they're unsure if she'll face charges. I spoke with the Inyo County sheriff and gave him an overview of your missing person case. I'm off today and tomorrow. It's a long drive. If you want to go, it's now or never."

They agreed to meet an hour later at Molly's Café in San Bernardino. They would leave Vega's Corvette there, figuring Lily's Jeep Wagoneer was better suited for the four-hour drive to Independence.

Lily arrived first. She was quickly seated by the waitress and was two coffees past by the time Vega arrived. His appearance turned heads in the small cafe.

"Holy fuck, Vega. I'll tell you now, we're not heading to Independence with you lookin' like this. Sheriffs in that part of the state will shoot first and save the questions for your next of kin."

"Morning. Coffee, please. Black."

"Did you hear what I said? I'm not taking you four hours up state with you looking like that."

"It's early to be chewin' my ass, Lily."
"Did you see the looks you got walking in here like that?"
"You care? I don't."

The waitress ignored the unkempt customer, figuring the pretty Mexican woman with him had the resources to pay for two orders of ham and eggs. Not her place to judge. Just serve.

Lily looked over Vega with the eyes of a reconstructive surgeon.

"The beard and hair? Gotta go. I'm serious, Vega. There's gotta be a barber here in town."

"Just tell me what you found out about Janice. Don't leave out anything."

Over a quick breakfast, Lily said Park Service rangers had received a report of vehicles burning in a canyon east of Searles Valley. They also saw that someone had attempted to dig a road through one of the dry creeks in that area, which is part of Death Valley National Monument. The Park Service didn't want that. They brought in an earthmoving machine to the western edge of the wash and left it there to block the road. They came back later and found that someone had set it on fire.

Deputies from the Highway Patrol and Inyo County were called in. They discovered a dune buggy and another vehicle further up the wash, each with a gun scabbard holding a rifle. The vehicles were reported stolen. Authorities continued to search the area and found a dozen people hiding in caves along one of the washes. They came out peacefully.

Lily opened her notebook, flipping through the pages until she found a passage she wanted to read.

"Listen to this. From a CHP named Purcell. I interviewed him last night over the phone."

We drove down Goler Wash. About halfway we met an old Army truck coming uphill. The driver was a miner named Paul Crockett. The passenger was a teenager named Brooks Poston. They indicated that some odd things were going on at Barker Ranch. They said the leader of this group staying at the ranch would put on a robe and preach. They said there were a large number of females there and that they had orgies and used drugs. They said the group had a fleet of dune buggies and that during the night they traveled the valleys up there as if they were re-creating the days of Rommel in North Africa.

"On October 12, they raided the ranch. Ten women and three men were taken into custody."

"Janice Showalter one of them?"

"Not yet. Let me continue reading."

"Wait. What about this ranch? Out in the middle of nowhere?"

"Purcell told me the ranch had been pretty nice at one time, but it was abandoned and is pretty run down. It's stone and stucco and sits up on a hill overlooking Death Valley."

"Go on."

"Here's what Purcell said when he and a Ranger went to the ranch."

We started walking up the hill on either side of this draw. Suddenly, I hear Dick whistling and waving me over. I dashed down and back up to his side of the draw, and I'm suddenly within a mass of young females, only a few males. Some are nude, some are dressed, and everything in between. They were trying to hide behind sage bushes, but you can't hide too well behind a sage bush. I could see further up the draw what looked like a dry camp. Dick took off running, and he disappeared. I said, 'Come on out!' I gathered them all together. When I inquired as to who these gals were and what they were doing, the spokesperson, a skinny red-haired girl who was buck naked, said, 'We're a Girl Scout troop from the Bay Area. Would you and the ranger like to be our scoutmasters?'"

"Girl Scouts?"

"C'mon, Vega, finish your breakfast. We got a long trip and back ahead of us. I'll continue Purcell's account on the way. After we find you a barber."

— • —

By eleven, with Vega freshly shorn and shaved, the pair traversed the San Gabriel Mountains through the Cajon Pass, which that day was relatively calm. Santa Ana winds that had howled down the pass the prior week were gone by the time their car reached the 3,800-foot crest. Lily picked up the story of the Barker Ranch arrests after they had descended into the high country on the other side.

"Purcell said the vehicles came back clean. Same with the shotgun they found. He and his partner were told to stay at the mouth of the wash overnight. That CHP would send a group of guys out there before dawn the next day. That morning, they raided the ranch and found more of these hippies hiding in caves and a nearby abandoned mine. In all, twenty-six were rounded up, including two infants."

"And Janice Showalter. How does she figure into this scene?"

"Don't know. They're still trying to sort it all out. She was arrested in the second raid."

Vega was antsy in the passenger seat. He was used to driving, not riding shotgun. Bits of hair that remained on his shirt collar itched like crazy. He pulled a pack of Pall Malls from the inside pocket of his jacket. He was about to light up when Lily slowed the car.

"Uh-uh. Not in my car. I don't want it to stink. When did you take that up?"

"Yesterday. Or the day before."

— • —

Highway 395 follows the east side of the Sierra Mountains north to Oregon. Once a rocky path worn by Yokut Indians and later wagon trains of pioneers, the two lanes of blacktop skirt both the highest peak and lowest point in the country. The route passes through long stretches of firebrick red Mojave Desert, sagebrush flats, and expanses of farmland before entering valleys of molten granite monsters at the base of the jagged peaks of the Sierras rounded by centuries of wind, rain, and snow.

It wasn't until they reached the dry lakebed of the Owens Valley that Vega asked Lily what she had heard about the Sharon Tate investigation, now in its second month.

"I'm told it's a clusterfuck. Keystone Cops stuff. The officer who was supposed to secure the scene until homicide arrived? Put his prints all over the place. It gets worse. The more officers visited the property, the more contaminated the crime scene became. Several guys tracked the victims' blood from inside to outside. A pair of horn-rimmed glasses was picked up from its place on the floor and set on a desk. Two wooden pieces of a gun grip found by the entryway were accidently kicked under a chair by one of the original officers on the scene."

"Jesus."

"It's bad, but I gotta say, what these guys saw would make your skin crawl. They're gonna have that crime scene playin' in their heads until they meet their maker. Shit, the whole fuckin' city is paranoid. Guns sales are off the chart. Bigshots hired guards and installed security cameras at their homes. Some are holed up at the Beverly Hills Hotel. I was at the supermarket the other day. These two women in front of me, in line, were comparing things. Not hairstyles. Not the price of food. But door locks. Door locks, Vega."

"I get it."

"Most pet shops were cleaned out of guard dogs. A Studio City kennel had to airlift German Shepherds in from Iowa to meet the demand."

"Suspects? I read they let the housekeeper go."

"He was a dead end. On some kind of narcotic when he was questioned. I'm told they believe at least two suspects are involved because the weapons used to kill the victims were a .22-caliber revolver and probably a bayonet. Likely part of a big dope transaction gone bad. Found hashish, marijuana, MDA, and cocaine at the residence."

"Not surprising. Hollywood."

"Yeah. The victims all were known for their party-going ways. Some film guy told a reporter that after hearing about the murders 'toilets were flushing all over Beverly Hills.' Said the entire Los Angeles sewer system is stoned."

Lily stopped briefly for a bathroom break in Lone Pine, although their courthouse destination was only sixteen miles ahead. Vega stretched his legs and back as he took in the majesty of the towering mountains to the west. Had Nancy been his traveling companion, he guessed she would be providing a lecture on the area's history and geology. Instead, when Lily returned, the subject returned to crime.

"The fuckin' country's going down the tubes, Vega. Mean streets are meaner. I was talking to a guy, former chief of detectives, about to retire his shield. He's been working homicide since the early forties. Told me there were about seventy murders a year in LA County back then. Now we're working on over four hundred. He said he was proud of the fact that, back then, ninety percent of the murders he investigated were solved within a year. The procedure, he said, was simple. Check out a victim's family, friends and associates. Find someone with a motive for killing him and in most cases you got the killer. Today, he said, the clearance rate is nothing like ninety percent. The problem, he said, is that so many of today's murders seem senseless. Drugs. Gangs. Everybody is getting whacked out."

The Jeep veered around an olive-green sedan that had slowed to pull off the road to admire the view.

"What frightens most people is the unpredictability. Three weeks ago a woman was crossing West Eighth. A car swerved out of its lane, struck her and knocked her to the pavement. The driver stopped, saw her trying to crawl back to the sidewalk, then backed up and ran over her again, killing her. He then got out of the car, grabbed her purse, and fled. Here's another. Guy gets stalled on the 101. Somebody stops to help. After trying for several minutes to get the car started, the Good Samaritan got pissed off, slugs the guy, robs him, then drives off."

"We're almost to Independence. Maybe we should go over how we want to approach Janice."

"One more. Saw a report that we found jagged bits of broken bottles lightly covered by sand…at the bottom of children's slides throughout parks in the city. Can you believe that shit! These fuckin' people are barely civilized."

CHAPTER THIRTY-NINE

Inyo County Sheriff Don Ward greeted Lily professionally. Ward's attitude turned frosty when she introduced Vega as a former patrol officer from New Jersey.

"Kinda far afield, aren't you?"

"It's a big country."

"Former cop? You're too young to retire from where I stand. Disability?"

Lily interrupted to point out that Vega had suffered several gunshot wounds, thinking it might soften the edges.

"Line of duty?"

"No."

"Didn't think so."

Again, Lily tried to salvage the initial meeting, which was quickly going sideways.

"As I mentioned in my telephone call, Mr. Vega is a private detective pursuing a missing person case from seventeen years ago. He believes that Janice Showalter, who is in your custody, is the younger sister of the missing woman. He...we'd like to interview her to see what, if any, information she may have about her sister's disappearance or possible whereabouts. You or one of your deputies are free to sit in on the interview in the chance anything she says relates to the reasons you are holding her for."

Ward turned his gaze from Vega to Lily.

"We got too much on our hands as it is. Don't need to muddy the waters any further. We still don't know what we got here. Have a seat. You need to know a thing or two about these people. The interviews we've conducted so far have resulted in some of the most goddamn tales we've ever heard. Stories about heavy drug use, sex orgies, attempts to recreate the days of Rommel and the Desert Corps by tearing over the countryside by night in dune buggies, stringing field phones around the area for rapid communication. The leader claims he's Jesus Christ. Seems to be trying to form some sort of a religious cult out here."

Rather than tell him they had already heard such accounts from a Highway Patrol officer, Lily allowed the rural sheriff to continue. Ward pulled a tape recorder from a drawer in the large oak desk he sat behind.

"Here's an example. This is an interview I conducted on October third, a week before the first raid at Barker's Ranch. The subject is Brooks Ramsey Poston, twenty years old. He was the first contact we made that indicated what we were dealing with was more than just vagrants panhandling and making a nuisance in our small towns."

Ward pushed the play button. The sound was scratchy and hampered by an echo from the walls of the interview room.

One of Charlie's basic creeds, is that all the girls are for, is to fuck, or make love. And that's all they're for, and that's – there's no crime, there's no sin, that everything's alright. That it's all just a game. Just like, games of a little kid, only it's grown-up games. And that, god', getting ready to pull down the curtain on this game. And start it over again, with his chosen people. And Charlie considers himself to be Jesus, the second coming of Christ. And that, he is to lead 144,000 people out onto the desert. From reading things into the Bible, from revelations. And he feels that the Beatles are the four-headed locusts that's mentioned in there. That are here to plague man with their mouths. And uh, he listens to all their records, while under the effects of LSD, or any other drug he can get a hold of. And he, puts into there, the meanings he wants in it. And he uses – he has, body control of his hands and his arms and his fingers, to the point, that, it's like watching something that constantly changes when he's moving. It doesn't ever appear to be the same on any two movements. And while everyone he's with is under the effects of these drugs he uses his hands and his fingers and says he can pass the motion on to you when you get tuned in to the infinite.

Ward stopped the recording, looking at his two guests for their reaction.

"Who's Charlie?"

"Charles Millus Manson. DOB eleven, twelve, thirty-four. Got a long rap sheet. Ex-con. Spent some time in…New Jersey."

The location was drawn out from the sheriff's mouth like a string of chewing gum.

"Ever run across him, Mister Former Police Officer?"

"First time I've heard the name."

"Puny guy. Five-two with eyes that seem to look right through you."

"Not ringing any bells."

The play button was pushed a second time.

Charlie's talked about his prison experiences, and where he's learned, many things, about, hypnosis, and what you can do with the power of the mind, from a man named Lanier Ramer, who was his cellmate. Uh, as far as I know, the whole group was there. Charlie and his people living in the back, myself and Juan, and the cowboys, living up front and doing the ranch work, for, approximately, three or four months. All summer, and a month, or maybe a month and a half into the fall. During this time, several people had come along, and he had persuaded them, in the same manner that he was Jesus. And everything that man did, was backwards to what it was supposed to be. And that making love was good and not bad. And that group orgies was the way to get tuned in. And he had convinced several girls, and he's got them tied up in this manner. And also by fear, because he's beaten up several girls, that I know of.

"What's the word on our girl?"

"Don't have much yet on her. No rap sheet. She's one of the older ones."

"What's she being held on?"

"All of them we got holding on auto theft. Prosecutor's taking his time, though. Here's more. I asked Poston about what's going on at Barker's place."

Charlie came back up from Los Angeles with eight people. And uh, they were all sporting knives then. And saying how bad it was getting in the city. He says the negros are going to revolt and kill all the white men, except the ones that are hiding in the desert. And he said it was getting worse and worse, and that he wanted to hide in the desert. And I believe he's on parole, and he's out of his parole area when he's up there. And uh, when he came back, he started, his games of trying to get me, to go back with him. And he said that, he'd release me from no agreements. That, I was still his, and that I should be able to do anything he said – and not think about it. Because that is what love does. Love doesn't fight. It gives up. And to give up would to be God. Charlie, or Charles, says that, giving up is to become God. And that, everything is God.

And that, eating meat is like eating yourself. And anytime there's an animal there, any meat that comes in is given to the animal. And if there's food enough, only for the dog to eat, the dog gets the food.

And the people are supposed to suck on each other. And get their nutriment that way. Because everything is an oral fixation, complex, or something. And he calls guns, phallic symbols – big phallic symbols that guys get their rocks off by shooting. And he says that, people who need guns are the ones that are gonna die. And people that have guns are the ones he's going to kill.

And he said that, I'd be willing to give my life up for you. And I'm willing to let you kill me, so that means I can kill you. And he's talked about killing a negro, militant leader in Los Angeles. And he's talked about killing, a guy named Shorty there too. Or having his people do it – cutting his head off and having the girls bury the body somewhere."

The recorder snapped off. Ward placed it back in the desk drawer.

"So you see what I'm talking about now? I got all these fruitcakes in my custody on grand theft auto and now there's testimony about a homicide of some guy named Shorty in LA. I've sent that information to detectives there but have not heard a peep. Not one goddamn thing. So you see, Officer Navarro? I was hoping that when you called that you were calling about Shorty's headless body. Nope. You called about a missing person, a woman who disappeared seventeen years ago. And now you want to interview her sister. You can see why I'm a bit outta sorts. I'm gonna let you interview Miss Showalter, and I don't need to be there 'cause I know you'll keep your questions to the case you're pursuing, not this other claptrap. Am I correct?"

Lily nodded.

"What about you, Mister Private Detective?"

"I understand the rules."

"Good. Gracie, she's my very capable assistant, has arranged a quiet room for you and Miss Showalter. She'll show you the way."

"Thank you, sheriff."

"One more thing. Officer Navarro? When you return to Los Angeles tomorrow, would you kindly ask around if they've found what's left of Shorty?"

Lily reached out her thank-you hand.

"I'll do you one better. I'll make a call or two tonight."

CHAPTER FORTY

In a ten-by-six-foot interview room, resting her chin on a metal desk that carried more chips and scrapes than gray paint, was Janice Showalter. Her hair was dark and matted. What could be seen of her face was etched with creases from the Death Valley sun. She looked older than twenty-eight but the resemblance to her sister, from the newspaper photo taken in 1952, was undeniable.

"Janice, I'm Aloysius Vega. I'm a private detective looking into your sister's disappearance back in 1952. This is Lily Navarro who…"

"Just so you know, I didn't kill her. She was already dead when I buried her."

"…is a Los Angeles police officer. She is here to assist me in learning about your sister."

Vega completed the introductions despite the interruption. Her statement quickly answered one mystery of the Showalter case. Mary was dead. He considered asking Lily to read Janice her rights, but decided it wasn't necessary. If she was culpable in the death of her older sister, that was for police and prosecutors to later determine. All he cared about was solving the mystery behind Mary's disappearance.

"We're jumping ahead here, but you indicated that your sister is dead. How do you know that?"

"I told you. I buried her."

Vega reached for the notebook in his jacket but saw that Lily was already ahead of him.

"Where is..."

"I hated her. But I didn't kill her."

Vega wanted to start the interview over. Beginnings should start at the beginning, right? These interviews need to be methodical. One starts by establishing a rapport, then outline the purpose of the interview before obtaining an accurate and reliable account of the crime from the witness. But Janice Showalter didn't want to bury the lead to her story. She didn't want the story to slowly unfold like an Agatha Christie novel.

"You said your sister is buried. Where is she buried?"

"The desert."

"That's a big chunk of land, Janice. Can you narrow it down? Is it near Palm Springs, where your sister lived?"

"Yes, but I wouldn't describe it as near."

"Is there another town nearby?"

"No."

"From the time you left Palm Springs, how long was the drive to where you say your sister is buried?"

"Maybe three hours."

"In which direction?"

"I don't know. It was dark."

"When did this occur? Do you recall the date?"

"I don't know the date. I was eleven at the time. I think a few days after her wedding."

"I see. This place where Mary is buried, can you describe it? Anything about the surroundings?"

"A cave."

Vega imagined there were dozens, maybe even hundreds of caves, mine shafts and lava tubes in the Mojave Desert. Each inhabited with bats, snakes, and other creatures of the night.

"Large or small? The cave."

"Big. Very big."

Vega made a note to call Nancy.

"Okay. This is helpful. Let's talk about how your sister died, okay?"

"Sure."

Vega waited for an explanation. Janice remained silent, still resting her chin on the table between them.

"Was it an accident?"

"I wouldn't call it that."

"Someone killed her?"

"I told you. It wasn't me."

"Who then? Who killed your sister?"

"The guy she married."

"Arthur Quail?"

"Uh-huh."

"Arthur Quail killed your sister?"

"Yes."

"How do you know that? That Arthur Quail killed your sister."

"I was there."

"Where did this occur?"

"At the cave."

"Can you tell me how…"

Lily slid her notebook to Vega, interrupting his next question. She took over the questioning.

"Janice, earlier you said you hated your sister. Why was that? Can you tell us?"

For the first time, Janice lifted her head off the table. Her eyes found Lily's.

"Because she didn't believe me. She never did."

"Didn't believe you? In what way? Why?"

"I told her not to marry him. I said he was evil. She didn't believe me. She never did."

"Why...why was Arthur Quail evil, Janice?"

"He raped me."

CHAPTER FORTY-ONE

The ugly story had its origins in Wyckoff when Janice was four. Her parents were arguing at the dinner table. Over what, Janice had no recollection other than it was loud and her mother was crying. Howard Showalter struck his wife across her face sending her sprawling onto the kitchen floor. With another sweep of an arm, plates of meatloaf, potatoes, and corn kernels toppled off the table onto the floor where Belinda Showalter lay bleeding from her nose.

"I remember him yelling for my mother to clean up the mess. She did, while he returned to his favorite chair, lighting up a cigar as he did each evening after dinner."

That night, as Janice and Mary got ready for bed, their mother told both girls to forget what they saw. Their father was out of work and it bothered him greatly. The following morning, after Mary went off to school, the argument flared again. Janice recalled her father screaming so loudly that she placed her hands over her ears and ran to her bedroom to hide. After the house became quiet, she returned downstairs.

"I saw their bedroom door was closed. I heard Mother crying and my father grunting and groaning. I was too young to know about sex, but they had a firm rule about never knocking on their bedroom door or entering when it was closed."

As the late morning wore on, Janice said she played with her dolls. Eventually bored, she dared to sit in her father's chair in the living room. She found his half-smoked cigar and a pack of matches. She attempted to light the cigar, following the steps she had seen her father do a thousand times.

"Next thing, I felt a terrible stinging on my fingertips. The matchbook was burning. I threw it down and sucked on my fingers, which hurt. It wasn't long before the room filled with smoke. It was coming from the bottom of the couch. I ran to their bedroom to let my parents know, but the door was still closed. Not knowing what else to do, I hid in the hall closet where we kept my snow clothes. I put those on and remained in the closet sucking my fingers until a fireman let me out."

To Lily's annoyance, Vega jumped in.

"Your sister was at school. Why weren't you?"

"I guess you weren't listening. I was four."

Lily poured a glass of water from the pitcher set to one side of the table.

"Here, drink this. I know this is a difficult memory to recall."

Lily waited for Janice to set down the glass before continuing.

"Thanks. She never forgave me for what happened. She blamed me for the fire. For killing them. She never let me forget. I hated her for that."

"I understand that, following the fire, you and Mary lived with your grandparents."

"For a short time. My sister went off to college before too long. She came back one time, for Christmas. She never returned."

Like a schoolgirl reciting state capitals, Janice clicked off the years that followed as a series of moves from one foster home to another after her grandmother died. Her grandfather told the state of Michigan he was unable to care for such a young girl. Her memories of her first foster home were limited to the smell of burnt bacon and thin, runny eggs. For the others, it was an unending circle of trying to fit in with a family not her own. After a year, sometimes less, Janice would drag her belongings in a plastic garbage bag to the next temporary home. Another throw-away child.

"What little I owned could have fit in a few shopping bags. Besides my clothing, I only had some school supplies. I learned to attach very little sentimental value to the items I owned. I had no choice with whom I lived or how long I would stay. Others controlled my life. I was continually told how lucky I was. How I was supposed to be grateful for the couple who supposedly 'chose me.' I did not want to call them mummy or daddy but was forced to. I wanted to be in a house where I had the same last name as everyone else and resembled the others. Instead of feeling like a family member, I was more like a guest, someone who had overstayed her welcome."

Lily asked why Mary hadn't visited during those years.

"All I know is that she didn't. Another thing I hated her for. She could have asked the courts to be my guardian. She didn't. She wanted me out of her life."

It was time for Lily to ask the inevitable.

"If you carried this hatred of your sister for all those years, why did you attend her wedding?"

"She called me out of the blue. I still don't know how she found me. The wedding invitation? I think it was her way of making up for lost time. She was starting a new life. She told me she wanted me to be part of it. I was eleven by then, and it sounded like a fairytale come true. She arranged for transportation to Palm Springs and set me up in her apartment."

"And that's when you first met Arthur Quail?"

"Yes. At first, he was very nice to me. Charming, in fact. Especially in front of my sister."

"Janice, I know this will be painful for you. Can you tell us what happened with Mr. Quail?"

"Like I said, he was nice to me at first. Rather than leave me alone in Mary's apartment when she went to work, he would take me with him as he drove from bank to bank, doing whatever it was that he did. We'd go to lunch together, McDonald's, cafes, whatever was convenient in these towns on his circuit. He would ask me about my favorite things, like movies, books, ice cream. He always made sure I got an ice cream cone before heading back to the apartment."

"Was Mr. Quail staying overnight at Mary's apartment?"

"I think he was before I arrived. I found some of his belongings there. But Mary insisted he bunk at his own apartment after I arrived. At least until the wedding."

"When did he first molest you?"

"It was a few days before the wedding. We were driving in the middle of nowhere when he pulled the car over on the side of the road. He said he had to go to the bathroom and the nearest gas station was still miles away. Rather than going behind a bush or tree or something, he stood on the side of the road across from the passenger seat where I was. I turned the other way when I saw him unzip his pants. I heard him peeing, but that stopped after a while. I wondered why he hadn't returned to the car, so I looked out the window. He was standing there with his pecker hanging out. I hadn't seen one of those before. Never saw my father in the buff or any of the foster boys, so my first sight of a penis was startling to say the least. It was stiff and he was massaging it. This was happening, I don't know, maybe five feet from where I was sitting. After I turned away, I waited for him to get back in the car. Neither of us said a word the rest of the way."

Janice said Quail's odd behavior increased the following day. Instead of asking about her favorite flavors of ice cream, he asked about her favorite color of underwear. He made comments about how in a few years her breasts would begin to grow. At times, he would place his right hand on her knee squeezing it gently.

"And you never told your sister about this?"

Lily glared at Vega for his question.

"Honestly, I didn't know what was going on other than he was being nice to me. My parents or my sister never sat down with me to talk about private places or sex, things like that. I was a very naïve eleven-year-old."

"Do you want to take a break?"

"I'm fine. Growing up, I thought about what he did. It happened. That's about all I can say."

"You said he raped you. When did that occur?"

"At his apartment, in Riverside. It was the day before the wedding. We had spent the day in that town. He stopped at two banks. I was given a ticket to watch this dumb movie called *Monkey Business*. He picked me up outside when the movie was over. He said he had to first stop at his apartment before we could head back to Palm Springs."

Once inside, she said, Quail told her to undress. When she refused, he grabbed her arms, pushing her toward his bedroom where he tossed her onto his bed, repeating his command. Frightened, Janice said she did what she was told. When she tried to pull a sheet over her nakedness, he pulled it to the floor.

"I didn't know what was happening, but he was angry and I was scared. He removed his clothes. He began to massage his pecker. He ordered me to touch myself between my legs. I hadn't gone through a period yet and I didn't understand what he meant. When he saw my confusion, he stopped fondling himself and put his face between my legs. He said, 'here, let me show you.' As he licked me, I remember feeling dizzy, like I was having an out-of-body experience. I closed my eyes and tried to imagine watching the ocean and birds."

After a long sip of water, Janice continued.

"Next, he dug his fingers into me. When I told him he was hurting me, he told me to stop squirming. That's when he threatened me. 'If you want to live, stop fighting.' That's what he said. But I couldn't. It hurt and I started crying. That made him stop. That's when he got up and stood by the side of the bed, facing me. His pecker was drooping, I could see that. He ordered me to kiss it, which I did. Seemed an easier thing to do than having his fingers dig into me. So, I did what he said. He told me to put it in my mouth. I didn't know what happened, but I didn't like it. I pulled from his grip and spit on his bed. He told me to get dressed, we were leaving."

"Was there penetration?"

Lily shot Vega another glance that screamed to keep quiet.

"No. That happened later."

Lily asked Janice to continue.

"He took me to his car. Showed me a gun he kept in the glove box. Said that if I ever said a word about what happened, to my sister, the police or anyone else, he would first kill my sister and then me. He described in detail what he would do. I believed him."

"So you never told your sister?"

"I called her at work one time. I told her she shouldn't marry him. That he was an evil man. She got angry and hung up."

"Tell us what happened at the marriage ceremony. Why you ran off."

"Sure. I managed to keep control of my emotions as we drove to the courthouse. But when the justice of the peace came out, the judge in his black robe, I got scared. So I ran off. To this day, I'm really not sure to where. I didn't have any money with me and I was wearing this pretty pink dress. Later that day I found my way back to the apartment, now their apartment. He answered the door. Said I had made my sister very angry and embarrassed, and she never wanted to see me again."

"What happened next?"

"I waited as he gathered up my belongings into my suitcase. He told me to wait in his car. It was unlocked. I did what I was told. I waited there for a long time. He finally arrived and drove to his apartment in Riverside. We didn't talk the entire way. He left me there the rest of the night and returned, I think, to my sister's place. I considered running off, but where would I go?"

Lily announced she had to take a bathroom break and asked Janice if she needed one. When Janice declined, Lily motioned for Vega to follow her out. They found their way outside to the stairs in front of the courthouse.

"Vega, I'm telling you to shut the fuck up in there. Janice opens up to me not you. Or haven't you noticed?"

"My case, not yours. Remember?"

"You listen! We have evidence, a confession of a rape from a victim. She deserves a little care and understanding ... something you seem to have lost along the way."

"You're forgetting that more than ten years have passed since she was molested."

"Raped!"

"Yeah, raped. But the statute of limitations has long passed. Meanwhile, I'm close to solving the murder of her sister. A crime that has no time limit. Penal Code Seven-Nine-Nine."

— • —

Gracie, the sheriff's assistant, was waiting outside the interrogation room when they returned. The courthouse would close in less than an hour. They were welcome to return in the morning if necessary.

Vega was anxious to learn more about Mary's death and the location of her remains. Lily had other ideas when they re-entered the room.

"Okay, Janice. We left off with Mr. Quail leaving you at his apartment and returning to Palm Springs and his new wife, your sister. Tell us what happened next."

For the next forty minutes, Vega and Lily heard a sordid tale of rape, kidnapping, and murder.

Janice said she remained in Quail's apartment, unsure of what to do. Going to the police was never considered because of the overhanging threat. When Quail returned the following morning, he raped her. This time there was penetration. The next day, Janice said, was a blur. She watched TV and slept. When Quail returned, he beat her.

"She must've said something to him. He slapped me across the face several times. My nose and mouth were bleeding. He tied my hands together with packing tape. A strip was placed across my mouth. Then he took me to Mary's."

Vega interrupted.

"Wait. When did this happen?"

"I don't know the date."

"Did any of Quail's neighbors witness this?"

"Not that I could see. Once he got me to the car, he tied my feet together and covered me with a blanket in the back seat."

Vega again.

"How did you know he took you to your sister's. You said you were under a blanket."

"When the car finally came to a stop, I heard tree frogs. I knew we were at Mary's apartment. The block there was teeming with those frogs. They sing all night long. A beautiful sound...even then."

"Go on."

"He got out of the door and the frogs stopped. He returned a short time later, then drove somewhere and parked again and got out. After about a half hour, he returned to the car. Instead of starting it up, he pulled me out onto the sidewalk. The blanket, which had slipped partially off, was wrapped over me again. He picked me up and carried me to another car. Mary's car."

"How did you know it was her car?"

"She was in the front seat. I caught a glimpse of her. Her head was tilted to one side. There was a gash across her forehead that was bleeding. I was thrown into the back seat with several bags of groceries. The car reversed then turned left. We were leaving town. I could tell by how quiet it was. The longer he drove the more the temperature dropped."

"Did he say anything? Was there any conversation between him and Mary?"

"No."

"What happened next?"

"I guess about three hours went by before we stopped and he ordered us out of the car. It was pitch dark. I heard coyotes crying in the distance."

Vega interrupted again.

"Did Quail stop the car at any other point along the way?"

"I forgot that part. The car stopped after an hour or so for gas. I heard him say something to my sister. I couldn't understand what, but it involved something in the glovebox. Next thing, the car moved forward. I heard the ding-ding of a service station bell. Someone got out of the car. Couldn't tell who. I heard the nozzle being inserted and, a bit later, it being removed and the gas cap replaced. We drove off. Next stop was when he ordered us out of the car. How was I going to get myself out? My hands and mouth were still taped. Eventually, he removed the blanket and the tape from my hands. But not my mouth."

Lily grabbed the notebook as Vega was furiously writing.

"I hope you have your own. The way you're taking notes, we're going to run out of room real fast. Don't you know shorthand?"

Vega removed a notebook tucked in his coat pocket, understanding that Lily was buying a breather. Janice was about to wander down an even darker road. Witnessing a killing, any killing, and then having to recount it in detail is about as nightmarish as it comes.

"Shorthand? No. The nuns taught us cursive. It's slower, but just as accurate. Maybe more so."

Lilly studied Janice before resuming her questioning. Her face remained devoid of any emotion.

"Ready to continue, Janice? They told us we could come back in the morning."

"The car's headlights were still on when I was able to stand. Flying bugs were darting about by the headlights. My sister was standing. She was naked. She was shivering. A lot. He was holding a gun. He kept it pointed at Mary, occasionally aiming it at me. He said nothing for the longest time, as if he was deciding what to do with us. I remember looking at my sister's body. I'm not sure I ever saw her naked. She was always very private. Anyway, I remember thinking how beautiful she was. She looked like a goddess."

Both Lily and Vega knew not to interrupt at this point. Janice would continue when she was ready.

"He removed the tape from my mouth and told me to suck on his pecker. I did as I was told. He kept the gun trained on my sister to ensure she was watching. She was. Her knees appeared ready to buckle. She kept whispering: Please. Don't. Not her. Not her. After he finished, he told me to fold my sister's clothes and put them in the car. He insisted that I fold them neatly. I thought that was weird. He then got out a flashlight and made us walk up this trail that took us to the opening of a cave."

"How long did it take you to reach the cave?"

"Maybe a half-hour. We stopped several times. My sister was barefoot and kept stepping on sharp stones and stuff."

"You were able to remain in your clothes?"

"Yeah. For some reason he...He walked behind us. Kept the flashlight pointed on Mary's butt instead of where we were stepping."

"Do you remember anything about the trail that stood out?"

"It was steep. I could make out the side of a mountain on one side and a cliff on the other."

"What side was the cliff? Your left or right?"

"Our left."

"What about any unusual markers?"

"There was a small grave at one point."

"At the start of the trail? Near the end? Midway?"

"Closer to the start."

"Did you see any markings on the grave?"

"No. But it spooked Mary. She screamed when she saw it. That pissed him off. He pushed her to the ground and held the gun to her head. Told her to shut up or he'd kill her. Or me. I don't remember which. When we reached the cave, he ordered us to kneel. He walked to the entrance, shining the flashlight inside. He picked up a rock and threw it inside. A few bats flew out. Then he shined the flashlight behind us, on the trail. There was nothing."

"Janice, what can you tell us about the entrance to the cave? Was it big or ..."

"Big enough for us to walk through. There were large boulders on either side."

"Please continue."

"He ordered us to stand up. My sister was unsteady. She was bleeding. From her forehead, knees, feet. She placed one hand on my shoulder to help her stand. She tried to plead with him to let us go. He said nothing. He..."

Vega interrupted.

"I'm sorry, Janice. Can you remember what your sister said? You said she tried to plead with Quail."

"I don't remember the exact words, but it was to the effect to let me go. That I didn't know anything."

"Did Quail respond?"

"No. He told us to enter the cave."

Vega and Lily waited for Janice to continue. Instead, she sat in silence. A silence that said more than words ever could.

CHAPTER FORTY-TWO

Vega and Lily understood that this moment, above all others in their interview, had the potential to shape the outcome of an eventual criminal prosecution. Which is why they waited for her to speak.

"I need to use the bathroom, if that's okay."

Lily jumped to her feet and signaled for the matron who was stationed down the hallway. After the two were alone, they discussed how best to use their remaining time, less than ten minutes.

"We can come back in the morning. The sheriff said as much."

"Janice may decide she's done talking with us. We need to quickly uncover a few pieces that are missing. For one, why didn't Quail kill Janice at the same time as Mary? Was he intending to keep her alive, maybe as his child bride?"

"Disgusting thought."

"And we still don't know what went down at the cave. How did Janice manage to survive? As I said, we're missing a lot of pieces here. Big pieces. We still don't know what we don't know."

— • —

If Janice had used the break to cry or vomit, it wasn't apparent. Once seated, she picked up the story in the same composed voice.

"I remember feeling frightened. I remember feeling sick. I also remember feeling just an overwhelming sense of anger at my sister. If she had listened to me just once, we...I remember how suddenly cold it felt as we entered the cave. And dark. His flashlight was the only source of light and he dropped it at one point. He was behind us and we heard it clatter on the ground. We stopped walking and turned to see what happened. He was feeling along the ground with one hand. When he found the flashlight I noticed he was bleeding and..."

"Where was the injury?"

"Uh, around his ear."

"Left or right?"

"His left...no, his right. Wait. He was holding the gun in his right hand. He picked up the flashlight with his left hand."

It was the first time that Janice appeared uncertain of the details. The injury, Vega knew, could be important evidence if it left a scar.

"Take your time, Janice. We want to..."

"The right. It was the right."

"Go on."

"He kept asking us to hurry up, to walk faster. We couldn't. It was too dark. We had to keep our hands out. In front of our face and by the sides to keep from hitting our heads. We crawled into one tunnel but turned back. Went nowhere. He was having a difficult time holding the gun and the flashlight. He kept shining it on the walls and ceiling in front of him, I think to avoid hitting his head again. He aimed the light toward another tunnel then told us to stop. He shined the flashlight on the ground, then to one side. There was nothing there. No wall. Nothing. Just a black hole, like a pit. That's when he fired."

CHAPTER FORTY-THREE

It took all of two phone calls and a state road map for Nancy Randall to identify the cave where Mary Showalter was allegedly buried. The first call went to the geology department at UCLA. After being transferred two times Nancy was placed with someone who knew the geology of the Mojave Desert. Nancy described the cave and the nearby gravesite and was told it likely was the Mitchell Caverns inside the Providence Mountains.

The second call was placed to her counterpart at the Los Angeles central library, who provided a quick history of the caverns and promised to mail Nancy a book written by Jack Mitchell, one of three men who filed claims on the property in 1930 and who put his name on the land.

Armed with this information, she called Vega at the Winnedumah Hotel where he and Lily had checked in. Named after a Paiute Indian, the hotel was built in 1927 to attract the movie stars like Roy Rogers, Gary Cooper, and John Wayne who were filming westerns in the nearby Alabama Hills.

"Mr. Vega, my contact at UCLA was certain the large cave with the nearby gravestone is the Mitchell Caverns in the Providence Mountains. It's a large limestone cave in the Mojave. The road map shows the Providence Mountains to be northeast of Palm Springs, about 160 miles away."

"That seems to match what Janice told us, both in her description of the cave and the time to drive that distance. Good work. How deep does it go?"

"I was told the opening itself is near the top of the mountain, at an elevation of 4,100 feet. From the entrance, that first level descends some fifty feet. Level two drops a hundred. If you make it down to the bottom, you're three-hundred feet underground."

"From what Janice told us, Quail took them in a tunnel that led to what she said was a pit."

"I'll see what I can find. Did she tell you what happened to Mary?"

"She did. Mary's dead. Buried there. I'll fill you in on the full story when we return. This Mitchell guy, he still work around there?"

"He died in fifty-four. Ida, his wife, passed just three years ago."

"This book, does it contain any diagrams or drawings of the interior?"

"I believe there are a few. The book is being mailed, so I should have it in a few days."

"Good. We should finish up here in the morning. I should be back late afternoon. We'll talk then. Thanks again."

— • —

After finishing two games of pool and a pitcher of cold beer, Vega and Lily sat at a table on the sidewalk outside the Pines Café, two blocks from the hotel. Lily had easily won both games. Few words were spoken as they played. Mostly gestures or nods as the balls ricocheted off a side cushion, on occasion disappearing into a pocket. Three old-timers hugging the bar ignored the two strangers as did those stopping at the small post office across the highway.

"What do you think she meant?"

"Who Janice? Which part? Not following you."

"At the cave. Mary told Quail her sister didn't know anything."

"Yeah, not sure what she was referring to. Grasping at straws, don't you think? Looking for some way to save her little sister."

"I guess. The two weren't very close, that's for sure."

"True. But Mary did try to break the ice by inviting Janice to the wedding."

Vega pulled an empty chair from a nearby table, putting his feet up as he drained the last of his beer, now warm.

"You look like one of those small-town sheriffs, sniffin' the wind for strangers riding in on horseback."

"I wouldn't mind that job."

"I bet you'd love it. A lawman with a badge and no one to challenge your methods, 'cept for maybe a circuit judge or two. C'mon, I'm hungry. You owe me a steak dinner and a back rub."

Lily stood but sat back down when Vega didn't follow her lead.

"She's a cold one."

"Janice? You think she's cold? C'mon, Vega. That person who sat across from us has been to hell and back. Several times. Her house burns down, her parents inside, at age four. Bounced around in foster care. Raped! Was there when her sister was murdered. And you think she's cold?"

"Different people react differently to trauma. Some become anxious, have trouble sleeping, constantly on edge. Others just withdraw. They're numb, emotionally blank. Cold."

"When did you become a psychologist?"

"Not me. Vivian. Doctor Dy."

"And her diagnosis? About you?"

"She said I was a jumble of all that."

"You still feel that way?"

"At times. Can we get back to my question? About Mary's comment to Quail? Everything seems to fit the evidence at the time. The stop for gas, blood in Mary's car, calls to Mary at the bank, the folded clothes. Except for that."

"Don't forget the flowers sent to her at the bank. The mystery suitor."

"As I said, we're missing a lot of pieces here. We still don't know what else happened in the cave. How or why Janice was spared."

— • —

After a dinner of bloody ribeyes and poorly made martinis, Lily and Vega zigzagged their way to the hotel. Lily tried playing *Row Your Boat* on the lobby piano. The back rub on one of the two queen beds lasted all of seven minutes before Lily rolled over and begged Vega to fuck her. Their brief lovemaking came with the ease and electricity of an attraction bound to go nowhere.

CHAPTER FORTY-FOUR

When they gathered the following morning, Janice appeared withdrawn. Shoulders hunched, she avoided eye contact. She flinched when Lily reached across the table, placing a hand on her wrist.

"We've asked a lot of you, Janice. You've been very brave and straightforward with us. We have a few more questions this morning. Only a few, I promise. Okay?"

Only a nod. When asked to explain what happened after her sister was shot, the answers were clipped.

She couldn't recall if she slipped off the ledge or jumped when the gunfire exploded next to her.

"I landed hard."

"My shoulder and chest hurt."

"I started crying. I bit my lip."

"The flashlight was way above me, moving back and forth in the darkness."

"He started shooting again."

"Bits of rock were spitting everywhere."

"I scooched against a wall I could feel behind me."

Encouraged by Lily to continue, Janice said she waited in the utter darkness until she felt it was safe to move. She waved her hands around to feel her surroundings. Without light of any kind, she touched the cool dusty ground and the wall behind her.

"I felt around for my sister as best I could."

Vega and Lily strained to hear more, the voice across the table had fallen to a whisper. She told them she crawled about in the dark after she felt certain Quail had left, eventually finding her sister's body.

"I just sat there, unsure of what to do. I undid my blouse and put it under her head. I knew she was dead, but it seemed something I should do. I don't know."

Deciding she needed to bury her sister in some fashion, Janice scrounged in the pitch darkness for rocks, clumps of dirt, anything she could use. She couldn't see her hands, only feel them as they scraped blindly across the cold ground. Every movement sent pain lancing through her side from the fall. She piled atop her sister's body whatever the cave would give up. It wasn't enough.

"But it was all I could find. I had to get out of there. The cave was making sounds. Animal sounds. Bats, I think. I don't know how, but I got to my feet and felt my way along the wall. I dipped my toe, testing the ground as I inched along. I was so scared. I didn't want to die there. I felt smothered. I don't know how long it took me. Climbing. Shuffling. Feeling my way. But I finally saw a sliver of light. I knew I was going in the right direction. When I finally reached the entrance, it was still night. But the stars and the moon were so bright, it seemed like daylight. It was light enough that I found my way down the trail to the parking area. The car was gone."

With some prodding from Lily, Janice finished her story. She walked the remainder of the night to the highway where she waited on the side of the road. Several cars passed before a truck pulled over. An elderly man asked what had happened and if she needed to get to a doctor.

"I lied. I said I was running away from home. That my parents were mean to me. That my father beat and raped me. He gave me a shirt to put on and drove me to a town called Needles where he was going to take me to the police. When we made a rest stop, I ran off. Anyhow, I got rides here and there but eventually got picked up as a runaway and returned to my foster home in Green Bay."

Anxious about their remaining time with Janice – one-hour tops, according to Gracie – Vega interrupted. He asked if Janice had ever been to McNeil Island Prison in Washington state. She hesitated before answering.

"I've...I've never been in jail. Until now."

"That's not what I asked."

"Why are you asking this? I don't understand."

"The reason I'm here is to find out what happened to your sister. You've told me that story. I believe you. After you're released, we're going to locate her remains so your sister can have a proper burial after I turn my notes over to the police. Arthur Quail deserves to pay for what he did to Mary and to you. To tie this all up in a neat package, I'll need to explain to police and prosecutors how I got involved in Mary's disappearance. Here's the short version. An inmate at McNeil Island claims that earlier this year he saw Mary with a trustee by the name of Alvin Karpis. Now we know that it couldn't be. Mary had been dead for seventeen years, according to what you told us. So this woman who was seen at the prison likely was someone who resembled your sister. Someone who obtained visitor access to meet with Mr. Karpis. So let me ask again. Have you ever been to McNeil Island, a federal penitentiary in Washington state?"

Janice looked to Lily before answering.

"Yes."

"Good. We're making progress. Was this in December of last year?"

"Yes."

"Any other times?"

"No. That was the only time."

"And did you meet Alvin Karpis?"

"Yes."

"And what was the purpose of that visit?"

"To thank him."

"To thank him? For what?"

"Charlie asked me to thank Mr. Karpis for the guitar lessons."

Vega thought for a moment before turning to Lily.

"Not sure I told you this. When I spoke with Karpis, he mentioned that he taught some inmates to play. He said his best student was a guy named Charlie."

Lily rolled her head back and forth. The story was getting odder by the moment.

"Did you reference Charlie's name when you filled out the visitor's form?"

"I did as Charlie asked."

"Had you met Karpis before that visit? Like a phone call or…"

"Charlie told me to write letters. He wanted me to become a pen pal. He said inmates like Mr. Karpis enjoyed the correspondence. I only mailed one. I mentioned Charlie's name and said I wanted to visit at Charlie's request. I received permission from the administrators three weeks later. Charlie was worried that Mr. Karpis would be released before I could get there. He read in the newspaper that he was getting paroled and would be sent to Canada."

"That was it? The only time you met Karpis?"

"Yes. He was a very nice man. After I thanked him, we talked for about an hour. About what he wanted to do when he got out. Where he wanted to go. He even asked me to come with him to Montreal. I couldn't. I promised Charlie I'd return. Mr. Karpis said he understood."

Vega decided against asking Janice how she thanked Karpis. He knew the answer.

Lily pushed the notepad to Vega. It was her turn to ask a few final questions.

"Tell me, how did you meet Charlie?"

For the first time in two days of interviews, Janice Showalter smiled.

"It was meant to be. In the stars, you know. I was working at the library at UC in Berkeley…"

"When was this?"

"Springtime, two years ago. I had recently moved from Wisconsin. I was engaged at the time. My fiancé was a student in Madison and was poised to take a position at the university. I could easily have fit into the role of faculty wife, but I wanted more. I read about Haight-Ashbury and all that was going on in San Francisco at the time. I left him, drove cross-country, and accepted a library position at UC. I rented a one-bedroom apartment with my dog Muffy. I was walking her on campus the day I met Charlie. He was playing guitar at Sather Gate when I walked by. He fussed over Muffy and we struck up a conversation. He played me some songs he wrote and casually mentioned he had no place to stay."

"Did you know at the time that he was an ex-con?"

Vega again.

"Not right away, no. But he later told me he had recently been released from prison on Terminal Island."

Lily's turn.

"Continue your story. About how you met Charlie."

"That same day, he said he didn't have any family members or friends in the Bay Area. I offered him my sofa that night. When we got to my apartment, he tried to hit on me, but I told him no. I offered my friendship, nothing more. I said goodbye the next morning, expecting that would be the last I saw of him. But when I returned from work that evening, Charlie and his guitar and everything he owned were in my living room."

"How did you react?"

"He promised to help me out, provide rent money, keep any bad guys away and not bother me for sex. I agreed and we got on quite well together."

At the door to the interview room was a deputy. Their time with Janice Showalter was already in overtime. They had to wrap up.

Vega asked Janice if she had an attorney.

"No. I was told they need to bring in more. There aren't enough public defenders in town."

Vega left two business cards and asked that she give one to the attorney assigned to her case.

"Tell him, or her, that I need to know when you're getting out. You're going to help me find your sister."

— • —

Sheriff Ward was on the telephone in his office when Gracie let them in. He motioned for them to sit down.

"That so? Doesn't surprise me a lick. Yeah, yeah, I'll let you know what else we find."

Vega and Lily sat quietly as the sheriff scribbled notes on a yellow pad after completing the call. He muttered.

"Seems our disciples were busy earlier this year at this ranch near Chatsworth where they used to film westerns. Arrested some of these same fine citizens in a raid looking for – guess what – stolen vehicles. This was in April. Charges didn't stick. Place was raided again in August, looking for suspects in an auto theft ring. Looks like Jesus and his followers high-tailed it north into my jurisdiction. Just my damn luck. Now, Officer Navarro, Gracie tells me you have information from LA regarding some homicides down there that might be of interest to me. Let's have it."

"There's the Sharon Tate case."

"Who?"

"Sharon Tate. Movie actress. Killed in her Beverly Hills home along with four others."

"Any of the victims a headless guy named Shorty?"

"No. But on a wall at the victim's house the words Political Piggy were painted. In blood."

"Officer Navarro, tell me why I should care."

"On the tape you played for us yesterday. Brooks Poston said that this Jesus guy, Charlie, told his followers there's going to be mass hysteria in the cities and the cops won't know what to do. There may not be a connection, but I thought you'd want to know."

"I appreciate the suggestion, Officer Navarro. Any other homicide cases in Los Angeles I should know about?"

Lily opened her notebook.

"One other. On August 6, detectives with the Los Angeles Sheriff's Department filed a homicide report on the murder of a music teacher who had been found dead in his Topanga Canyon home a week prior. His ear was severed then stitched with dental floss. He also suffered chest wounds caused by a large knife. These were fatal and delivered approximately three days after the wounds to the ear. It appears he was tortured."

"I take the victim's not the headless horseman who goes by Shorty."

"Victim's name is Gary Hinman. Appears he was killed during a break-in at his home. The place had been trashed as if the perpetrators were looking for something. Drugs, likely. They made an arrest in the case. Found the five-inch knife and other incriminating evidence in the possession of one Bobby Beausoleil."

Sheriff Ward asked Lily to spell the name.

"B-o-b-b..."

"The last name, please. We rural folks went to school. We're familiar with the spelling of Bob, Bobby, even Robert. It's those French-sounding names that are a bitch."

"Sorry. B-e-a-u-s-o-l-e-i-l."

After jotting down the name, Ward asked Gracie to join them.

"Bring me the notes on the Kitty girl. Our visitors here may have something. Detective Navarro? Mr. Vega? You may want to hear this. At Barker Ranch, they came across two young girls who told us they wanted to get away from Mr. Manson. The girls claimed they weren't being held against their will but wanted to get back to their family and friends. One little freckle-faced girl, she's all of seventeen, is pregnant. Her name is ... thanks, Gracie."

After putting on reading glasses, Ward read from the yellow legal pad he was handed.

"Kathryn Rene Lutesinger. Goes by Kitty. DOB eight-fourteen-fifty-two. Blond hair...let's see, parents live in San Carlos. She...let me cut to the chase here. This pretty little girl, as I mentioned, is pregnant. When we asked who the father was, she said he was a rock-and-roll musician down your way. Name is Robert Kenneth Beausoleil. How's that for a coincidence? I think your homicide folks in Los Angeles might want to have a little talk with her. What is the name of the lead detective on this Hangman case?"

"Hinman. Gary Hinman. He's the deceased. My notes have the names of two detectives on the case: Det. Sgt. Paul J. Whiteley and Deputy Charles Guenther. Both are with the LA County Sheriff's Office. Want me to spell their..."

"I'll give Detective Whiteley a call right now. Gracie? Get me the sheriff's office for the County of Los Angeles. Now that I have work to do, I'll have you on your way. Thank you and safe travels. Please shut the door on your way out."

As Vega and Lily left Ward's office for the long drive back to Palm Springs, deputies were escorting down the courthouse stairway a small, long-haired man in handcuffs. He grinned.

CHAPTER FORTY-FIVE

The following week was busy with preparations. Vega contacted Korshak, who promised to relay the news to Roselli. The attorney insisted that any skeletal remains found in the caverns would have to be confirmed as Mary's before the case would be turned over to Palm Springs detectives.

"I don't want my client brought into this until we are assured that it is the girl, understood?"

Korshak said he had a contact in the Los Angeles County coroner's office who would perform the analysis.

"I don't trust nobody else. You get me the bones, I'll take care of the rest."

Vega brought Scott Jarvis into the loop, promising the Post reporter an exclusive. Besides the reward money, Vega sought publicity for his agency when it reopened.

"That's the deal, Jarvis. But nothing gets out, to your readers or even your editors, until Mary's identity is confirmed. Not a word. You burn me, I'll cut your heart out."

"Jesus, Vega, that's awfully harsh. Have I ever broken a deal?"

"Things are riding on this in a big way."

"I get it. No problem. One more thing. I need to bring one of our photographers with me when we go there. Bound to be some dramatic shots. Bones, caves…"

"Forget it. I'm taking only four with me: Lily, Mary's sister, Nancy, and you. You want photos? You take 'em."

— • —

The first setback was reported by Nancy. Mitchell Caverns were closed. Opened as a state park only a decade earlier, funding cuts ordered by Governor Reagan were needed to offset a budget crunch.

"What does closed mean? No access? No Boy Scout to issue a parking pass?"

Nancy said she had no idea but would find out.

Lily delivered the second and third obstacles, both of which were crushing to Vega's plans. LAPD canceled vacations and time off for all uniformed officers. No exceptions, she told Vega.

"Something's up. I don't think it has to do with the Tate case. Whispers are it involves the Panthers. Whatever, I'm out. Sorry."

Lily had arranged for time to pick up Janice Showalter on Friday, when she was scheduled to be released from custody. The Inyo County prosecutor had declined to press charges against her and two other women. Other members of the Barker Ranch cult remained in confinement.

After vomiting a few vulgarities, Vega said he'd make the drive to Independence himself.

"Don't bother. There's another problem."

"What?"

"She's gone. Janice and two other gals were sprung today. In the interest of justice, the prosecutor said. No one has a clue where she is. I spoke to her PD. He has no idea where she took off to. Stuck her thumb out on the highway and disappeared."

"North or south?"

"I don't understand."

"Which side of 395 was she standing with her thumb out?"
"No fuckin' idea."

— • —

Not surprisingly, the task of gathering gear for the cave exploration was left to Nancy. She quickly inhaled two books on spelunking and was dispatched to Ladd-Higgins, a hardware store owned by actor Alan Ladd. The star of Shane had decided that Palm Springs needed more than one hardware store. He partnered with a local builder to purchase land and construct the building.

Oftentimes Ladd could be found behind the cash register, as he was when Nancy arrived. He quickly hopped off the counter and was about to assist her when the phone rang.

"Excuse me a minute. We're short-handed today. Manager's sick. I'll be right with you."

Ladd took the phone call before yelling the order to someone in the back of the store.

"Ladd-Higgins, how can I help you? Sure. We got it. I'll send it right over. See yah, Frank...Hundred feet of green plastic hose to Sinatra's place. Pronto! He needs it right away."

His attention back on Nancy, Ladd jotted down her list of equipment before sprinting to an aisle where he collected two coils of twisted Manila rope, each a hundred feet in length. He quickly found most of the other items: heavy gloves, flashlights, two small coils of lightweight braided rope, painter's kneepads, a cloth laundry bag, and extra batteries.

"Rock climbing?"

"Nope. Exploring a cave. Fossils."

"Careful. Lots of nasty things in these caves. Not doing this alone, are you?"

"Nope. Two strong men are there to help."

A sliver of tangerine sky stretched across the eastern horizon as the trio left Palm Springs on a late October morning. The sun would soon reveal its crown above the flat desert expanse, igniting a firestorm of color framed beneath a sky turning from black to neon blue. By the time Nancy's Toyota Corolla began its ascent to the high desert, the valley floor behind glistened in new daylight.

Vega agreed that it made the most sense for Nancy to drive. His Corvette was not built for four passengers and the load of supplies they were bringing. Jarvis said he needed to take notes along the way. He had already filled two notebooks from the stories Vega and Nancy had provided about the lives of Mary and Janice Showalter and was eager to learn more on the three-hour drive.

"Where do you think she's headed?"

"Who, Janice?"

"I certainly wasn't inquiring about Mary's whereabouts."

Vega said he had no clue. Janice had indicated to authorities in Inyo County that she wanted to leave Manson's group.

"Maybe back to Berkeley. She was working at the university before she was lured away by Jesus and his followers. Like Nancy, a librarian."

"I still don't get how these young girls got so taken with this ex-con. Seems creepy."

Sex, drugs, and rock-n-roll, Vega told the newspaperman.

"It's the Sixties, don't forget."

"Not for long. Two months and, bingo, we begin the Seventies."

Nancy, who had been quietly focused on the roadway, said it was more than drugs and sex and music.

"This guy, Charlie, he appears very adept at exploiting insecurities. The drugs, the sex, his followers, it all creates the promise of community. Of belonging. That's important to most young people.

They don't realize he's not only an ex-con, he's a con man. Not the first. And I promise he won't be the last. Montreal."

Both men looked at her, puzzled.

"Montreal what?"

"That's my prediction. About Janice. About where's she's headed. You said she made a comment about liking Mr. Karpis. She's obviously in search of some sort of male companionship. And she's attracted to danger. First Charlie, then Alvin. Criminal minds from different generations."

Jarvis said it could make for a good book or movie.

— • —

As they passed through Twenty-Nine Palms, Vega asked Nancy to pull to the side of the road.

"According to police, it was a gas station along here where Mary's credit card was used by a woman to gas up. If Janice was telling the truth, and I believe she was, she was shackled in the back seat. So, it was Mary who entered the service station and paid. The description the attendants gave match what Janice said. Mary was wearing a scarf and her forehead was cut."

"I still want to know how she was able to get a credit card under her maiden name. Banks still won't issue one to me or other unmarried women."

Vega told Nancy he'd make sure she had a card under the agency once it reopened.

"Thanks, but that's not the issue. The issue is discrimination. It took nearly one-hundred-fifty years for women to get the right to vote."

"Maybe you should burn your bra."

Nancy glared at Jarvis.

"If you're referring to last year's protest at the Miss America pageant, you're mistaken. Not a single bra was burned. Newspapers, your profession, made that up. The women outside the event, on the Boardwalk, crowned a sheep and filled a trash can with makeup, ladies' magazines and mops. No bras were burned. Get your facts straight. And, by the way, I personally have no problem wearing a bra, putting on makeup or mopping a floor on occasion. I am against the type of discrimination that prevents me from having my own credit card. It's my money!"

Rather than accepting the put-down silently, Jarvis opened his mouth.

"Get your facts straight. It's not your money, it's the bank's. Until you use it, of course. Then it's your debt."

Fearing that Nancy was about to order her back-seat passenger out of the car, Vega suggested they continue to Amboy where he'd buy them breakfast at Roy's.

— • —

Over large servings of eggs, ham, and potatoes, Jarvis raised the first of two unanswered questions about their odyssey.

"What happens if we can't find her bones?"

Vega swallowed a helping of hash browns before answering.

"We keep looking."

"How long?"

"Until we find them."

"And if we can't? Our flashlights can't burn forever."

"We brought extra batteries."

"C'mon, Vega. Quit avoiding my question. There's a possibility we won't be able to locate what's left of her. We don't know exactly where in the cave her body landed. And it's been seventeen years. Rotting flesh attracts scavengers. Coyotes, birds, snakes, blow flies. Her bones could be scattered all over the place."

Vega inspected his friend.

"We don't need the entire skeleton. Just the skull or jawbone. Even a tooth."

"Still, there's the possibility..."

"Let's deal with that possibility if and when it becomes a reality. Okay? Let's finish up and move out. We still have an hour or so ahead of us."

It was left to Nancy to ask an even tougher question, one she knew would never have the right moment to be asked.

"What if your vertigo returns? In the cavern?"

Vega examined his assistant before he set down his fork and paper napkin, leaving at the table his companions and the remainder of his breakfast. He paid the tab at the counter, then made his way to the parking lot where he raised a right hand to his forehead, shielding his eyes from the already intense morning sunlight. He stood for what seemed like several minutes – perhaps a lifetime – staring at Roy's famous Atomic-age sign, a gigantic and neon-colored beacon of civilization staked into the vast desert floor, a hundred miles from anything. A light that would burn all night, even as a heaven full of stars would dim and then extinguish.

CHAPTER FORTY-SIX

Route 66 took them thirty-five miles to Essex, a threadbare town that was once a maintenance camp along the tracks of the Atchison, Topeka and Santa Fe Railway. They turned left onto a primitive road named after the town.

"Those are the Providence Mountains on the left. The caverns are about twenty miles ahead."

Nancy's were the first words spoken since they left the restaurant. She decided to break the tension by explaining to Jarvis what she had learned about the caverns from Jack Mitchell's book.

"Jack and Ida came to the desert during the Depression, arriving here with a sack of beans, a rifle, and not much else. The Bonanza King mine was up in the nearby mountains. In the 1880s it was producing about two-thousand ounces of silver each day. Operations closed in 1920 after all the silver had been mined. With a quick partner, Jack bought an ore mine nearby and eked out a living mining low-grade ore."

Exploring the mountains one evening, Nancy explained, Jack noticed a cloud of bats leaving a cleft in the rocks. He spotted the entrance, clambered over boulders, and found himself in a small cave. It took a half-day's work before he found a passage that would lead to a cave within the cave. After exploring the caverns further, he and Ida thought they might make a better living making the caverns a tourist attraction. They built a trail leading up to the opening and stairways and paths inside the mountain. Called it the Cave of the Winding Stair.

"It was their principal business in the thirties, forties, and fifties."

Jarvis asked how they came up with the name.

"What Jack found was a series of caverns like a five-story underground building. As if the mountain had been hollowed out with a series of passageways and shafts that led deeper and deeper. Some of those shafts are like stairways that lead down to the next level."

"Ever think of becoming a reporter, Nancy? Jesus, with your ability to remember every single detail, the newspaper would never have to publish a correction."

"What interests me is science. Astronomy, technology, medicine. The natural sciences as well. I hope someday to make a discovery, a discovery that will help the human race."

"Makes my career seem insignificant."

"Can we get back to the caves?"

Vega, his first words since breakfast.

"What is it you want to know?"

"For one thing, it's unlikely that we'll need to explore more than what you call the first floor. Janice told us that it wasn't long after Quail took Mary into the entrance that he killed her. So I'm more curious about what that first level is like. Did Mitchell's book contain any diagrams or photos?"

"No diagrams, some old photos. He wrote that once inside there's a mammoth chamber that descends to an area of calcite crystals hanging from the ceiling and dozens of stalagmites rising from the floor. After that, several paths lead in different directions. One led to a larger chamber. Others went a short distance and ended. He explored them all but wrote extensively about one that descends at a seventy-two-degree angle for one-hundred-twenty-five feet.

There was a ledge there, with the floor about twelve feet below... We've arrived."

The Corolla came to a stop before a wooden gate that closed the entry to the parking lot. A veil of saddle brown dust drizzled over the car, trapping its passengers until it coated the hood and roof. After unpacking the trunk of backpacks that contained both clothes and gear, the trio walked around the gate toward the trail that began across from the small parking area. They stopped briefly at the small headstone that marked the grave of Benita Mora, an infant who died in 1912.

"Know anything about her or why she's buried here?"

"Just what's etched on the stone."

The trail that stretched up the side of the mountain was steep, making for a rugged climb for Jarvis who, at thirty-six, was only a year older than Vega but carried an extra sixty pounds above his belt. As a result, they made several stops on his behalf. Nancy offered to carry his backpack along with hers, which he declined.

As they trudged up the side of the mountain, the appearance of creosote, Mojave yucca, and cholla cactus marked the higher elevation. The limestone rocks along the upper trail were replaced by volcanic rock. Below them, the valley was visible for several miles.

After three more rest stops, they rounded a ridge where the twin openings to the cavern lay ahead. Nancy said the Chemehuevi Indians called them The Eyes of the Mountain. To Vega, they appeared more like the dark sunken orbits of a human skull.

CHAPTER FORTY-SEVEN

First to reach the entrance, Nancy stopped abruptly before entering. The buzz was almost imperceptible, before it quickly rose to a furious rattle. The sound cut through the mid-morning stillness, freezing everyone where they stood. Ahead, Nancy raised a hand, palm open.

"Snake?"

She nodded slowly, unwilling or unable to answer. After surveying to her right then to her left, her head tilted to one side, as if wanting her left eye and ear undistracted by the other pair. Then, just as suddenly as it had started, the dry electric buzz that filled the air seemed to weaken then stop. No one moved in the stillness that followed.

Nancy inched backward, one slow and uncertain step at a time. Her eyes remained fixed on a small pile of brown and tan rocks near the entrance to the cave. Outstretched hands caught her softly as she backed into Vega. She turned to face him and Jarvis, her eyes wide and unblinking, her breath caught somewhere between her lungs and throat.

"Mojave Green. A fat one."

"Like a Western Diamondback?"

Waiting until her heartrate settled, Nancy explained that the two are similar in appearance except for the Green's wider stripes and larger diamonds.

"Its venom is more lethal. A bite delivers a cocktail of enzymes and peptides that can quickly shut down your body and tenderize your insides. You'll die here. Never make it to a hospital."

Jarvis looked behind at the rocky path that wound down the mountain. The parking lot was visible, about the size of a postage stamp, a half mile below.

"I'm not going in there. No fuckin' way."

Vega met the remark with a glare, one he learned from Fat Frank Majuri, designed to bore into the deepest recess of the soul.

"We're not going back. We came here to find Mary's remains. Got it?"

"But how do we get past that green snake?"

Vega grabbed the P210 from his shoulder holster.

"We kill it."

"Wait!"

Nancy blocked Vega from passing her on the narrow trail.

"It's behind a pile of rocks. You miss, or even hit the damn thing, the bullet's going to ricochet and hit one of us. The sound alone is going to wake up every critter inside and outside the cave. Let's push the rocks – they're small – down the side. Okay? We can use his walking stick."

Nancy grabbed the ocotillo cane from Jarvis, handing it to Vega.

"I'll point him out. Use this to wedge the rocks over and down. Just stay about three feet away from the snake. About the length of the stick."

"You guys sure you know what you're doing?"

Vega said he trusted Nancy's plan.

"Let's go."

The two inched up the path to the entrance. Nancy pointed to the cluster of rocks. Vega stuck the cane out, triggering the snake's instinctive warning, a sound of coiled tension sent directly to the detective's spine. He jabbed violently at the rocks, sending several tumbling loose down the steep slope. His teeth clenched with each thrust, his left arm held out for balance, as more rocks disappeared over the side in a dusty crash.

"He's gone! Stop!"

The tiny avalanche hit a wall of large rocks halfway down the slope. Nancy peered over the side of the trail, listening for the snake. Nothing. Just the final clicks of small stones cartwheeling to a stop and the quiet settling of sand and silt.

Vega returned the cane to Jarvis, who appeared to finally exhale.

"Jesus, Vega! You looked like Athos dueling the Duke of Savoy."

— • —

After tossing a handful of rocks into the cavern and hearing only soft echoing, the trio stepped through the entrance. Sunlight from the entrance allowed them to make their way down a narrow, winding slope. As the outside light faded, each switched on a flashlight. The three beams of light searched ahead, above and below, revealing an uneven floor and narrow crevices that veined the ancient walls.

Vega led the parade, with Nancy directly behind. The air was cool and fresh, not the mustiness they expected. No one spoke, fearing any sound other than the gravel crunching beneath their boots would alert any creatures to their presence or bring down rocks from overhead.

The dark was a primal black. A void that swallowed their shadows and made each step a guess. It wasn't just the absence of light. Each felt the presence of something deeper, something older, as if both light and time were buried here millions of years ago.

Ahead, their flashlights found openings to two tunnels. Vega recalled Janice saying, *We crawled into one tunnel but turned back. Turned out to go nowhere.* He kicked himself for not asking her the simple "left or right" question. Rather than confer with his accomplices, he got to his knees, ducked his head, and crept into the opening, avoiding a jagged rock in the ceiling. Nancy and Jarvis followed.

Ten yards ahead the tunnel opened to a small cave. Able to stand, Vega swung his flashlight in a broad arch. The walls and ceiling ahead contracted. The way forward was blocked. When Nancy's light was added to his, a narrow crevice was revealed. She stepped around Vega, making her way to the thin fissure that appeared barely wider than her waist. She aimed her flashlight through the gap, straining to follow the beam. There was no way to judge how deep it was or what was on the other side, assuming there was another side.

"I can squeeze through. It seems to open up on the right after a few feet."

Her observations were whispered, the tone each assumed was necessary. She gently dropped her backpack and canteen on the cavern floor and inspected the gap a second time. She turned sideways, pressed her arms to her sides, and wedged through. The flashlight in one hand flickered once, then vanished.

The cave was still. Vega and Jarvis stared at the crevice where Nancy had been a moment earlier, expecting her to reappear at any second. She didn't. Vega approached the opening, shining his light as far as it would go. The passage veered right as she indicated, then disappeared. He listened but heard nothing on the other side.

Jarvis kept his flashlight on Vega and tried to contain his alarm. His heartbeat thundered in his ears, each thump a grim reminder of another scare. A near fatal one. He pressed a hand against his sternum and tried to slow his heart with a prayer. Not now. Not here. Please, God.

"You okay?"

"I...I truly hope so. I..."

"Here. Sit over here. There's a rock that looks halfway comfortable. I'll grab some water."

Jarvis found the rock, but his panic didn't lessen when he sat. Was it just fear? Or was it starting again? Out here. The middle of nowhere. Last time there was a hospital. Here, nothing.

"Listen, you gonna be okay? I need to go after Nancy. I'll..."

"Stay here. I'm...scared."

"Of the dark?"

"No. It's my heart. I never told you. I suffered a heart attack back in sixty-five. At my desk in the newsroom. I..."

Vega shined his flashlight in his buddy's face.

"You're sweating, but your color looks okay."

"How can you tell in this light?"

"I can't. Catch your breath and drink water. I think you're overheated."

Jarvis didn't protest further. He sipped from his canteen, watching nervously as Vega approached the crevice and tried to cram his five-ten frame into the narrow passage, a losing battle. The newsman cast a nervous glance over his shoulder, thinking he heard a noise. He did. It was Nancy, crawling toward them.

"Forget it, Mr. Vega. You'll get stuck. That other tunnel, the one we passed? It connects. It's wider. Much wider. You won't believe what's on the other side."

— • —

After crawling back several yards, then entering the second tunnel, their flashlights revealed a vast limestone cavern. Rows of stalactites hung like enormous white fangs from an unseen ceiling. Towering stalagmites rose from various pits. Some had fused into stone columns that stretched upward into darkness their flashlights were unable to penetrate.

Once on their feet, the trio stood in awe of the immensity of the ghostly spires carved over millions of years. Jarvis said it reminded him of a church organ in an ancient cathedral. Shadows danced behind the formations as Nancy and Vega painted the cones with their flashlights, giving the impression of movement in their surreal surroundings.

They wrapped one rope around the base of a thick limestone column, using the line like breadcrumbs as they explored the vast cavern. Jarvis said he felt better after drinking half his canteen. Nancy encouraged him to take more photos of the formations that surrounded them as they explored more of the cavern.

"It's taken more than fifty million years to shape these rocks. The hand of God at work."

Jarvis said he thought it was caused by dripping water.

"You don't believe these formations are evidence that God, or a god, exists?"

"I'm a journalist, Nancy. There is no objective or verifiable evidence to support a belief that god exists."

"I thought journalists are taught to be open-minded. Or am I wrong?"

"I remain open-minded about those who believe in god or a supreme being. However, the burden of proof lies with those making the claim that god exists."

"What about you, Vega?"

The detective paused to swallow from his canteen before answering.

"I guess we'll find out, one way or another, after we die."

— • —

After exploring for another twenty minutes, Vega said they'd gone too far.

"Think about it. Quail hadn't taken them very far before he killed Mary, according to Janice. And she was able to find her way out without a flashlight. We need to double back. There must be another tunnel we missed."

They picked up the rope as they traced its path in reverse. Slower now, they stopped to examine each crevice they had passed. Nancy was the first to spot a likely path to the grave of Mary Showalter. A thin passage that was overlooked on their initial trek seemed obvious on their return. They moved in single file, the rope again a lifeline in their wake. Vega led, the beams of his flashlight revealing only the next few feet.

The passage narrowed further, forcing them shoulder to shoulder against the stone walls. Before long, they had to turn sideways to fit, dragging their backpacks through the pinched opening.

The trail widened as it veered sharply to the left, leading to a narrow ledge where the stone floor gave way to a vast, black chasm. Spanning the void were two wooden planks, each warped with age. They stretched from one side to the other with no railings. On the far side, the path resumed, disappearing into a low tunnel.

Vega stepped cautiously to his left where the floor appeared to give way to a large pit. His light disappeared down the seemingly bottomless chasm before revealing what appeared to be a partial opening on the wall below his feet. From it, a rocky shelf jutted out maybe eight feet, hanging over what looked like an open wound in the earth.

"This may be the place. It looks to drop off about twenty feet to the…I'll call it a shelf. Janice survived the fall and was able to find her way back up. Let's tie one of the ropes around one of these columns. I'll climb down."

"You sure you don't want me to do it, Mr. Vega? I'm lighter than you. Likely by seventy or eighty pounds."

Unsaid were her fears about her boss's spells of vertigo.

"No way. I'm going down. Just make sure to find a strong column and tie a secure knot."

Nancy removed a coil of Manilla rope, looping one end around a thick stalagmite and cinching it with a bowline knot. His heartrate in check, Jarvis searched his backpack for his Nikon 35mm. Vega, meanwhile, stuffed his hands into thick gloves and adjusted the painter's kneepads on his blue jeans. He tugged on the rope several times before approaching the edge.

"If I find anything, throw me the bag."

He knelt, bracing his left palm on the ground like an anchor before sitting and swinging his legs over the edge. The heel on one boot kicked the wall beneath where he sat, sending loose gravel into the void.

The first flicker of unease arrived behind his eyes. Then the ground seemed to tilt a fraction beneath him. Vega knew better than to look down. But he already had and was unable to shake the memory of that brief glimpse. He closed his eyes. But it was too late. His stomach flipped. The walls of the cavern began to sway as his feet dangled over the void. There was no up or down, only a choking sensation of falling into forever.

"Mr. Vega. Are you okay?"

Any answer was trapped in his throat. Icy waves of vertigo shivered up his spine. He froze, locked in a moment of silent panic. Unable to stand, he scooted backward, inch by inch, pushing with his heels, sliding on his backside like a child afraid of the deep end of a swimming pool. When he finally was far enough from the edge to breathe again he sat, hunched over, sweat cooling on his brow.

Nancy and Jarvis didn't say a word. Each knew Vega was unable to go forward. One of them would have to go next.

"I used to climb trees all the time. Mom said I was part monkey."

Nancy's comment broke the uneasy silence. She handed Vega her canteen and began to unwind the rope that coiled around his waist and legs. She was already looping the rope between her legs and over one shoulder when Vega scratched out a reply.

"You sure, Nancy?"

"I need your gloves. Not sure where I left mine."

Breathing easier with the edge now a good five feet away, Vega slowly peeled each glove off, one finger at a time. Rather than handing Nancy each glove, he put them on for her, easing her fingers into the thick canvas, tugging it snug over her knuckles. She watched him quietly as he fitted the second glove.

"Be careful. Whatever is down there is ... not worth your life."

Their eyes met for a moment before she crouched, then crabbed her way toward the pit. After letting her legs dangle over the lip she tested the rope a final time, then turned to one side and was gone.

Vega took one look at Jarvis, who sat frozen a few feet back. The reporter hadn't moved. It was up to him to help Nancy. Every part of his body told him not to. His spent limbs. The nausea twisting in his gut. But she had gone over the edge and he couldn't bail out now.

Mustering his remaining strength and nerve, Vega belly-crawled toward the pit, a flashlight in one hand. The vertigo had subsided but was still there, lurking at the edges of his vision, ready to emerge from the shadows. But he kept inching forward.

Vega stopped a foot from the edge, lying flat, chest heaving. He pointed the beam of one flashlight down before pushing himself forward the final few inches. He steeled himself before looking over the edge of the vast pit and its endless dark. As he leaned over, a whisp of vertigo brushed the back of his neck. It wasn't just fear of falling, it was the sense that the void summoned him.

He spotted Nancy's silhouette in the small circle of his light, descending slowly into the dark. Her gloved hands worked the rope with practiced ease. Each move was measured, like she'd done this a hundred times before. He kept his eyes locked on her, forcing himself to watch, to stay anchored.

Twenty-some feet down, her boots found footing on the ledge jutting from the wall beneath Vega. She tested it twice before letting her full weight settle. Still gripping the rope with one hand,

Nancy surveyed the ground to her left and right before she reached for her belt.

No flashlight.

She'd left it clipped to her backpack in the scramble to take Vega's place. Tilting her head back, she looked up into the beam that showered her in pale light. In a voice that was low but clear she called to Vega.

"Light. Toss me my flashlight."

Vega twisted to his left and whispered to Jarvis to find Nancy's flashlight and bring it to him. After sweeping his own flashlight over Nancy's backpack, Jarvis rose stiffly, unhooked the instrument, and crawled across the cavern floor to hand it to Vega. He crept back to his seat of safety like he was walking to shore on a frozen pond.

Vega found Nancy looking up and gently underhanded the flashlight. She reached up a gloved hand, the fingers open to catch it. She missed. The flashlight hit the limestone floor with a sharp crack, bounced twice, then rolled off the ledge. They both watched helpless as it pinwheeled into the deeper dark. A second later, it hit something far below with a distant clack, followed at first by silence.

Then came the sound.

The dry buzzing, faint at first, then multiplying. The unmistakable chorus of disturbed rattlesnakes.

Nancy froze, her eyes still fixed on Vega. Above, he kept his flashlight on her and signaled for her to start climbing up. She shook her head ever so slowly. No.

The fury of buzzing echoed off the limestone walls, impossible to track. Jarvis climbed to a higher rock, once again clutching his heart. The little sound he made seemed to stir more snakes – or at least that's what the echoing implied. Then, slowly, the sound began to ebb. One by one, the rattles fell quiet. A final few continued before fading into stillness. The tense silence that followed was worse.

Still on his stomach, Vega flashed his light below Nancy's feet, which were pinched against the rope, a few feet off the ground. Vega shook his head, a silent signal that no snakes were spotted. They were either all collected far below or elsewhere on the shelf.

Getting another flashlight to Nancy was paramount. Vega rolled away from the edge and shimmied backward to where Jarvis waited.

"She needs your light."

The reporter swallowed hard. But he nodded, once. He handed the flashlight to Vega like he was passing over a piece of himself. Vega took it, then rummaged through Nancy's backpack for another rope, a thin cord. He secured the flashlight in several knots then crawled back to the edge, where he lowered it carefully. She caught the swinging light, untied it, then bathed her surroundings with its glow.

Around her, the silence held. There were loose mounds of rock to her left. She took one step, then a second toward the pile. It looked too deliberate, though one end looked like it had been swept aside. She took two additional uneasy steps, hesitated, and listened. Nothing.

The cavern wall leaned over the pile, forcing her to crouch as she delicately approached. As she rested on her heels, her flashlight exposed something pale jutting from the rubble. At first, it looked like a shard of limestone, long and slender. But the end was rounded, the unmistakable ball that would form the socket for an upper arm bone.

What remained of Mary Showalter had been found. Buried in silence for seventeen years, the cavern had at last surrendered its secret.

Nancy knelt motionless for a moment, the flashlight trembling in her hand. The discovery cut through her nervous composure. She considered the horror of Mary's final minutes, and the sister who risked her own survival to gather rocks in the darkness, placing the stones as best she could to form an earthen grave, unmarked, sealed inside a mountain in the far reaches of the Mojave Desert.

Nancy raised a hand to her forehead to begin the sign of the cross. Just a quiet gesture. She whispered nothing. There was nothing to say.

Carefully, she turned her flashlight to the end of the grave where the rocks had been scattered. More bones. Tiny fingers here, a shoulder blade there. A ribcage cracked open and spread like broken wings. A ghastly trail caused by creatures who stripped Mary like vultures, dragging her piece by piece from where she once laid whole.

Nancy untied the gray laundry bag from her belt and began the grim task of selecting bones to return to the living world. She found the skull across the cave resting on its side, the jaw unhinged. Over what would have been Mary's left ear, a small hole.

As she reached for the skull, her boot clipped a rock, sending it rolling to where it clattered against another rocky pile. There was a sound. A faint rattle. She froze. The silence returned. Or did it?

She was about to leave. Tie the rope around her and escape this crypt when her flashlight caught a reflection. A glint. Barely more than a pinprick from the shadows behind Mary's grave. There it was. Did it blink? Nancy froze, adjusting her grip on the flashlight. The light swept to the spot. It flashed again.

She couldn't make it out from where she crouched. A small animal's eyes low to the ground? Or metal, half-buried in the rubble? The reflection offered no answer. It didn't blink. It didn't move.

— • —

Thirty-some feet above where Nancy crouched, Vega remained on his stomach, staring into the abyss. A part of him wanted to look away, but he remained rooted at the chasm's edge. Thoughts, half-formed, wandered from Nancy. Memories surfaced. Moments of loss. Regrets he had tried to forget. Words left unspoken. Choices made, then abandoned. Faces blurred by time.

The tumble of a rock below returned his attention to Nancy. He followed the beam of light that pierced the darkness to the shelf below. Anxious for her return to safety, he fought the urge to call out. Even a whisper could set off snakes once again.

Jarvis remained seated on an uncomfortable rock, frozen in place, consumed by the dark that enveloped him. Attempting to evade his own thoughts, he fixed his attention on the slim column of light that Vega pointed into the chasm.

At first, he thought it was a shadow he saw, some trick of the light thrown on the rope alongside Vega where he was stretched out. But then the shadow shifted somehow, slow and deliberate. Vega hadn't noticed. He remained sprawled at the edge, his flashlight beam waiting for Nancy, unaware of the danger creeping just a few yards nearby. Jarvis wanted to shout – something, anything – but his mouth went dry.

— • —

Nancy leaned toward the reflection, every nerve of hers stirred. Clutching the bag of bones and the flashlight in one hand she reached a gloved hand toward the object, which appeared to be wedged between the rocks on the grave. She carefully removed one rock. It was a finger. Detached cleanly from the palm, the lone digit lay there like a twisted white root. Above the knuckle, a tarnished diamond ring clung to the bone, placed there at Mary's wedding by the man who would kill her two days later.

Nancy collected the finger, adding it to the bag, and stepped quietly toward the hanging rope. She looped the rope around her as she had done before, looked up at Vega's face and nodded her readiness. Vega pushed himself up, crouching on one knee. He gripped the rope in both hands, arching his back with each tug. Every pull a reminder of the fragile lifeline he held.

Nancy was midway to the top, dangling over the deep pit when Jarvis shrieked and the rope suddenly slackened. She dropped several feet before the line tightened. She lost her grip in the sudden jerk and fell backward, saved only by the rope wrapped around her thighs and waist.

She dangled in the black void, still grasping the bag of Mary's bones. Unable to right herself, she cried out for help. Her shout woke the nest of rattlesnakes that had been hiding in the dark. The buzzing from the shadows came in a deadly chorus that echoed in waves off the limestone walls. She hung helplessly in the dark, swaying back and forth, fighting the urge to scream again.

Minutes later, what seemed to Nancy like hours, hands grabbed her ankles and hauled the rest of her slender torso upward. Vega stretched over the edge, leaning forward to reach an arm. Instead, he grabbed her by the belt and pulled her up the last few feet in a flurry of gravel that tumbled over the edge, disappearing into the void.

Nancy and Vega collapsed onto the rocky floor with their hearts racing and chests heaving. The cavern continued to pulse with the sound of rattlesnakes stirred to fury. The buzzing raged from everywhere, vibrating in waves that prickled the skin.

Nancy and Vega remained flat on their backs, chests rising and falling in shallow breaths, eyes darting left and right, neither daring to move. After several heart-stopping moments, the buzzing began to fade, one rattle dropping out, followed by another. The quiet that followed the threat didn't release the tension. Vega kept one hand on the flashlight. Holding it upside down, he carefully swept it in a slow circle. If any snakes were there, he trusted – prayed really – that Jarvis would say something.

He didn't.

DARKNESS GETS THERE FIRST

With his other hand he reached to Nancy without looking. His fingers found hers, curling around them. She laced her fingers through his, gripping tightly. Neither of them spoke. Slowly, they helped themselves up. First one elbow, then the other, until finally both were sitting. They scanned the dim light for any sign of the deadly reptiles before Vega stood, helping Nancy to her feet. With a final look around, they approached Jarvis and collected their backpacks and canteens.

Nancy glared at both men, then whispered.

"What happened? You nearly got me killed!"

Jarvis said he saw a snake near Vega's foot when he was pulling her up.

"It was moving. I saw it!"

Reading their skepticism, Jarvis doubled down.

"The snake was there. That's my story and I'm sticking to it. It'll add great drama to my story."

Vega saw that Nancy was still clutching the laundry bag. She nodded when their eyes connected.

"Let's go home."

PART 4

Someday it will all seem like a dream

CHAPTER FORTY-EIGHT

Aloysius Vega burrowed under a checkered woolen blanket as he waited for the first spray of sunlight to paint the northeast face of San Jacinto. The air that morning had the type of chill that brought clarity. The stillness felt fresh, untouched by the winter heat that would arrive later that day. A day unhurried by anything but the wind. Headlines and the demands of the day could wait. Until then, nothing more was required.

The lounge chair fabric whined as Vega shifted his weight. If the movement bothered the cat, it was not obvious. The gray tabby remained curled near the detective's feet as it had since the two stepped outside before six. Their daily routine began after the family across the street packed their belongings and left without the cat.

With the leanness of a feral cat, green glass eyes, and fur streaked with dark racing stripes, the cat was content to follow Vega while he was home. It laid claim to the entire territory, including the space under the detective's bed where it would remain at night until it was time to wake the detective.

He named the cat Koma.

The bones found in Mitchell's Caverns had been identified as those of Mary Showalter. After cleaning the skull and jawbone of bat droppings, dirt, and insect dung, the teeth were compared to her dental records. Dr. Thomas Noguchi, the Los Angeles coroner who had performed the autopsies of Marilyn Monroe, Robert Kennedy, and Sharon Tate, made the positive conclusion at the request of Sidney Korshak. The results had been turned over to investigators in Palm Springs, who reopened the seventeen-year-old case under a searing blush of embarrassment after the *Desert Post* reported the still-unexplained disappearance of the police files.

Vega was questioned by detectives about his role locating Mary's remains. He testified under oath that Janice Showalter shared information about her sister's death and the man responsible for it. Lily and Nancy were also questioned. All three were expecting to be called before a grand jury.

Arthur Quail remained free as police and prosecutors constructed a case based, so far, on second-hand testimony. The *Post* and other newspapers refrained from naming Quail, referencing only "a person of interest."

An All Points Bulletin was issued to locate Janice Showalter. At Lily's urging, the search was expanded to Canada. Meanwhile, Korshak worked his contacts in the Department of Justice to schedule a hearing before the U.S. Parole Commission on reducing John Roselli's prison sentence based on the information he provided to help locate Mary's remains.

After completing the necessary paperwork to claim the $50,000 reward from CV Savings & Loan, Vega deposited the winnings into the Vega Detective Agency account. A portion was then transferred to Vega's personal account. A teller reminded the detective the reward was considered taxable income.

— • —

Despite the favorable publicity from locating the remains of Mary Showalter, only a smattering of new cases found their way to the Vega Detective Agency.

A local attorney referred a woman who was convinced her landlord was rearranging furniture in her apartment unit while she was at work. Vega spent two work weeks staking out the Palm Springs apartment. When he explained that no one had entered the apartment, the woman offered a vital tidbit of information she had not previously mentioned.

"He must have some machine that makes him invisible. He's a space alien, after all."

Another case had Vega following a sixty-year-old accountant whose wife suspected him of sleeping with his secretary instead of working late. The husband was indeed cheating, but not with the secretary. Instead, he would leave the office in the evening and set out for a local bar favored by homosexuals. After a few drinks, the man and a partner would head to the back seat of his car. When Vega produced damning photographs of the nightly trysts, the wife burst into tears and paid the invoice on the spot.

When an insurance company hired Vega to do surveillance on a nurse who filed a disability claim against her employer, Desert Hospital, Nancy asked to accompany him. That night, Vega's young assistant not only observed that the nurse was not restricted physically but was able to use her body in a coordinated manner.

They followed the nurse from her home to Sugar's, a strip club where she was employed as an entertainer. Because the club had a posted prohibition on photography, Nancy and Vega entered and were seated near the stage where a lazy red spotlight rested on a silver pole at the center. They ordered drinks and watched the performance so they could testify the nurse was pole dancing topless should the case go to court. If Nancy was shocked, she kept it to herself. She told Vega she looked forward to sending their expense report to the insurer.

— • —

Mostly, in the days following Thanksgiving, Vega remained in the office reviewing notes from the interviews with Janice Showalter, both his and those taken by Lily. The reward money now banked, it was left to police and prosecutors to convict Quail and close the books on Mary's murder.

Yet, nagging questions needed answers, like a loose thread that had to be tugged.

Vega kept returning to the account Janice provided, where Mary pleaded with Quail to spare her sister at the entrance to the cavern.

I don't remember her exact words, but it was to the effect to let me go. That I didn't know anything.

The inference, Vega came to believe, was that Mary held a secret that her husband, the bank examiner, shared. Once phrased as a question, he now announced it to himself as a statement:

"Mary was aware of the fraudulent activity."

Vega jotted down the questions that would need to be answered before he could stamp the agency's case file as resolved.

What was the extent of Mary's knowledge?

Did she conspire with Löwenstein?

Or did she help her husband uncover the illegal activity?

Both? Involved but put the blame on Löwenstein?

What happened to the money that was never recovered?

Which customers lost money in the scheme?

Next, Vega listed those he needed to interview, some for the second time. Topping the list was László Löwenstein. The inmate was at the center of the embezzlement scheme and worked alongside Mary Showalter for several years. Also on the list were Blackpool, the manager of CV Savings & Loan, and Erika Lake. Several tendrils from the case curled toward the former actress. Her accounts at the bank had been handled by Mary. She stepped in to witness Mary's wedding to Quail. And she had propped up the reward amount by a cool thirty grand.

Vega was about to ask Nancy to call Blackpool when his assistant shrieked.

"Oh my god, no!"

Quickly making his way to her desk in the lobby, he found her in tears, holding a letter.

"What on earth..."

"I'm being... we're being sued!"

Vega pulled the letter from her hands. The letterhead was marked Hartley Weil & Associates of Irvine. The three-page document alleged the Vega Detective Agency had violated the terms of its license with the State of California and had also slandered its client, Arthur Quail. It named both Vega and Nancy as defendants.

"I'm so sorry, Mr. Vega, this is all my fault. I shouldn't have..."

"Quiet! I need to read this. Blow your nose for Christ sakes."

Vega shoved a nearby chair to Nancy's desk and sat next to her as he read the complaint.

The letter alleged that Nancy Randall operated as an unlicensed private investigator in violation of California's Business and Professions Code when she interviewed Arthur Quail on June 16 at the Hillsdale Inn in San Mateo and again that same day at Castaway Restaurant. A complaint was being made to the Bureau of Security & Investigative Services with a demand that Vega's license be revoked as the head of the agency. A cease-and-desist order was requested in the interim, to effectively bar Vega and Nancy from continuing their activities regarding Quail.

Additionally, the law firm was seeking that Nancy be charged with a misdemeanor for her actions, punishable by fines of up to $5,000 and potential jail time of up to one year. The letter also accused Vega of slander by making false statements about Quail to law enforcement personnel investigating the death of Mary Showalter, causing enormous injury to him. The firm was seeking damages of half-a-million dollars.

The remainder of the letter detailed the basis of the claims, including Quail's statement recounting his questioning by Nancy, both privately one-on-one and in public at the Castaway, in front of his professional colleagues and restaurant patrons.

Vega turned to his assistant, now red-eyed and puffy.

"First, I want you to write down everything that was said by both you and Quail at the restaurant. That iron-clad memory of yours will ensure that authorities know who is telling the truth. Second, find the business card for Sid Korshak. Send his office the letter? Use the Beast and have him call me after he's had time to review it. Okay? Pull yourself together. I need you to be fully engaged."

"You're not going to fire me?"

"Nope. If this sinks the agency, we both go down."

— • —

"The slander complaint is absolute horse shit."

Korshak's phone call came less than a half-hour later. The gravelly voice, like the voice of God, was impossible to ignore.

"These fuckers are rookies trying to shake you down. Either that or they got their law degree at some dime-store college like...Like I said, the slander accusation is horse shit. The testimony you and Miss Randall gave to police was given under oath. That's considered privileged communication. Defamation only deals with unprivileged statements. Got it?"

"I do. What about the complaint to BSIS?"

"That's problematic. I'll want to confirm with Miss Randall her conversations with Quail and how she presented herself."

"Nancy has a photographic memory. She cannot forget. She remembers everything in detail."

"That's helpful and can be tested if necessary."

"Absolutely."

"About this correspondence. You may have noticed that it threatens to file a complaint rather than stating it as a done deal. That's a game they're playing. They want money – now – in exchange for dropping the complaint. And for you and Miss Randall to, shall we say, be rather absent-minded when you're called before the grand jury. From what you just told me about Miss Randall, that's near impossible. Here's what I'm gonna do. Make a friendly call to Hartley Weil and persuade them of their misguided ways on behalf of their client. I'm sure they'll comply. If not, well…Don't worry. They'll comply. My advice to you, Mr. Vega, is to get Miss Randall a license. Capisce?"

"Got it. Thanks. Any news on getting Roselli out?"

"There's progress. Have a pleasant evening, Mr. Vega."

— • —

I appreciate you reaching out again, but I'm not comfortable continuing this conversation. I don't have anything more to add."

Tobias Blackpool was about to hang up when Vega asked what he considered to be a straightforward question about the bank's former examiner, Arthur Quail.

"When did he begin knocking on the door of CV Savings?"

"I don't understand your question."

"I'll rephrase it. When was Arthur Quail assigned by the FDIC to examine your books?"

"I don't recall. That was two decades ago, Mr. Vega. I don't know how you expect me ..."

"Was it before you hired László Löwenstein or after?"

"My answer, I'm afraid, is the same. I don't recall."

"I'm sure you must have access to those dates. Employee records, audit reports."

"Personnel records are private, as I'm sure you understand. Savings and loans such as ours are required to retain audit reports for at least seven years from the release date. It's unlikely that we have the records going back further. If we had, those too would be considered private."

"I understand. Does the FDIC keep copies?"

"I have no idea, Mr. Vega. Now, as I said earlier, I have important matters to attend to."

"One final question. After that, I'll be on my way. How many individual accounts were tapped by Löwenstein?"

"A dozen. Goodbye, Mr. ..."

"A dozen accounts or a dozen customers?"

"Accounts. Now..."

"The names of those customers, may I..."

"No."

"Was Erika Lake one of the customers who..."

A sharp, mechanical click announced the conversation had ended.

CHAPTER FORTY-NINE

Vega was ushered to the shaded terrace where Erika reclined in a teak chaise under the shade of a pergola draped in climbing wisteria. Beneath the canopy, sheltered from the direct glare of early December sunlight, she held an unopened book in her lap. A silk robe, champagne-colored and sheer, veiled the Batiste black swimsuit beneath. Her gaze drifted toward the large mermaid presiding over a pool that stretched long and low across the manicured yard. A statue sculpted in the image of her late daughter.

"You haven't already forgotten Eva, have you, Aloysius?"

"It's difficult to forget someone held for a heartbeat."

Turning to face her visitor, Erika remarked how much better he looked without the long hair and beard.

"I doubt Eva would have approved. Please, sit. Care for an iced tea? Something stronger?"

"I'm fine. I have a few questions regarding Mary Showalter."

Instead of answering, Erika held up the book, Mario Puzo's *The Godfather*.

"Have you read this, Aloysius? Quite good, I'm told. Evans said he bought the film rights from the author for peanuts. Said the manuscript hadn't even been completed at the time. Apparently the author had a gambling debt that was overdue. Evans said *Godfather* will be one of two of the biggest books of the decade. Right up there with *Love Story*. Speaking of which, I'm leaving for Boston. Filming is underway. Evans wants me there. Says I'll bring a touch of magic to the set. I'll be there through the holidays. You do know they married. He and Ali. The epitome of Hollywood glamor: a young rising actress, a powerhouse producer. This is his third. I actually think he's lost interest in other women."

Vega said he hadn't read either book. He tried to steer the conversation back to Mary Showalter, the reason for his visit.

"I thought you turned that awfulness over to police. You don't have confidence in their ability, do you?"

"They haven't shown me much."

"You expect Mr. Quail to be acquitted?"

"Acquitted? I'm not sure he'll make it to court. All they have is second-hand testimony from me and Lily regarding what Janice said about how her sister died. It's a stretch unless she turns up. The questions I have today relate to your role in this matter."

Erika's eyes widened at first. Her mouth parted. No words, just an expression of shock and wounded pride.

"My role! What do..."

"Easy. I'm not trying to indict you in Mary's murder."

"Well, that's a relief."

"But a few things don't add up. And I'm not going to go away until I get answers from you. Be straight with me, Erika. I want the truth."

The sunglasses that obscured her eyes were pushed to the bridge of her nose, revealing a vaguely amused look. Tilting her head, and in a voice mimicking a Southern belle, she rolled out her response slow and syrupy.

"Well, I do declare. My dear Aloysius has returned. I did so desperately miss his certitude."

"The account you held at CV Savings..."

Returning to her normal tone, measured and deliberate, Erika explained that she and her then-husband had several accounts at the time. Vega asked if any had been looted by László Löwenstein.

"One, as it happened."

"For how much?"

"I believe it was close to $80,000. I'm curious why you want to know."

After explaining how he believed that Mary Showalter was involved in Löwenstein's scam, Erika shook her head.

"Not the Mary I knew. Once she got wind of what he was up to, she brought it to the attention of her boss, Mr. Blackpool."

"And you know this how?"

"Mary told me."

"And you believed her?"

"I did. I do. If she was guilty of anything, it was in protecting me."

"I don't understand."

"You see, Aloysius, Mary informed me that one of my accounts had been ... I believe the term she used was manipulated. When she told me which one, I told her I could not be involved in any investigation. That my privacy had to be protected."

Puzzled, Vega asked Erika to explain.

"Must I? You already know the answer."

— • —

Much like the time it takes for the morning sun to loosen the grip of a stubborn Pacific Coast fog, Vega sat quietly as he assembled memories from two years earlier. From a case that eventually brought him here, to the estate of Erika Lake, then known as Erika Vanderpol.

New in town, and freshly licensed as a private investigator, a newspaper article caught his eye. A Hollywood director had disappeared and was last seen at a house he was building in Indio. Al Archer made his reputation in the 1950s and early sixties with low-budget horror or science fiction films. Among his works were *Hell's Biker Devils, Satan's Stewardess,* and *Horror of the Blood Demons.* They developed a cult following among fans of cheesy horror films and drive-in movies.

Vega eventually located Archer's body, only to discover the film director had coerced a young girl into starring in an underground stag film. The aspiring actress was Erika. When she gained a few credited film roles and her name began appearing in fan magazines such as *Modern Screen,* Archer decided that blackmail offered a steadier income than stag film residuals. He demanded and got a monthly payment from the young actress.

After Erika left Hollywood and married shipping tycoon Eugene Vanderpol, Archer upped the ante considerably. The payments continued to grow over the years. Erika made no attempt to bring in the police. Money wasn't the issue. Her reputation was. As one of Palm Spring's most visible socialites, Erika kept her secret from her husband and the world that surrounded her.

The scheme was nearly exposed by police investigating Archer's disappearance. Checking his bank statements, they traced the large recurring deposits to a bank in Palm Desert. Erika's name was on the account. She admitted that Archer was blackmailing her but told investigators it was over a photograph of her passed out drunk with her skirt hiked up. Vega was brought in to find and secure the original 88 mm film, which he did. Rewarded handsomely for safeguarding her reputation, Erika promised to repay him in other ways. He became her confidante and occasional guest at social events. She paid his hospital bills – twice – after he was severely wounded.

DARKNESS GETS THERE FIRST

— • —

"**You do remember the** Archer affair, Aloysius. I believe you dubbed it The Gimlet Eye caper. I never understood why."

Like coastal cliffs sharpening into form as the fog lifts, the collision of that case and Mary Showalter revealed itself.

"Your account at CV Savings, it was used to fund the other bank account, the one in Palm Desert."

"That's correct. Each month Mary was instructed to transfer a set amount to the other account. The pass-through was another means of protecting myself."

"Did Mary know the purpose of those transfers?"

"Of course not. She never asked and I certainly never had reason to give her that information. She understood the privacy her job required."

"Yet she informed you about the fraudulent activity at the bank. That couldn't have been kosher."

"It wasn't, and she knew that she could be fired for that. Or worse."

"So, why did she risk all that for you?"

"I really can't say. I was young, she was young. I think she liked having a former movie star as a client. I shared with her a few stories from my time in Hollywood. Then, as you know, I helped her out in a pinch, at her wedding."

Without his notebook, Vega gambled that his slip-shot memory would contain what he was hearing until he could write it down later. Where was Nancy when he needed her?

"Did you ask Mary to protect your account from the examiner?"

"I did. She never asked why and I never asked how she intended to conceal it. She said only that she would not lie under oath. She later told me investigators never asked about that particular account. Likely, the large transfers never stood out. I made sure over the years to use that account for payments other than to Mr. Archer."

When Vega left the estate an hour later, it was with a clear understanding of Erika's relationship with Mary Showalter. Her reasons for avoiding the fraud investigation made sense. The interlocking narratives were plausible. But Mary remained an enigma. Vega hoped a meeting or at least a phone call with Löwenstein would clear the remaining veil of Pacific fog.

CHAPTER FIFTY

I wasn't aware you had an appointment."

The two FBI agents stood when Vega arrived at the agency the following morning. A glance at Nancy indicated the dark-suited duo had arrived unannounced.

"Everything is an appointment, Mr. Vega. Especially the ones we don't want to disclose. We need to talk. Let's use your office."

"Help yourselves to the coffee while you're at it. Nancy, make sure Sid Korshak's number is handy. I may need some legal muscle with these guys."

"You're not under arrest. We have a few questions ..."

"Glad to hear."

"...about the death of a federal inmate."

The words hit Vega before he had time to brace. He blinked, uncertain as to what he just heard. His thoughts scrambled to catch up.

"As you said, my office."

The two agents displayed their badges when they sat across from Vega.

"Don't bother. We're old friends."

"Regulations."

"Okay, let's cut to the chase. Who died and why do you think it has something to do with me?"

"We understand you've been looking into the 1952 death of Mary Showalter and the fraudulent activity that occurred at her place of employment, CV Savings & Loan."

"No secret. Been all over the local newspaper."

"You discovered her remains in the desert, in a place called Mitchell Caverns."

"It wasn't just me. I had help. I'll ask again. What's this about and what does it have to do with me and a dead con?"

"Last time we were here, you refused to discuss the reason for your trip on March 7 to McNeil Island and your visit with John Roselli."

"That's correct. And I have no intention of discussing it now. Is that the reason you're here. Roselli's dead?"

The two agents exchanged a glance. A flicker of something crossed their faces followed by the instinctive effort to regain control, to act as if nothing had slipped through.

"John Roselli is still breathing. He's sick. Emphysema. He's being cared for in the infirmary."

Surprised that he was relieved, Vega asked what inmate they were talking about. His exact words were: So, who's the stiff in pinstripes?

"We're here regarding László Löwenstein. We understand you've been asking questions about him. Back on March 13 and just yesterday with the manager of CV Savings & Loan, Mr. Tobias Blackpool."

For a moment Vega just stared, trying to decide whether he'd heard correctly.

"Löwenstein? He's dead? The circumstances?"

"Had you been in contact with Mr. Löwenstein?"

"What? No."

"The superintendent's office at McNeil said you were attempting to contact him. That you were wanting to arrange a phone call."

Vega exhaled with the realization that his last hope of resolving the circumstances surrounding the death of Mary Showalter had perished with Löwenstein's final breath.

"That's correct. I asked my assistant to contact the prison to arrange a phone call. C'mon, guys. I got nothing to hold back. How'd he die?"

The agent who had been quietly taking notes spoke for the first time.

"Stabbed. There was a disturbance of some sort between two groups of inmates. Several were injured. Inmate Löwenstein was airlifted to St. Joseph Hospital in Tacoma where he was pronounced dead."

Vega said he didn't understand. Löwenstein was a meager bank employee, not a gang member or some hardened con.

"From what they told us, there was a scuffle involving white and Negro inmates at a minimum-custody annex."

"Summit House?"

"I believe that's correct. They're still piecing together what triggered the melee and Löwenstein's participation. Right now, all inmates are confined to their cells."

Vega buzzed Nancy in the lobby area, asking her to bring three coffees and her notebook. He needed a pause to sort through what he intended to tell the agents. Was there reason, any at all, to hold anything back?

CHAPTER FIFTY-ONE

WILD CULT BLAMED IN TATE SLAYINGS

By Jerry Cohen
Times Staff Writer

Police believe they have solved the Sharon Tate murder case, and that an occult band of hippies, directed by a leader who calls himself "Jesus," committed the five killings.

Members of the band – a mystical hate-oriented tribe of 20th Century nomads – also are suspected of the La Bianca – or "copycat" – killings and at least four other comparably grotesque butcherings.

The suspects slew their victims, police believe, both to "punish" them for their affluent lifestyle and to "liberate" them from it.

The killers invaded the Tate and La Bianca households, it is suspected, because they learned about the victims' affluence through friends or relatives of those slain.

Police have found no evidence of association between the suspects and the victims prior to the murders, it was reported Monday.

The cult leader, Charles Manson, 34, who also refers to himself as "God" and "Satan," is in custody along with a man and two young women. A third young woman is being sought out of state, but her whereabouts is believed known.

Vega read the LA Times article standing barefoot on his front porch and in pajamas. He was drawn to the first of two mug-shot photos displayed on the right side of the article. A man with Beatle-style hair was smiling off the page. Underneath, his name: Charles D. Watson.

"Sonofabitch!"

Watson had been arrested two years earlier in Indio by Riverside County deputies. He was taken into custody as a suspect in the murder of Archer, the cheesy film director. The charges were dropped after Vega's investigation of the case. After he found the body and confronted the real killer, Watson was freed.

The same guy was now in custody in McKinney, Texas, on an unrelated charge, according to the article. But he was accused in the complaint filed by Deputy District Attorney Vincent Bugliosi of killing the 18-year-old found in the car outside the Tate residence.

Vega flipped to page three where the article continued, searching anxiously for more information on Watson and the missing woman. He soon read the fugitive was named Linda Kasabian, not Janice Showalter.

The article went on to repeat the gruesome details of the string of slayings before detailing how the young women in Manson's self-styled family considered themselves his slaves, willing to do his bidding without question. A related headline promoted how arrests of the clan in Independence for auto theft led investigators to unravel the Tate-LaBianca murders. Another interviewed the father of one of the women charged. Joseph Krenwinkel remarked how his "stable and conservative" daughter Patricia changed after she met Manson. I'm convinced, he said, that Manson was some type of hypnotist.

Vega reentered the house when the kitchen telephone rang. It was Lily.

"Did you see the news? I told you..."

"I'm reading it now. You called it. That group. You saw there's no mention of Janice."

"Yeah. It doesn't help us, but I'm glad she's not involved in these atrocities."

"It's early."

The conversation stalled as if both were weighing what to say. Lily broke the silence first.

"Listen, I called in a score in the DA's office. They reached out to Pierce County about your guy Löwenstein. Pretty much what the newspapers reported. Bad blood between the races. Your guy apparently got caught in between."

"Nothing the guards saw, or surveillance cameras caught that indicates a set-up?"

"Nothing I've heard. Investigation is ongoing. I gotta go, Vega. More tactical training alongside SWAT guys."

"SWAT?"

"That's what they're calling this unit from Metro. Heavy hitters. For use in riots, that kind of action."

"Expecting another Watts?"

"Something's up. Boy Scout stuff. You know, be prepared? Talk later."

CHAPTER FIFTY-TWO

Vega and Nancy spent December 5, a Friday, before the grand jury in Riverside. The nineteen men and women serving on the panel listened to their testimony for three hours, occasionally interrupting the assistant prosecutor, who was not District Attorney Jack Cady. Not an encouraging sign, Vega whispered to Nancy as the session convened.

"They're not taking this seriously."

The questions directed at Nancy were straightforward, primarily about her conversations with Quail in San Mateo. When one of the jurors remarked about her ability to recall with precision what was said, Nancy explained that she had what scientists term eidetic memory.

"I'm able to vividly recall images from memory without any aid."

The diversion from her testimony unsettled the young prosecutor, Carl Nubio, who struggled to get jurors refocused on the case before them.

When it came time for Vega to testify, Nubio treated him like a hostile witness. He questioned the way Mary's case came to his attention. The magazine clipping was made to appear like a device from a mystery novel. He questioned how Vega could be certain that Janice Showalter was Mary's sister. Vega pointed out that the identification was made by law enforcement officials in Independence.

Later, Nubio attempted to challenge Vega's recollections of his interview with Janice, pointing out to jurors that the detective had suffered an injury a year ago that had put him in a coma. Irritated, Vega shot back.

"Detective Navarro and I took copious notes during those interviews. You have access to those notebooks. You have our written statements. If there's any discrepancy between the two of us, I've yet to hear it."

"Right, right. Now, Mr. Vega, you're aware that Miss Showalter took off after being released by Inyo County officials."

"I am."

"And you're aware that, as of this date, she has not been located. Correct?"

"I believe so."

"Then let me ask you this, Mr. Vega. If your account is correct, that Janice Showalter told you she witnessed the fatal shooting of her sister, and the brutal way she was led to her death in Mitchell's Caverns, don't you think Miss Showalter would want to help bring the killer to justice?"

There it was. The question of the hour.

"You would think so, Mr. Nubio. I'm as disappointed as you that Janice hasn't come forward. But we should keep in mind that she suffered...suffered at the hands of Arthur Quail. She said she was raped and kidnapped by the man. Forced to watch as Quail put a bullet through her sister's skull. He then tried to kill Janice as well. People are afraid of monsters, Mr. Nubio, real or imagined. And don't forget that Janice spent the last two years in the company of Charles Manson. From what we've all read, he's some crazed Svengali, able to lure young women into his cult and get them to do the most horrendous crimes. Janice Showalter told officer Navarro and me she didn't want to return to his so-called family. So, to answer your question, I'm disappointed but not surprised she isn't here, sitting in this chair, telling all of you what she witnessed."

Nubio attempted to regain the floor, but Vega cut him off.

"And if you don't believe me. And if you don't believe Officer Navarro. Fine! But you can still put the screws to Quail's neighbor, Abraham Barnheiser, who covered for Quail the night she vanished. Who covered for Quail as he repeatedly raped an eleven-year-old girl in the adjoining apartment. Sit him down, right here, under oath. Make him squirm. And Quail? Guys like him think they can outsmart anybody and everybody. You know the thing about guys like him? They think they're smarter than the system, the evidence, sometimes even themselves. But even the smartest ones make mistakes. Not because they're careless. Because they're human. Humans slip up. Humans can crack. Sit him down right here, where I'm sitting. Ask him how he knew about this cave in the Mojave Desert. Ask him how he got that scar on his right ear."

"Mr. Vega, the police have questioned Arthur Quail. They've questioned Mr. Barnheiser. Seventeen years ago, and again over the last several weeks. His account of his whereabouts holds up."

"Then why the fuck am I here? If you don't have the balls to file charges, don't waste my time. Don't waste the time of these good men and women. Jesus! You sure you don't work for the PD's office?"

The final hour of Vega's testimony was subdued. Reversing course, Nubio tried to bolster the merits of the circumstantial case he was handed. Possible motives: covering up his rape of Janice, benefitting from Mary's life insurance as paltry as it was, sexual deviation. He displayed for jurors photographs of Mary's skull and the bullet hole that Dr. Noguchi said was made by a Smith & Wesson .38-caliber handgun. Inferences were made about Quail's sexual appetite and comparisons in physical attractiveness between him and his new bride.

It was all for show. The grand jury was unlikely to return a true bill, sparing the DA's office from a public trial they were likely to lose. Palms Springs police wanted to avoid the embarrassment of further exposure of the missing case files and a murder they failed to solve not once but twice.

CHAPTER FIFTY-THREE

Indictments came down on Monday. The charges were issued by the Office of the Los Angeles County district attorney, not the one in Riverside. The grand jury in LA returned seven counts of murder and one of conspiracy against Charles Manson and five members of his cult in connection with the murder of Sharon Tate and six other victims.

Among those charged was "Tex" Watson, the man Vega helped walk free.

The detective's fingers felt heavy as he read the account on the front page of the *Times*. Watson, the indictment charged, was the ringleader of the group that massacred the actress and six others. According to Deputy District Attorney Bugliosi, Manson told Watson to go to Tate's house in Benedict Canyon and kill everyone there. On the evening of August 8, Watson, along with Susan Atkins, Patricia Krenwinkel, and Linda Kasabian, did just that. The following night, Watson, Leslie Van Houten, and Krenwinkel entered another residence. Once again Watson was the leader of the massacre, personally delivering savage death blows to Leno and Rosemary LaBianca.

Grief, rather than rage or remorse, welled up inside Vega. He knew the evidence against Watson hadn't held up in the Indio case. Watson did not kill Archer, the Hollywood director. That was fact, not conjecture. Yet, the satisfaction that truth had triumphed couldn't deaden the ache that in freeing one innocent man he had somehow enabled the slaughter of seven others.

Vega allowed the newspaper to drop to his feet as he stepped off the front porch to return to the kitchen where Koma waited for breakfast. Outside, the edge of the front page curled in the slight breeze, waving the day's other headlines like a tired flag.

Headlines about the trial of an Army lieutenant accused of leading the My Lai massacre. About murder and mayhem at a rock concert at the Altamont Speedway near San Francisco. About a deadly four-hour gunfight in south central Los Angeles between 350 police and six members of the Black Panthers armed with an arsenal of automatic weapons and grenades. The confrontation coming only two days after a similar raid by Chicago police, where Fred Hampton, deputy chairman of the Illinois chapter of the Panthers, was shot to death at point-blank range while he was sleeping.

CHAPTER FIFTY-FOUR

The first gunshot tore through the dark of the bedroom like a lightning strike, shattering the silence with a sharp crack. Wooden splinters exploded as the headrest jerked backward. The second came a second later, louder, more violent, like a hammer slamming into sheet metal.

Both gunshots missed their mark. The intended victim had been asleep, but his night had been restless. Sheets tangled around legs like seaweed, leaving him sprawled on the right edge of the bed, one arm hanging limply over the side. The uneasy sleep had saved his life.

In a blur, Vega rolled off the bed, hitting the floor hard on his bad shoulder as the mattress exploded above him. Fully awake, his heart slamming against his ribs, he rolled instinctively beneath the edge of the bed, wedged between the baseboard and the nightstand where he kept his revolver.

In the sudden silence, clarity. Someone had fired at him while he slept. Not a warning. Not a message. Kill shots. He lay frozen, eyes wide open in the dark, listening. Whoever pulled the trigger was still there.

Two more cracks, sharp and vicious, ripped into the mattress with muffled whumps, sending a cascade of white down into the air, tangling with the acrid scent of gunpowder.

In the momentary stillness, the gunman stood in the doorway, his hand reaching out in the darkness for the light switch on the wall. The blinding light was quickly followed by a wild shriek. A streak of gray fur launched itself from under the bed at the intruder's leg. Claws pierced skin beneath the thin polyester trousers, digging into the leg like razors. A second scream followed as the animal clung to the limb, tearing at the fabric and raking the flesh.

The intruder stumbled backward before slamming the cat with the gun. In that instant, Vega vaulted to his knees, grabbed his gun off the nightstand and began firing. He emptied four rounds into the man's chest and upper abdomen. The attacker pitched to the floor, the gun pinwheeling off his fingers.

Vega stood barefoot on the tiled floor, one hand still clutching the gun, the other limp at his side twitching. His ears rang with the echo of the gunplay. His mind wrestling with the fight and the message it was meant to send.

— • —

Red and blue lights announced the arrival of the first patrol car. Radio chatter spilled into the quiet street as two uniformed officers stepped out, hands resting near their belts, eyes scanning the house with its front door open. Neighbors peered nervously from behind curtains as sirens grew near.

One officer peeled off toward the front of the house. He kept low, one hand resting on his revolver. From his angle, he had a clear line on the front door. The second officer took a position behind the car's hood. He squatted, taking a look behind him as a second patrol unit arrived, before turning his attention to the open front door.

"Mr. Vega! Exit the house and with your hands in clear view!"

Silence held for a beat. Then Vega stepped slowly into the porch light, hands raised and fingers spread. He knew the drill. He stood there waiting their next command, clad only in blue boxers, his chest soaked in sweat.

"Walk down the driveway and stop halfway. Keep your hands up."

Vega complied without a word. When he reached the mark, he stopped and was quickly approached from behind by a young officer holding a lengthy silver flashlight, as lethal looking as the holstered gun covered with his other hand. After a quick pat down of his briefs, Vega was walked down the driveway to the other officer.

After they sat him back of the patrol car, door open, he was asked what happened in there. Vega's voice was hoarse from sleep and louder than needed. A piercing whine refused to fade from his ears.

"As I told dispatch, guy broke in somehow. I was asleep in the bedroom. Came in shooting. Missed. I returned fire. He went down. He's flatlined. Don't know the guy. Body's down the hallway just outside the large bedroom. His gun is on the floor. Mine's on the nightstand. There's a cat in there. Wounded. I called a vet."

As officers from the second unit kept an eye on Vega, the two patrolmen called homicide before approaching the house. Once inside, with the air thick with the unmistakable scent of cordite, they first spotted the cat sprawled on the kitchen table next to a tall glass of vodka and orange juice. Its fur was matted with blood along one side. It lay motionless but its side was rising in weak, uneven breaths. Neither patrolman approached the animal, both heading down the lighted hallway where they began to evaluate and secure the crime scene. Work that would last until dawn and beyond.

— • —

The would-be assassin was quickly identified as Andres Cardoso of Whitewater. Riverside County police were familiar with the 34-year-old and his record of drugs, theft, and assault. The petty crook had no record of burglary or criminal activity with a firearm.

The assault charge followed a fight at a local bar. Cardoso came out on top, not surprising given that he was a gifted boxer.

Sponsored by a local gym, he compiled a record of fourteen wins and three losses. Ten of his victories were knockouts. Injured in a motorcycle accident when he was 31, Cardoso had to hang up his gloves. In the years that followed, he did odd jobs, including dealing methamphetamines and stealing Social Security checks.

Cardoso had no obvious ties with the Mexican gangs in Los Angeles or the Imperial Valley. A former girlfriend told investigators he became obsessed with the cult film *Hell's Biker Devils*. The drive-in movie, directed by Al Archer, portrays an outlaw motorcycle gang that roams the Mojave Desert preying on tourists and getting into fights with other gangs.

"He must've watched that flick a dozen times. After that, all he wanted to do is ride motorcycle, shoot guns, and fuck me in the ass."

The weapon used to execute Vega's bed was a Ruger Mark II traced to a 1967 home robbery in Desert Hot Springs. Detectives followed that lead to the Berdoo Canyon Shooting Area near Desert Hot Springs. Cardoso spent much of his time there, according to gun enthusiasts they interviewed in the off-road area.

Despite the pieces they were putting together, investigators were unable to advance a motive for the shooting or connect Cardoso and Vega, who insisted it was a hit job.

"He wasn't some burglar. He was hired to kill me."

Homicide detectives asked how he could be certain.

"Because burglars sure as hell don't fire into a bed without checking for cash or jewelry first. Cardoso didn't enter my house looking for stuff. He was here for me."

"You've made enemies before, Mr. Vega. Maybe a pissed-off husband. A bad divorce case. A jealous client. You dig up dirt for a living. Someone probably just wanted to scare you."

"Scare me? Five rounds straight into the bed where I was sleeping? That's not a warning shot. That's a kill order."

"Okay. Let's play along. Give us names of who would want you dead."

"Just one. Arthur Quail."

— • —

A day after the crime scene tape was removed, and Cardoso's body remained shelved in a cooler at the coroner's office, the scene at Vega's home on South Monte Vista still looked like a war zone. Bullet holes pockmarked the bedroom walls. Splinters from the headboard littered the floor along with gray plaster dust. Foam stuffing curled out from the mattress like pale intestines. Blood on the floor tiles had been cleaned, but the sterile smell of bleach hung in the air.

Vega's handgun remained in the evidence locker along with Cardoso's and other seized evidence. Koma, meanwhile, remained at the vet. The cat suffered a broken tibia and was refusing to eat after surgery. The doctor wanted the feline to remain under observation for another few days to ensure that its injury was limited to the hind leg and that its appetite returned.

Despite offers to assist with cleaning from Coralina and Nancy, Vega kept the house closed. He didn't want the women to see the carnage and had not ruled out that Quail would hire another contract killer. To prepare for that possibility, Vega retrieved a SIG P210 from a locker in the garage. It would be kept within grasp whenever he was in the house or out and about.

— • —

When Vega and Lily finally connected by telephone, she needled him mercilessly about his life being spared by a cat.

"You are one lucky bastard. The guys at LAPD are calling you Detective Whiskers, the cat's meow."

"Hilarious."

"You gonna give him a medal or extra kibbles?"

"I thought you called to see how I'm doing?"

"That too. First, how's the furry hero doing?"

"Should be home tomorrow. Got a giant cast on one leg. Eating well and shitting like there's no tomorrow. Turns out it's kinda deaf. Congenital thing, the vet told me. Gunshots didn't help."

"I hear you emptied your gun on the guy."

"I saved two."

"Justifiable homicide. Castle doctrine, right?"

"That's what they tell me."

"First kill, right?"

"First time I squeezed the trigger outside of the range."

"Ever the Boy Scout. Anything more on this guy? Cardoso?"

"Petty thief. Former boxer. Some punk after a payday."

"Quail put him up?"

"That's my take. Dunno who else has it out for me."

"You seem to attract them."

"I survived. That's all that matters right now. What about you? Sounds like it was one helluva firefight with the Panthers. More than five-thousand rounds exchanged?"

"Something like that. They came at us with Tommy guns, shotguns."

"Thirteen armed men and women against, what, three-hundred LAPD? You also brought in a tank."

"You going left-wing permissive, Vega? You saw what happened in Watts. Jesus."

"Don't get your ass out of joint. Just reacting to what I read, that's all."

"I told you, it's getting more than crazy out there. Panthers, Bloods, Crips. Drugged-up psychos"

"Gangs have been around for a long time, Lily. You know that."

"No shit. But they used to stay in their communities, supposedly protecting those communities. Now they're mobile. They don't stay in their communities. They move about. They keep trying to expand territory. They're committing crimes all over the city. Got these drive-by shootings. People gunned down on front lawns and porches. Shit, Vega, people can't eat dinner at night. They eat on the floor, they're scared. Kids are afraid to sleep in their beds. It's a different day, Vega."

"Noted. Watch yourself out there. Don't get caught in the crossfire."

Lily laughed.

"Yeah, right. Seems the world is gunning for you. Three attempts on your life in three years? That's not life-affirming. Maybe you should try another field. Something simple, like herding cats."

CHAPTER FIFTY-FIVE

The motive for the attempted hit on Vega presented itself when detectives interviewed Cardoso's mother. She lived in a mobile home a half mile from her son. Hunched on a sagging couch inside a sun-faded tube of aluminum and dust just off a dirt road outside Desert Hot Springs, her eyes still red and raw, Carmen Cardoso spoke at length about her son's troubled childhood, absent father, his success as a bantam-weight boxer, and his troubles with drugs after his accident.

"He changed after that accident. Started with pills after, then harder stuff. Heroin, maybe. I don't know for sure. He kept things from me. Didn't want me to worry."

She wiped a tear from her cheek, her eyes holding a memory for the moment. One she took pride in.

"Andres wanted to do right. Said he was going to get clean. Said he had plans. Big plans. Told me he was going to buy me a house. A real house, he said, not this old place."

A wet Kleenex twisted in her bony hands.

"I don't know where he thought the money would come from. He tried to get the banks to loan him money, but they refused."

Following the interview, a lone Palm Springs detective, armed with a subpoena, took on the tedious task of contacting the thirteen banks and financial institutions in the valley. He retrieved completed loan applications from a dozen. Others had no record of Cardoso. Each loan application was denied because he lacked steady employment or assets that could be used for collateral. The amounts Cardoso sought ranged from $10,000 to $30,000.

The detective, Bose Fairfax, was unable to find any bank accounts in Cardoso's name. On a hunch, he checked his notebook for the mother's maiden name. He recalled she had provided that as part of her account of Andres' upbringing. After locating the name – Sosa – he sought and was granted another subpoena.

Fairfax's return to the banks yielded several accounts in that surname. Only one, however, was held by Carmen Sosa. The address matched her property in Desert Hot Springs. The account had been opened at CV Savings & Loan on December 5, six days before the attack on Vega. An initial deposit of $100 had been made that day by Andres Cardoso. A second deposit was made four days later in the amount of $3,000. That same amount had been withdrawn on December 10, also by the son.

The large deposit arrived as a Western Union money order. The sender's name was listed as Cardoso's, which was more than odd. Why would he pay for a money order rather than just deposit cash into his mother's bank account?

Fairfax ran the ten-digit transfer number and followed the trail to a Western Union office on Trabuco Road in Mission Viejo, three miles from Arthur Quail's front door.

— • —

Armed with another search warrant and accompanied by another Palm Springs detective, Fairfax met with two Orange County sheriff's deputies after arriving in Mission Viejo on December 15. The makeshift team assembled at a back table at Carmaleta's cantina. They agreed that the first stop would be the Western Union office where they would attempt to confirm the identity of the person who took out the money order. Confronting Quail would come afterward, when he returned home rather than at his FDIC office in Irvine.

The two detectives from Palm Springs met with the lone Western Union employee an hour later. The young man stood out like a roadside flare. His wild tangle of orange curls fell past his shoulders, a style he explained was necessary for his night gig, playing bass in a rock band, the Electric Weathervanes. He confirmed he was on duty the day the $3,000 money order was placed.

"We don't get orders of that amount very often so, yeah, I remember the guy."

Detectives asked for a description of the customer before placing on a table five photographs, one at a time, like a five-card stud. Cardoso. Quail. Vega. And two clowns cooling their heels in a cell in Palm Springs.

Weathervane patiently studied each before rejecting all five headshots.

"You certain none of these men placed the $3,000 money order on December 9?"

"Absolutely."

Fairfax returned the five photographs to the folder. Outside, he informed the Orange County deputies they no longer were needed. There would be no call that evening at the Quail residence.

— • —

That evening, the 49-year-old detective sunk into his favorite chair, the muted Lakers-SuperSonics game flickering from the corner of the den. He reached for the last of the second Manhattan his wife had grudgingly fixed. In his lap, a notepad was turned to the page with the description Weathervane had provided. He read it again, letting the words sink past the fog from the long day. Something stirred in the back of his mind, a face half-remembered.

Damn. He knew this guy. Somewhere their paths had crossed.

But the name wouldn't come. It hung there in the room, just out of reach, like the lingering scent of menthol from the final Kool he stubbed out before heading for bed.

CHAPTER FIFTY-SIX

The morning air was crisp, carrying a faint scent of the Nacapule Jasmine that Vega had planted behind the pool along the cinderblock wall that enclosed his back yard. Remaking his backyard had unearthed a welcome peace following the turmoil of the preceding weeks. He found quiet satisfaction teasing weeds from the sand and gravel that posed as soil in the Coachella Valley.

Overgrown oleander that had dominated the yard was removed, allowing him to refashion the inherited landscaping with more color. Desert milkweed, Mexican gold poppies, and purple-flowered bougainvillea gave the yard a welcoming personality.

Vega slouched on the lounge chair next to the pool, quietly reading the first chapter of *The Godfather*, which Erika had gifted. Only twenty-three pages into the novel, he paused at the author's description of Luca Brasi, "a man to frighten the devil in hell." The passage reminded him of Fat Frank, the only member of the Califano family to attend the historic summit of mobsters held at a home along McFall Road in the Catskills.

Vega's time with the family had only been five years ago, but it could have been fifty. Not just a stretch of time, but a separate existence. The man he'd been back then lived in a different world. Strangely, a more peaceful world. A world untouched by gunfire as he slept. Before surgical scars tattooed his flesh. Before mortality became impossible to ignore.

He caught himself thinking about that life. About Sundays when his wife made breakfasts of panettone, baked eggs, and sausage. About autumn, when they walked along the bleached planks of the boardwalk after the summer crowds and humidity had left, leaving the gray ocean horizon to locals like them. About his dreams of earning a gold shield. Dreams of a family of his own. Before a stillbirth and subsequent divorce and his firing changed it all.

It all felt foreign now, like a story someone else had told long ago.

— • —

Vega scanned the yard for Koma thinking the tabby had gone around the side of the house searching for a stray gecko, dragging its cumbersome cast along for the hunt. The thing was too damn long. The plaster and tape were filthy from the cat's backyard adventuring. Koma didn't seem to care. It hobbled from the kitchen to the living room, tail flicked high, pausing only long enough to glare at any chair leg that got in the way.

About to get up to look for the animal, Vega found Koma dozing near the end of the lounge chair, curled up on a folded bath towel, the same one that served as his bed in the living room, where Vega slept each night until new bedroom furniture arrived. He watched the cat's breathing, slow and shallow, its flank rising and falling in a steady rhythm. Afraid even a soft touch would wake it, Vega was content to watch Koma sleep, knowing it was a hard-won rest.

Setting down the coffee mug, his shoulder barked, a sore reminder from when he rolled out of bed as the gunfight erupted. The gunman was dead but the man who ordered the hit was still out there. He placed the mug on a folding lawn table where it shared space with the SIG P210.

Next door, a lawn sprinkler came on, each spray tick, tick, ticking like a stopwatch. Overhead, a red-tailed hawk circled high and lazy in a wandering breeze. Its screech the voice of a waiting hunter.

CHAPTER FIFTY-SEVEN

Monday morning, as Palm Springs residents shook off sleep and returned to the new workweek, police and sheriff's deputies assembled near the CV Savings & Loan on North Palm Canyon Drive. A small team boxed in the building as Fairfax and another detective and partner entered the front door once the business opened. They left the building ten minutes later, accompanied by the manager, now handcuffed.

Tobias Blackpool angrily denied he had hired Cardoso to kill Vega. Evidence said otherwise. His appearance matched the description given by Weathervane, who would later confirm the identity. Blackpool's desk calendar and that of his secretary showed that he was out of the office on December 9, the day the money order was sent to Carmen Sosa's bank account. A teller confirmed Sosa's son withdrew the identical amount the following day.

Police had probable cause for the arrest, though it would be up to a grand jury to indict Blackpool with solicitation of murder and conspiracy to commit murder. Prosecutors would later allege that the manager of the savings and loan blamed Vega when the FBI and FDIC began to re-examine the 1954 bank fraud and embezzlement case after Mary Showalter's body was identified. Fearing his role in the scheme would be uncovered, prosecutors said Blackpool panicked, hiring Cardoso after learning of his need for money.

— • —

After completing the multitude of requisite forms after booking Blackpool, Fairfax made a house call at 372 South Monte Vista. Over more than one Manhattan, the police detective outlined the elaborate embezzlement scheme to Vega, who mostly listened. There was ample evidence that pointed to the bank manager as the one behind Cardoso's attempted hit.

Vega absorbed the news, and a realization he had been wrong. Again.

"That's a helluva story, I'll hand you that. Blackpool struck me as a bean-counter in a tailored suit. Someone who wanted me dead? Nah. You did good. You followed the money, pushed past the fog."

"Thanks. I heard you don't think too kindly of my department."

"What? You? No. Just one. Turner. We go back."

"He's connected."

"I heard. You certain Quail had nothing to do with this? He killed Mary, raped her sister. I figured he had motive and the nerve to kill me. Guy's pure evil."

"Listen, there's nothing linking him to Cardoso or the attempted hit on you. I buy what you said he did to those girls. Proving it is another matter. As for the embezzlement? I don't know if he was involved. That's up to the feds to figure out."

Vega got up from the kitchen table to get more ice. He stopped before he got the bucket, snapping his fingers.

"That's what Mary was referring to. She pleaded with Quail to spare Janice because she *didn't know anything*. She meant Blackpool's role in the scheme. Quail was aware of it. He covered it up as part of his initial report. Probably split some of the money with

Blackpool. They worked together, branch manager and bank examiner, to pile all the blame on the little guy, Löwenstein. Mary somehow found out about it and the role her new husband played. Maybe Quail was careless. Spilled something to his new bride. Pillow talk. Or maybe Mary was sharp and figured it out. Either way, she wasn't around when Löwenstein went down."

Fairfax said it was an interesting theory, one that FBI agents investigating the embezzlement case ought to consider.

"I'll leave that to you. My friends at the FBI aren't exactly friendly these days."

Fairfax covered the mouth of his glass with a hand.

"I'm good. More than good. I gotta drive home."

"You can have the chair over there. I'm on the couch. Bedroom's still a mess."

"Nah. Wife would have me castrated. Gotta go."

Vega escorted his guest to the front door.

"Your first name? Shorthand for?"

"Almost as inspired as yours. Parents named me Bosley. After a few fights in grade school, I asked everyone to call me Bose. They did. Could've been worse. Mom wanted to name me Atticus. Hoped I'd become a lawyer."

"Thanks for stopping by. It meant a lot."

"You deserved to hear directly. You found Mary. I fingered Blackpool. Someday, maybe, we'll get Quail."

Fairfax stepped gingerly along the sidewalk toward his car, parked in the moonless dark across the street. Something in the way the detective walked off struck Vega. A grainy flicker of memory floating up uninvited. Something about the beginning of a beautiful friendship.

CHAPTER FIFTY-EIGHT

The final days of December sagged under the weight of the decade. The Sixties were burning out, leaving behind a scorched trail of drugs, cultural revolution, political assassination, and war. The triumph of technology and imagination from the Apollo moon landing dimmed as the relentless body count from Vietnam continued to haunt the nightly news. The pending trial of Charles Manson overtook the music and karma that had once defined the decade. A petty criminal from the margins – a drifter with messianic delusions, a hypnotic stare, and a cult of cutthroat disciples – became a grotesque reminder that monsters still roamed the Earth.

For the Vega Detective Agency, 1969 had yielded its own depressing headlines: the cold trails, missing evidence, disappearance of the star witness, and a perverted killer still roaming free. Not to mention Vega's personal descent into darkness and the attempt on his life.

Christmas Eve, however, proved different. Vega gathered his colleagues at Melvyn's Restaurant at the Ingleside Inn. Dinner was on him. It was, he told them, a gift for their support and dedication.

Dining on New Zealand rack of lamb with purple Okinawa mash and braised artichoke, the group celebrated joyously. It wasn't just solving the mystery of the vanishing bride. A sense of purpose was rediscovered. The Vega Detective Agency would continue, rescued by three women bound to its founder.

Assembled around a white-cloth table beneath crystal chandeliers, within the gaze of Modigliani portraits, conversations spilled easily from each of Vega's guests. Playful comparisons were made between the little black dress Nancy wore that evening to her predicament in the caverns, where she dangled upside down over an abyss while clutching a bag of bones.

Jarvis offered as many Palm Springs scandals as the whiskey sours he downed. From the arrest of actor Tom Neal after he fatally shot his wife for refusing his advances to Sinatra's charming sidekick, Jerry the Crusher, who earned his nickname from crushing Coke bottles in his bare hands.

Nancy, tipsy from several glasses of Valle Freres Chablis, recited the entire dinner menu from memory. Lily offered the tale of a bank robber who put a five-dollar bill on the counter along with his note demanding cash.

"I guess he wanted to look like someone looking for change. Anyhow, the teller read the note, ducked, then pulled the silent alarm per procedure when there is no gun. Puzzled, the robber just walked away ... without anything, even his fiver. We never caught the guy, but he could have done twenty-five for losing five dollars."

Vega allowed himself a rare smile as he watched his mismatched colleagues. The policewoman who twice had saved his life. A newspaperman who enjoyed pastrami on marbled rye as much as a page-one byline. The modest teenager with a timestamp memory inevitably progressing to heartbreaker.

And, of course, Coralina.

The room seemed to bend in her direction. She was laughing when he let his eyes drift toward her. A new mother, beautiful and intelligent, someone who understood his soul more than he could. He recalled kissing her for the first time, and her whispered advice.

"Do not forget these moments, Aloysius. Someday, it will all seem like a dream."

In the morning, after celebrating Juliet's first Christmas, a steamship ferry would take them to Catalina Island where they would stay through the start of the new decade. The trip was her idea, though he didn't argue. It was there, two years ago, outside their rooms at the Zane Gray Hotel, where they kissed. Separate rooms were booked at the hotel once again. Nancy had agreed to accompany them, to care for Juliet while Coralina and Vega spent time together.

As waiters began to clear their plates, each of the five raised their emptied wine glass a final time, proposing the occasion be repeated in a year. Vega agreed to make it a tradition.

Coralina turned his way. In the time that passes between heartbeats, their eyes locked. A moment poised between their past and whatever the future was shaping for them. Her dark brown eyes searched for a smile of recognition or even the smallest flicker in his eyes that said he remembered he loved her. She held her smile, graceful under the weight of anticipation.

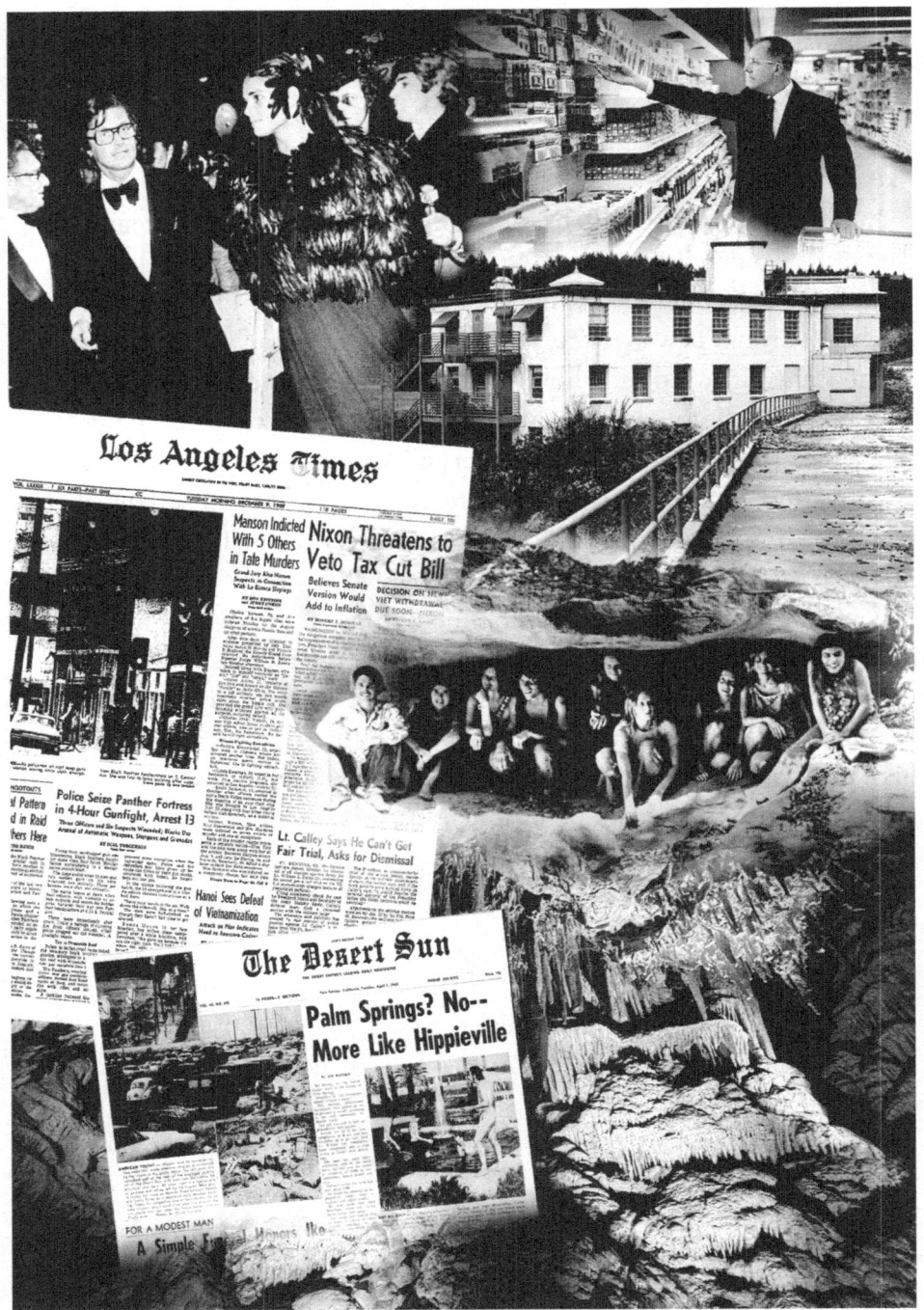

Echoes from 1969: (clockwise from upper left): Robert Evans and Ali MacGraw; Alvin Karpis shopping for groceries in Canada following his release; McNeil Island Prison; members of the Manson family; limestone formations deep in the Mitchell Caverns; and front pages of the Desert Sun and Los Angeles Times.

ABOUT THE CAST

Non-Fictional Characters

Alvin Karpis, whose self-described profession was "robbing banks, knocking off payrolls, and kidnapping rich men," led the life of an infamous but reformed man in Montreal after his parole. He granted interviews, gave lectures, wrote an autobiography, and even appeared in beer commercials. In 1973, he relocated to Torremolinos on the Costa del Sol in Spain. Little is known about his life there. Neighbors said he had very few friends, rarely went out, and gave the impression of being an ordinary pensioner. The one-time Public Enemy Number One died of a heart attack in 1979 at age eighty-two. Only two women were present at his burial in Malaga's San Miguel cemetery.

John Roselli was transferred from McNeil Island to the Federal Medical Center in Rochester, Minnesota, where he was treated for pneumonia and digestive disorders. His lawyer and friends with pull were eventually able to get him transferred to a minimum-security federal institution in southeastern Arizona where his health improved. Paroled in 1973 at age sixty-eight, he moved to Florida to live with his sister. Three years later the decomposing body of the Mafia kingpin was found by fishermen in a 55-gallon steel fuel drum floating in Dumfoundling Bay near Miami. Roselli's testimony before Congress regarding a CIA plot to assassinate Fidel Castro is believed to have led to his murder.

James Carty, former city attorney for Woodland, Washington, and prosecuting attorney for Clark County, continued to correspond with Alvin Karpis after his release. Carty died in 2001.

Robert Evans, the extravagant film producer whose glamorous lifestyle at times overshadowed the movies he made as head of production at Paramount Pictures, died in 2019 at age eighty-nine in Beverly Hills. He was responsible for reviving the fortunes of that moribund studio by overseeing hits such as *Rosemary's Baby, Love Story, The Godfather,* and *Chinatown.* His marriage to Ali MacGraw ended after four years when she left him for Steve McQueen.

Sidney Korshak, the Chicago labor lawyer who became one of Hollywood's most influential fixers, died in 1996 in Beverly Hills at age eighty-eight. His ability to arrange loans of millions of dollars from the Teamsters' infamous Central States Pension Fund helped finance the growth of the Las Vegas casino industry.

Truman Capote regularly hosted large and noisy parties attended by some of the biggest socialites and celebrities of the day at his Palm Springs home at 853 E. Paseo El Mirador. His novel *Answered Prayers* was never completed. One of the chapters, however, appeared in *Esquire* magazine. The thinly veiled fiction outraged his rich friends, destroying his friendships, reputation, social standing, and his desire to write. The celebrated author died in 1984 just shy of his sixtieth birthday from liver disease complicated by multiple drug intoxication.

Don Ward served as deputy sheriff for Inyo County until 1975. He died of cancer at age 49 in 1976 and is buried in Independence under a military headstone. Despite his pivotal role in the initial arrest of Charles Manson and his followers, Ward received little credit for his work. Los Angeles Prosecutor Vincent Bugliosi disparaged the contributions of the small-town deputy in his best-selling book *Helter Skelter:* "Ward's interview (with Paul Crockett and Brooks Poston) had nothing to do with those murders, only the activities of the 'hippie types' who were living in Goler Wash."

Charles Manson, one of the most notorious murderers of the 20th Century, was convicted of nine brutal killings, including seven committed by his followers on two consecutive August nights in 1969. He died in 2017 at the age of eighty-three after spending most of his life behind bars. His right-hand man, **Charles "Tex" Watson**, remains incarcerated. He has been denied parole eighteen times.

Kitty Lutesinger, Bobby Beausoleil's girlfriend and Manson family member, told Inyo County investigators that Susan Atkins had been involved in the murder of Gary Hinman. It was the initial break in the Tate-LaBianca murders. After a series of arrests for minor crimes, Lutesinger went on to teach middle school science and serve as a principal. Now retired, she lives in Colorado.

Fictional Characters

Aloysius Vega recovered fully from his injuries and the after effects of his four-day coma. He remained head of the Vega Detective Agency for two decades. In his spare time, he golfed and enjoyed his role as Uncle Al. His tabby, Koma, wandered off in 1972 and was not seen again.

Coralina Sanchez returned to limited duty at the detective agency in 1970. She later obtained a degree in criminology and eventually remarried. She returns to Catalina Island every year on the same date, often visiting with her family.

Nancy Randall began working full time at the agency in 1970. On weekends she participated in small lecture groups studying computers via videotaped lectures from Stanford University. Her unique skills caught the attention of legendary computer scientist John McCarthy, who is credited with coining the term "artificial intelligence."

Lily Navarro never was admitted to LAPD's SWAT team. It wasn't until 2008 that a female police officer joined the unit. Navarro eventually earned a gold shield, becoming LAPD's first female Latino officer to make detective grade. She spearheaded successful investigations into corruption in the department. Her work earned her plaudits from the press and hostility from many uniformed officers.

Erika Lake was on hand for the grand opening in 1971 of Eisenhower Medical Center. Erika continued to live at her estate on West Hermosa Place while spending summers traveling or at her condominium in Manhattan. She maintained a relationship with Vega as his covert advocate and occasional benefactor.

Scott Jarvis worked at *The Desert Post* until 1989. He remained on the crime beat, which eventually was renamed public safety.

Bose Fairfax retired in 1998 after a distinguished career with the Palm Springs Police Department. Bose and his wife moved to Eagle, Idaho, where he spent his final years bass fishing. He died of natural causes in 2023 at the ripe age of 94.

Tobias Blackpool was convicted of the felony crime of solicitation of murder and sentenced to nine years in prison and fined $10,000. Upon release from the California State Prison in Folsom in 1979, he began serving a concurrent sentence at the federal penitentiary in Victorville for tax evasions and his role in the fraudulent activity at CV Savings & Loan. Paroled in 1998, he opened a pawn shop in Yucca Valley. Blackpool died of heart disease in 2004.

Arthur Quail remained at the FDIC following an internal investigation by the agency's Office of Inspector General regarding his audit of CV Savings & Loan in 1954. Though found innocent of any wrongdoing in the matter, he was subsequently passed over for several promotions at the federal agency. He resigned in 1976 to form his own financial consulting agency. He died in 1999 at age 79 from cardiac arrest. Quail was among several neighbors initially questioned by police in the disappearance of a twelve-year-old Mission Viejo girl in 1971. The case remains open.

Janice Showalter left the United States, changed her name, and vanished much like her sister. Over the years, rumors reached the Vega Detective Agency that she had been sighted in Costa Rica and Spain.

The remains of **Mary Showalter** were reinterred at Desert Memorial Park in Cathedral City on behalf of the Vega Detective Agency. Her gravesite is adjacent to that of Lawrence Crossley, a Palm Springs businessman and the town's first black resident. In addition to his success as an entrepreneur, Crossley spearheaded efforts to ensure the Agua Caliente Band of Cahuilla Indians was properly given Section 14 land, awarding each member property and cash.

ACKNOWLEDGEMENTS

"In journalism just one fact that is false prejudices the entire work. In contrast, in fiction one single fact that is true gives legitimacy to the entire work."
— *Gabriel Garcia Marquez.*

I am often asked why I choose historical fiction as a genre for my stories. After nearly half a century in journalism where facts rule, my imagination was impatiently waiting its turn. Historical fiction offers freedom to mix fact and fiction while still grounding the narrative in a specific place and time.

For *Darkness Gets There First,* the place once again is Palm Springs. The time is 1969, among the most historic and turbulent years in memory. Neil Armstrong took one small step for mankind. The Vietnam War raged overseas and at home. Woodstock. Altamont. Stonewall. Hippies. Civil Rights. Student unrest. Zodiac. Manson.

Reconstructing that time – and blending it with a storyline that begins where I left Aloysius Vega at the end of *Wrong Side of the Wind* – required both imagination and research. Among the people and organizations that helped:

McNeil Island – Ann Kane Burkly, author of *McNeil Island,* and Crystal Hicks from the Washington State Library were essential resources on the former prison. Courtney Elliott of the National Archives in Seattle provided information on John Roselli's time at the federal prison. Also helpful were *The News-Tribune* of Tacoma, *Bellingham Herald,* and *Seattle Times.* The federal prison closed in 1976. It operated afterward as a state prison until 2011. Some of the buildings are currently used as a civil commitment facility for sexually violent predators.

Alvin Karpis – The James E. Carty Collection at Washington State University in Vancouver was the primary depository of information on Old Creepy's time at McNeil and his subsequent release arranged by the Clark County attorney. Interviews published by *The Montreal Star, Vancouver Province, Sur,* and Associated Press shed light on Karpis upon his release and his life in Montreal and Spain. For the curious, there are interviews with Karpis on YouTube.

Charles Manson – The notorious cult leader has been the subject of countless books and articles. His arrest at Barker Ranch and subsequent jailing in Independence were chronicled in newspapers and magazines. The tape-recorded interviews conducted by Inyo County Deputy Sheriff Don Ward, along with investigative reports by California Highway Patrol officer James Pursell, provided key details that helped complete the picture.

Mitchell Caverns – *Keepers of the Caves,* a revised edition of a book by Jack Mitchell, was the principal source of information on the history of the caverns. I toured the limestone formations in June of this year with my good buddy Steve Bonswor to obtain a first-hand look at the Mojave treasure.

Palm Springs – *Palm Springs Babylon* by Ray Mungo and *Palm Springs Confidential* by Howard Johns helped provide personality and color of the playground of the rich and famous during the 1960s. Articles in several magazines and newspapers about **Robert Evans** were helpful in finding the Paramount producer's voice. His intoxicating autobiography, *The Kid Stays in the Picture,* was essential reading. And that "hippie invasion" in 1969? The backlash was severe, according to *The Desert Sun.* Outdoor concerts were banned for over a decade. Tahquitz Canyon was closed to visitors for more than three decades.

Coma – *Guide to the Comatose Patient* by Eelco F.M. Wijdicks of the Mayo Clinic was my principal source of information about the mysterious condition. The book explains the many causes, the different stages of unconsciousness, and offers advice on how families can deal with what often feels like an unending roller coaster ride.

My wife and my sister – Diane Perry and Susan Fuhrman Perry – helped me shape *Darkness* into its final form and provided first-line editing. Laurie D. Kroes, my former colleague at the *Journal-American* in Bellevue, Washington, once again applied her considerable editing skills to my manuscript. Any remaining mistakes of grammar or fact are owned by the author.

My sincere thanks to Anita Williams, whose exceptional artistry brought the cover and pages of *Darkness* to life. Special thanks to Steve Bonswor and Bill Abel, retired law enforcement officers now my neighbors in La Quinta. They offered advice and corrected my initial descriptions of police procedures. Mike Sherk, a historical and genealogical research specialist in Independence, helped locate information on Don Ward.

I've begun work on my sixth novel. It's a story shaped in many ways by my years as a journalist in the Pacific Northwest. At its heart, the story explores the secrets we live with, the truths we bury, and the weight of decisions made by a local newspaper. The draft is in its early days, but the characters are starting to speak and I'm listening.

Thank you for your continuing support, readership, and reviews.

John Spencer Perry
August 2025

ABOUT THE AUTHOR

John Spencer Perry was born in Wilmette, Illinois, and lived there and in Oregon, Washington, and California. He attended Cañada Junior College in Redwood City, California, and received a bachelor's degree in journalism from the University of Oregon in Eugene. He spent forty-six years in the newspaper business in the Pacific Northwest, as a reporter, editor and publisher. Those newspapers include: the West-Lane News in Veneta, Oregon; the East Oregonian in Pendleton, Oregon; the Journal-American in Bellevue, Washington; and the Valley Daily News, South County Journal and King County Journal in Kent, Washington. Before retiring in 2017, Perry served as Chief Operating Officer for EO Media Group, a family-owned company with eleven newspapers in Oregon and Washington. In 1980, he served as senior editor of the best-selling book *VOLCANO: The Eruption of Mount St. Helens*. Perry published his first novel, *Desert Fire*, in 2020. *The Gimlet Eye* followed in 2021 and *The Liar's Paradox* a year later. He and his wife, Diane, live in La Quinta, California, with their two cats.

Made in the USA
Coppell, TX
10 February 2026

71741943R00197